# The Postmistress

MAGGIE SULLIVAN

Maggie Sullivan loves to travel, is an avid reader – never going anywhere without a book – and her abiding love is watching football. She is also a freelance university lecturer and has a keen interest in drama and theatre.

Maggie was born and brought up in Manchester, after living abroad for several years, she settled in London where she still lives.

Also by Maggie Sullivan

*Christmas on Coronation Street*
*Mother's Day on Coronation Street*
*Snow on the Cobbles*
*The Land Girls from Coronation Street*

· OUR STREET AT WAR ·

# The Postmistress

MAGGIE SULLIVAN

One More Chapter
A division of HarperCollins*Publishers*
The News Building,
1 London Bridge Street,
London SE1 9GF

www.harpercollins.co.uk

HarperCollins*Publishers*
1st Floor, Watermarque Building, Ringsend Road
Dublin 4, Ireland

First published in Great Britain by HarperCollins*Publishers* 2020
This edition published 2021
1

Maggie Sullivan asserts the moral right to
be identified as the author of this work

A catalogue record for this book
is available from the British Library

ISBN: 978-0-00-841986-8

Set in Sabon LT Std by Palimpsest Book Production Limited,
Falkirk, Stirlingshire

Printed and bound in Great Britain by
CPI Group (UK) Ltd, Croydon CR0 4YY

This book is produced from independently certified FSC™ paper
to ensure responsible forest management.

For more information visit: www.harpercollins.co.uk/green

This book is dedicated to Julie Leibrich, a true *ayshet chayil* – a woman of valour, a woman of worth.

# Chapter 1

**Greenhill, Spring 1939**

'Looks like we're definitely headed for war if what's writ in these papers is to be believed,' a gruff voice said.

The shop bell tinkled as Vicky Parrott pushed open the front door of the Post Office that gave onto Greenhill's narrow High Street and she stood for a moment on the doorstep looking to see who had spoken. The Post Office was wedged between Boardman's newsagent, tobacco and confectionery shop and Thompson's the butcher shop and, as Vicky looked up, it was Lawrence Boardman who was coming towards her waving the *Daily Express*.

'Here y'are,' he said. 'I kept your copy back as the

delivery boy was late in this morning. Thought you might want to read it over your first cup of coffee.'

'I had that a while since, but thanks. I know my dad will want to see it.' Vicky stepped outside and took the paper from him. She couldn't help a groan escaping as she scanned the dramatic pictures accompanying the front-page stories. The outlook did indeed seem very grim.

The Great War had had such a devastating effect on the small Lancashire town, and on the Parrott family in particular, that she couldn't bear to acknowledge that hostilities might be starting up again. Wasn't that supposed to have been the war to end all wars?

Vicky wasn't religious in any way. How could she keep the faith after all that had happened to her and her family? Nevertheless, she found herself unconsciously offering up a prayer to whatever gods there might be that the reporters' predictions would come to nothing. She glanced across the road to where the river continued to glide silently behind the rusted railings, looking for all the world as if nothing were amiss. And indeed, when she looked in one direction it really did seem as if nothing had changed, for all she saw was the peaceful scene of the schoolhouse with clusters of carefree children chasing each other around the playground. It was only when she turned to look in the other direction and her eyes focussed on the old cotton mill in the distance that she was reminded that it had recently been turned into a munitions factory, manufacturing ammunition and important parts for hand weapons and shells.

She shook her head to rid it of the unwelcome images that were suddenly crowding in and she tried to hang on to the stillness she usually enjoyed at this hour of the morning, the peace and quiet of those few splendid minutes before the daily bustle began. At least the High Street looked peaceful. She imagined Greenhill was like any other Lancashire mill town, with its cobbled streets that would soon be thronging with shoppers and the gentle smoke that curled from the distant chimneys so that they looked like they had been etched onto the backdrop of the craggy moorland hills. The only hint of war was an army recruitment poster in a shop window and her lips quivered with a fanciful smile as she thought of what Dot Pritchard had always been so fond of pointing out. Kindly Dot, who for ten years before her marriage had been such an important part of Vicky's life, had only been a young lass herself when she had taken on the task of looking after Vicky and her little brother Henry after their mother had died from Spanish flu. Dear Dot, who at the age of eighteen had so willingly taken on the potentially arduous role of substitute mother, showing them nothing but love. Vicky could hear her voice now.

'It might all look harmless,' she used to say, 'but we've no way of knowing what goes on behind them closed doors.' She'd have a knowing look on her face and she'd tap the side of her nose and this had always made Vicky laugh as her imagination went into overdrive.

This morning, apart from the newsagent, there was no one about but the dairyman, Billy Pritchard, Dot's father. The street was quiet save for the occasional whinny from his old horse while Billy was busy delivering fresh pints of milk to each doorstep, just as he always did. Meanwhile, the work-weary nag scented the air, plopping yet another steaming pat of fertiliser onto the cobblestones.

'Ne'er mind eh, Pretty Polly?' Lawrence Boardman brought Vicky out of her reverie as he handed her the newspaper. 'You know what they say, while there's life . . .' He turned his face skyward. 'And looking on the bright side, it might well be another sunny day.'

Vicky cringed at his use of the soubriquet. She was far too old at twenty-five to be referred to as 'Pretty Polly' even as a tease; it was a childhood nickname that harked back to her early days at the old schoolhouse and she thought it should be left there. The only person she hadn't minded using it after she left school was Stan . . . She stopped. There was no time for such memories now. It was a new morning and she needed to face it brightly, as she tried to do most mornings. She pasted what she hoped looked like a patient smile onto her face as she turned to go inside. 'Thanks for the paper,' she said and the doorbell jangled once more as she went back into the Post Office.

'Victoria, is that you?' The familiar rasp of her father's voice, followed by a throaty cough, greeted her as she lifted the counter and went through to the small living room behind the shop front, calling, 'Yes, it's only me, Dad!'

But the room was empty. None of the clutter on the small table had been disturbed. Only a disembodied voice wheezed over the banisters from the top of the stairs. 'Who was that in the shop? Why have you opened up so early? I haven't had my breakfast yet.'

Vicky rolled her grey eyes heavenward, an ironic smile tugging at her lips as she stood in front of the mirror over the fireplace where she had left all her kirby grips the previous night. She pulled her long dark hair off her face, gathering as best she could the wispy tendrils that seemed determined to escape and, sweeping them round her fingers, deftly pinned it all into a neat bun at the nape of her neck. She tried to pinch a bit of colour into her cheeks and succeeded in highlighting the high cheekbones that she was always being told were her best feature. At least the world hadn't stopped turning and her father was his usual irascible self.

'There's nowt to fret over, Dad. It was only me checking the weather,' Vicky said, disguising a sigh as she tossed the newspaper onto the table, knocking her father's favourite pipe to the floor. It hadn't had any tobacco in it since his lungs had been so badly damaged by mustard gas in the Great War but he liked to suck on it – like a baby's dummy, she always said – and she couldn't get him to part with it. She tutted as she bent to pick it up, fortunately still in one piece. She stared down at the grim front-page headlines again with the gruesome pictures of tanks and soldiers on the march and she groaned. Here they were, talking about a new war, while she was still dealing with the consequences of the old one. Life was so unfair.

'I've already put the water up and Mr Boardman next door's sent in the paper,' she shouted up to where she could see her father on the small landing at the top of the stairs. 'Shall I mash you some tea?' But the only response she got was the sound of more coughing followed by the slam of his bedroom door.

The tiny gong on the pretty clock on the mantelpiece that had once belonged to her mother pinged nine times and, on the final stroke, Vicky stepped into the Post Office, just as she always did. She pulled up the blind on the front door and swung the 'closed' sign round to read 'open'. Dr Roger Buckley was already on the step, as he was most mornings, the first customer of the day. If she was honest, she looked forward to seeing him though she wouldn't have dreamt of saying so. He was a good-looking man with a high forehead, a strong, smoothly shaven chin, and a perfectly chiselled nose, she considered him to be like an early-morning tonic, and she knew from the admiring glances his velvet-brown eyes and dark slicked-back hair drew from most of the women in the neighbourhood, that she wasn't the only one who thought so. The village's most eligible bachelor, some said, though in fact he was a widower with a child and Vicky liked him best when he dropped in to the Post Office at the weekend with his little daughter, Julie. If she had time, Vicky would stop and chat to the bright six-year-old and, if she wasn't busy, she'd let her wind the date stamp to the correct reading then press it into the ink pad before she stamped it onto any piece of scrap paper she could find. Julie was like a ray of sunshine, Vicky thought, though talking to her sometimes made Vicky tearful, thinking of things in her own life that might have been . . .

This morning being a weekday, Roger Buckley was alone, on his way to work, and she greeted him with a spluttering chuckle when he almost tumbled inside as she drew back the bolts and flicked the latch to open the shop door. She had always thought it unusual for a doctor to be buying stamps for his own business letters, particularly when she knew any number of her neighbours would have loved to become his secretary. But he had once told her that he liked to deal with his correspondence himself at the start of each day before climbing into his little Austin 7 and chugging up and down the streets of the village, visiting his patients. Vicky checked the weight and counted the letters as he placed them, one at a time, onto the scales and she carefully tore off the correct number of postage stamps.

'I wonder what it feels like to see your own picture every time you stick a stamp onto an envelope,' the doctor suddenly said.

Vicky looked at him sceptically. 'You don't imagine the King attends to his own correspondence, do you?' She giggled at the thought.

'No, I don't suppose he does.' Dr Buckley laughed. 'I imagine he has a personal secretary to see to such matters.'

'Perhaps you should think of doing that,' Vicky said, 'then you wouldn't have to spend so much time rushing around each morning before you even start seeing patients.'

He laughed again. 'As it happens, I don't mind beginning my day a little earlier than necessary. He lowered his voice and leaned over the counter. 'It gives me a chance to see what my neighbours look like when they're well without having to wait for them to appear at the clinic when they're not.' She realised he was staring directly at her and his sharp brown eyes seemed to soften, enhancing the smile on his lips so that she had to look away. 'Of course, you could be right,' he said, 'though at the moment I'm not convinced that writing out a few bills and reports would justify me shelling out a whole extra salary for a secretary – unless you're offering to do the job for free?'

Vicky caught the friendly teasing tone she so often

heard in his voice and felt the blood rush to her cheeks. She couldn't maintain eye contact and had to look away. He had a disconcerting way of meeting her gaze that she found unsettling, so she busied herself straightening some papers before tossing the stamped letters into a large sack that hung beside the counter, ready for collection later in the day. 'Anything else I can help you with?' Vicky asked, still not daring to look at him.

'Just a fresh pad of Basildon Bond paper and a packet of matching envelopes, please, and then I'd best be off.' The doctor smiled at her and raised his hat. 'May you have a day filled with customers,' he said, and Vicky couldn't help but smile back.

'And may all your patients get well soon.' Roger Buckley was surprised when she responded so sparkily and he smiled as he nodded in agreement. Then his thoughts turned to his first visit of the morning. He was on his way to the greengrocer's shop three doors down from the Post Office where fourteen-year-old Ruby Bowdon had recently returned from hospital having survived polio, and was now recuperating at home, awaiting his advice about how best she should approach her rehabilitation.

'I'd better be on my way to make sure that she gets off on the right foot, so to speak,' Roger said. He raised his hand to the brim of his brown felt trilby hat and left.

A prolonged series of coughs from the living room

behind her made Vicky look round before greeting the next customer.

'Victoria,' her father's voice rasped with some urgency. 'Was that Dr Buckley? Only, I could have done with him having a listen to my chest. I think I might need some more of that linctus he gave me last time he called.'

Vicky excused herself for a moment from the counter to put her head round the door that led through to their living quarters. 'I'm sure he doesn't carry such things around with him, Dad,' she whispered. 'And you can probably get it from the chemist. I can always ask Mr Stone if you run out but I think there may still be some of the old one left. I'll come and have a look as soon as I've got a minute but I've got a line of customers to serve first.'

'Then you'd better pray I'm still here by the time you get round to it,' he snapped. 'I'm warning you, I won't be able to help out today – or any other day, for that matter – unless you find me some of that cough mixture stuff, sharpish.' Her father was wheezing badly as he spoke. 'My chest feels like a washboard this morning.' And with that he pulled the door shut.

Vicky felt a stab of guilt when she heard his slippers scuffing on the thin carpet as he shuffled across the sitting room to the couch in front of the fireplace. She was trying to gauge the seriousness of his words and didn't know what to do first. With a sigh, she decided to turn back to the queue that had now formed. She puckered her lips and raised her brows by way of apology but the villagers knew her and her father well enough. There were a few disgruntled murmurs from people in the queue who were mostly strangers to the village, the rest were chattering amongst themselves and not objecting at having to wait.

'Good morning, sorry to keep you,' Vicky said to the first in line, recognising Violet Pegg, the teacher from the infants' school. 'I hope I've not made you late?'

'Don't worry.' Violet glanced at the watch on her slim wrist. 'Mrs Diamond's taking morning assembly today for my Infants as well as her Juniors so I should be back in time.'

'What can I get you? The usual, is it?' Vicky asked.

'Yes, please.' Violet giggled. 'Sounds like you're offering me a pint down at the Stoat and Weasel. But a stamp for Canada will do very nicely instead, thanks.'

'Put your letter on the scales so's I can check it.' Vicky licked the stamp and dropped the airmail envelope with its readily identifiable blue and red border into the collection sack, while Violet fumbled for the coppers in her purse.

'Actually, before you go I've got something to show you,' Vicky said, opening and closing the till in one practiced movement. She reached up and released several sheaves of flimsy blue paper from a large bulldog clip above the wicket. 'Head office has just sent me these new air letters and I thought they might be of interest.'

She pushed one over the counter for Violet to examine. 'It's one piece of paper that you fold up and seal,' she explained, 'and then it goes straight into the pillar box.'

'That's handy, but what about a stamp?' Violet asked.

'That's already printed on it, so it's cheaper than buying paper and envelopes and a regular stamp.'

'Now that certainly sounds like a good idea. I'll take one so I can try it next time,' Violet said, delving back into her purse. 'I reckon that with all the money I've spent on stamps over the years I could have booked a passage to Canada for a first-hand visit.' Violet giggled.

'But the King and Queen have beaten you to it,' Vicky said. 'I see they're off to Quebec soon.'

'That's where my pen-friend lives – I'm jealous,' Violet said.

'Don't they speak French there?' Vicky looked impressed. 'Don't tell me you write in French?'

'We used to when we first started writing, while we were both still at school. But now he's moving to Toronto and his English is far better than my French so we've switched.'

Vicky deposited the extra money in the till drawer. 'You've been writing for years, haven't you? It really is amazing.'

'Here!' The woman who was next in the queue suddenly interrupted and Vicky was caught unawares she'd been so engrossed in her conversation with Violet. 'We're all very impressed that you can write in a foreign language, love, but do you think you could be moving on for now?' The woman spoke directly to Violet.

'I agree, Betty,' the woman behind her said. 'I only wish I had the time to sit and write letters but we've all got to get to work this morning, even if you don't!' She indicated the people in the rest of the line and there were nods and mutters of agreement, though mostly good-natured.

'Oh dear, yes, I'm sorry,' Violet said. 'Who knows, maybe one day I'll get to meet him and then I won't have to keep posting letters.' She grinned at the two women behind her. 'Thanks for this, anyway.' She waved the flimsy letter towards Vicky. 'See you again soon.'

'Let me know how you find it,' Vicky called after her then she turned to the next in line. 'So sorry, Mrs Wellsley. I didn't mean to hold you up. We got carried away,' she said. 'Now, how can I help you?'

When Vicky heard the clock in the sitting room registering midday, she finished the final transaction of the morning and ushered the last customer out. Then she flicked the closed sign into place on the front door and pulled down the blind with a sigh of relief. It was dinnertime and she couldn't help wondering where the morning had gone. She felt a stab of guilt as she went behind into their living quarters and saw that her father had fallen asleep on the couch. She'd forgotten that she'd promised to look for his medicine, but at least he looked peaceful and he wasn't coughing now. He was sitting in an awkward position, though, his head uncomfortably lolling forwards onto his chest. He jerked awake as she passed through into the scullery and began tackling the small pile of breakfast dishes.

'What's happened? What time is it?' Arthur Parrott said, his voice sounding croaky and he started coughing almost immediately.

'Nothing's happened.' Vicky began to rummage in one of the wall cabinets, displacing bottles of Dinneford's Milk of Magnesia and Dettol, while being careful not to touch the TCP disinfectant that would stink the place out. Her father wouldn't thank her if she had that smell on her hands when she was making up their dinnertime sandwiches.

'Sorry, I couldn't get away to come and check sooner but it's been bedlam out there today. A constant stream, though I'm sure I don't know why. Seems like everyone's suddenly writing letters or sending parcels.'

'They must be worried that if there's going to be a war they won't be able to send owt,' Arthur said. 'And who knows? Maybe they won't.' He coughed, briefly this time, though as he did so he rubbed his hand across his chest as if to soothe the pain.

'Sorry, Dad,' Vicky said, replacing the bottles in the cabinet, 'but it looks like you'll have to take an aspirin for the minute if your chest hurts. There doesn't seem to be any linctus left.'

'Well, I need some,' Arthur grumbled. 'You'll have to go to the chemist after you've shut up shop tonight. Tobias Stone might not be the friendliest on the parade but at least he'll let his neighbours pick up medicines after hours, provided it's not too late.'

Vicky sighed. 'Why don't you ask Henry to go while I see to the tea? I'm sure he'll be back in time. You never seem to think to ask him. Don't you think it's time he helped out a little more here?' She snapped the words out but at the look on her father's face she wished she hadn't, and for a moment she worried that she'd gone too far.

'What, ask him to do woman's work after he's put in a hard shift at the foundry?' Her father looked aghast at her suggestion and gave another hack.

Vicky was stung into responding, 'Oh, I see – it's all right to ask me, even though I'm on my feet all day in the Post Office, and never mind everything else that I have to do?' She couldn't seem to stop now that she'd started. She was aware that her voice had begun to rise.

'Don't you get shirty with me, young lady. You can't compare your work to his. You should be glad to have such a cushy number.'

Vicky closed her eyes, thinking of all the household tasks that she still had to do. She knew it was the same for most of the other women of Greenhill and that she should really be counting her blessings for she wasn't as badly off as some, but when she was consumed by depression she found it difficult to hide her feelings. She couldn't help thinking about the past and the effect it had had on her. But she knew she couldn't afford to lose her temper completely, for then she would say things she didn't mean and there would be no way back. She loved her father, of course she did. After all, he had done his best in a situation that had proved to be hard on all of them. It wasn't his fault what had happened to Stan, or what had happened to her, and in the end he hadn't thrown her out onto the street as he had threatened to do. He had provided a roof over her head and made it possible for her to pursue a job she actually enjoyed. It was just that sometimes she wished Henry would take on more responsibility and not leave so much to her. She took a deep breath and counted to ten in an effort to calm down as she saw her father's features harden and he took a step towards her. He wagged his finger in her face and his voice suddenly dropped, making his words sound menacing and deliberate.

'You, my girl, are doing your duty. Nothing more, nothing less, and don't you ever forget it.'

Vicky's shoulders slumped for she knew he was right and there was little point in denying it. Life had not been easy for any of them. 'You know, Dad, I've never objected to doing my duty as you call it, it's just that . . .' As she clenched and unclenched her fists, Vicky suddenly realised that this was a fight she had been spoiling for ever since she had been hauled out of school at the age of fourteen and told that, as Dot was now leaving to get married, it was her job to look after her little brother. She had so desperately wanted to continue her education, to stay on at school and perhaps go to secretarial college. But she hadn't felt able to argue then and she didn't feel able to say anything now. Not when she had been guilty of contributing to the family's misfortunes. All she could do was to try her best to make amends. 'You must know I do my best to do my job and to look after you and the house and . . . whatever else is needed,' she said, 'but I don't see why—'

'It was hardly my fault that I came back from the war like this, I can bloody assure you of that!' Arthur cut in, wheezing heavily, though he still managed to carry on talking. 'Any more than it was anyone's fault that your poor mother caught that damned Spanish flu right at the end, even though she'd managed to see out the war. But what was your bloody fault was . . . was . . .'

Vicky could see that he was struggling to get the words out now, but as he spoke Arthur stood up and to her astonishment began fumbling with his belt. Fortunately, he didn't have the strength to disengage the buckle before he fell back onto the couch, overcome by a terrible coughing spasm. As far back as she could remember, her father's physical strength had not been able to match his temper, though he could still hurt her with his tongue lashings. But for once her tears were frozen. She didn't need reminding of what she had done.

'It's no less than you deserve when I think of the shame you were on the verge of bringing onto this family!' Arthur shouted at her. 'You're no better than you should be.'

'That was three years ago,' Vicky said softly. 'But you certainly make sure I keep paying for it, don't you? While all the time your precious Henry gets away with murder. When are you going to face up to him and tell him to start pulling his weight?' As she said this, her father began to cough again and this time she was afraid he wouldn't be able to stop. She became really scared as his eyes began to bulge and it took all her strength to prop him up on the couch and loosen his collar. She ran into the scullery for a cold compress and tried to dab it on his forehead, but he shrugged her away.

'I should have thrown you out when I had the chance. You and your wanton ways,' Arthur gasped between wheezes. 'I swear to God, you'll be the death of me. But maybe that's what you want?' Without warning he pushed Vicky's hand away. He swung his legs round and stood up unsteadily, lurching in the direction of the stairs. 'Call me when my dinner's ready,' he said and heaved himself upwards one step at a time.

Vicky could feel her eyes burning but she was determined not to let her father see her cry. She had a problem. Arthur's breathing seemed to be getting worse. Maybe she should ask Dr Buckley to come and have a look at him, find out if there was anything else he could do. She would even pay him, if necessary, if an extra visit wasn't covered by Arthur's GPO Health Insurance scheme. Roger Buckley seemed to be the only person her father really trusted, the only one apart from her and Henry that he would allow inside the house.

She sat at the table for a few minutes, rubbing her eyes with the heels of her hands. She could only feel sorry for what her father had suffered as a direct result of being so badly gassed during the Great War. But on a practical level, the remnants of his injuries put a great strain on her and now she feared that the symptoms were escalating. Today was the first time Arthur had refused to come to help out in the Post Office – and if he wasn't able to work behind the counter, then she would need to look for some help. It was a full-time job and she could no longer cope with it while at the same time having to be housekeeper, shopper and general factotum as well, no matter what she felt was her duty. And what would she do when Arthur needed more nursing? How would she manage then? Whether she would be able to carry on looking after him if his health continued to deteriorate at the rate it had recently was a question for Dr Buckley.

Perhaps she should contact her bosses at the GPO and sound them out about getting an assistant? Unless, of course, she could ask Henry. Maybe she should approach her brother and try to make him see how much she would appreciate his help, urge him to at least shoulder some of the responsibility.

The trouble was that as the threat of war became more immediate, so more people wanted to stop and chat about it. She hated being rude to her customers, but it was becoming almost impossible for Vicky to encourage them to pay for their purchases and be on their way. She was named as the postmistress, although the certificate of trading was in Arthur's name, but she could hardly spell out to her customers, most of whom she had got to know well over the years, that she needed time to be able to see to all her other chores as well. It was even becoming difficult to lock the door for an hour at midday as she was entitled to do because there always seemed to be someone who had something important that needed to be dealt with immediately. She could understand if it involved sending an urgent telegram but it rarely did, so why buying a postage stamp or writing paper and envelopes couldn't wait for an hour Vicky was unable to understand; she only knew she felt as if she was being pulled in all directions . . .

Henry came in later than usual that night, through the back door they used as their personal home entrance, and he ran straight up the stairs to the room he shared with his father, ignoring Vicky's greeting and her enquiry regarding his tea.

'Where's Dad?' he called down over the bannisters.

'Down the garden,' Vicky said, invoking the euphemism the family used to describe a visit to the lav.

'Damn, I need him to be here.' Henry came down the steep stairs slowly. He sat on one of the chairs at the table and hid his face behind the sports page of the evening paper he'd brought in with him. Then he jumped up and paced back and forth in the small living room.

'Why don't you go and wash your hands and I can serve up your tea?' Vicky said. 'It's better than you wearing out the carpet. We don't have to wait for Dad.' She was wondering if she might be able to pin Henry down before their father returned, talk to him about taking more responsibility for looking after Arthur.

'I'm not ready to eat yet,' Henry said 'I'll hang on till Dad gets here. I've got summat to tell you both and I'm not saying it twice.'

'I thought you were looking agitated. What's wrong?' Vicky asked, as he circled the table for the third time. Her brother's restlessness seemed to fill the room and she was beginning to feel the waves of his anxiety wash over her.

Thankfully, it was not for long. Henry had sat down and stood up again several more times when, to the relief of them both, there were the distinctive sounds of Arthur making his way down the path and through the backyard. Vicky saw it as her cue to bring in the large earthenware dish from the oven and begin ladling out the steaming juicy layers of spicy meat, potatoes and vegetables that comprised her own special version of hotpot that she knew they both loved. She brought in three large bowls from the scullery and began to fill them before placing them on the wooden mats she had laid on the table.

'Hurry up, Dad,' she called out. 'Yer tea's ready. It's yer favourite and I'm just serving up.'

Arthur ran his hands briefly under the cold water tap, then he rubbed them down the front of his heavy drill trousers in an attempt to dry them.

'We've been waiting for you because Henry's got something to tell us,' Vicky said.

'Oh, and what's that?' Arthur asked as he sat down. He turned to face Henry, but as he did so his face seemed to drain of blood. It was then that Vicky gasped, covering her mouth with her hands and looking from one to the other as she suddenly realised from reading her father's face what it was her brother had come to tell them.

For a moment nobody spoke. Vicky automatically handed round three sets of forks and spoons but no one attempted to eat from their fast-cooling plates. Henry picked a corner off one of the slices of bread that had been piled onto a plate in the centre of the table and almost unconsciously began to roll small fragments between his index finger and thumb. Then he nervously gathered the tiny grey pellets into a cairn-like pile beside his plate on the oilcloth. He didn't look at her or his father as he spoke.

'I'm going to join up. Sign on for the army. I thought you ought to know,' he said eventually.

The silence that followed was broken only by the sound of Arthur wheezing. His brows knitted then his lips twitched into an uncertain smile. Henry looked up at that moment, his eyebrows raised in query as his gaze met Vicky's but for once she didn't know what to say.

'Look . . .' Henry filled the void when neither Arthur nor Vicky spoke. 'There's no question about whether this war's going to happen. I've no doubt in my mind that it will, and it will be soon. Meaning that it will be over soon, but the thing is . . . I want to be part of it. I want to be there to stick it to the Germans, so that we can shut them up for ever. I say we need to show them who's boss, get it over and done with before they've got a chance to invade any other countries . . . And that might include Britain. Whichever way, my bet is that war will be declared sooner rather than later.'

'But—' Arthur started to say but Henry cut him off.

'No, Dad, I don't think there are any buts. It won't be like last time. This time it really will all be over by Christmas. Hitler's off his rocker, thinking he can take on the world, and I say that the more of us join up early, the easier it will be to show him that he can't.'

'When will you . . .?' Vicky's voice croaked as she struggled to control it.

'Not sure yet, but it will be soon.'

For the moment she forgot the speech with which she had been preparing to confront Henry. Now all she could do was fear for the life of her little brother and worry about how she and Arthur would manage with him gone.

'What about your job?' Vicky managed to say eventually as it dawned on her that they would be down to a single wage coming into the household. But Henry was not thinking along the same lines.

'What about it? I hate the bloody foundry,' he said vehemently. 'I'd have left no matter what. In fact, I've already handed in my notice so there'll be no delay in me actually signing on the dotted line.'

'You mean you . . .?' Vicky said.

'I'll be volunteering, yes. I don't imagine I'll have any problem passing a medical so I'm not waiting for any kind of forced conscription, if that's what you're thinking. I'm taking fate into my own hands and doing summat useful for my country at the same time.'

He beamed as he spouted what Vicky knew to be the message on some of the recruitment posters she'd seen pasted up around the town. She felt a cold shiver that was more like an electric charge shoot down her spine. 'You mean you can't wait to get away. To leave us here to our own devices?' she finally managed to say.

Henry looked puzzled. 'What do you mean? You're capable of managing perfectly well on your own. You don't need me.'

Vicky wondered if there would have been a different outcome if she had managed to get her two penn'orth in first before he'd made his announcement. What would have happened if she'd had a chance to tell him of her fears and concerns? Would she have made him change his mind? She had to admit that she doubted it but she asked the question anyway. Turning to face Henry and using as quiet a voice as possible she said, 'And how am I to cope if Dad gets really sick? I do worry about him, you know.'

Arthur had picked up his empty pipe from the table and was pulling hard on the stem as if it were lit. 'You don't have to worry about me, girl. I shan't be any bother,' he said quickly as if to show her he'd heard her whispered words. 'Of course he must go and fight for his King and country,' he said with a satisfied smirk.

'How can you say that? Look where fighting for your country got you.' Her voice was twisted in a sob. 'And where did fighting get my poor Stan?' Vicky stopped, angry that she couldn't disguise her voice breaking. 'And I didn't notice the King or your country stepping in to do much once you were wounded.'

'I was unfortunate. But Henry's got a chance to be the hero I never was,' Arthur said, a broad smile on his face now.

Henry blushed but didn't respond.

'And you and me will manage, lass, you wait and see.' Arthur patted Vicky's leg under the table.

Vicky screwed up her eyes tight but to her chagrin scalding tears still managed to make serious tracks down her cheeks.

'So once again it's me that's left with all the responsibility, me that will have no choice, no life.' She thought she had whispered the words so that only she could hear them but Arthur's response was swift and cruel when he gave a scornful laugh.

'You've not shown any interest in having a life for the past however many years, so why suddenly the concern now? You don't even respond when someone does take an interest in you.'

Vicky looked puzzled but her father didn't elaborate. Instead, he went on, 'And once upon a time you were prepared to throw your life away completely for a fella – and you would have too, if the war hadn't stopped him in his tracks.' Vicky could feel the colour rising from her neck to her cheeks and up to the top of her head as she glared at her father.

'All I can say is, I'm glad you're not thinking of doing that now, sis,' Henry suddenly said and he reached across the table and squeezed her hand. 'We'll be needing the likes of you to keep the home fires burning and all that. Isn't that what they used to sing about in the Great War, Dad?'

'They did indeed,' Arthur said and he began to hum the first line of the well-known song. 'Besides, you should be thankful your life's turned out so well, given the kind of start you had. There's lots of girls would give their eye teeth to have what you've got right now: a good job, a home, a family.'

Vicky could only stare at him, her thoughts momentarily bound up with all that she had lost, though she switched her gaze as Henry stood up and pushed his chair back.

'Well, I'm off to tell my mates.' He grinned. 'See if I can shame them into joining me. I've got a feeling I might be the first, but I know I certainly won't be the last.'

Arthur slowly got up from the table. He went over to Henry and patted him on the shoulder. 'I'm proud of you, son,' he said. 'I'm sure you're doing the right thing.' Then he turned to glower for a moment at Vicky. Unexpectedly, she shuddered. It was the kind of look that had frightened her when she was a little girl, when her father had just come back from the war, just after her mother had died. And it frightened her now to think that in her father's eyes she would probably always be second best. As if to underline the sentiment, Arthur turned his attention back to Henry and beamed at his son one more time.

'You don't worry about us, lad,' he said. 'You go and do what you've got to do.' And he patted him one more time on the back, 'We'll manage, same as we always have.' And with that he slowly made his way up the stairs.

# Chapter 2

'Daddy! Daddy!' The little girl squealed with joy as she ran across the hall and into her father's arms. Roger Buckley put down his doctor's Gladstone bag that suddenly felt heavy and he opened his arms wide to accommodate the sturdy six-year-old.

'Julie, my love. What a wonderful welcome, as ever,' he said. He kissed the top of her head and stroked her gleaming black hair that hung straight to her shoulders. It was smooth and sleek just like her mother's had been. Such moments always brought a tear to his eyes.

'Don't touch my hair, you'll mess it up,' Julie said, patting it down with her hands.

Roger didn't mind that his daughter was unusually vain for her age about her hair. He found it strangely comforting. He loved to see her comparing it with the well-thumbed photos of Anna that, at Julie's insistence, adorned her bedroom. If she deemed it to be so much as an inch longer than the hair in the photographs, she insisted that her granny cut it.

At that moment Freda Buckley appeared and, as she opened the door from the family's living quarters that led into the hall, Roger was greeted by the appetising smell that suggested his mother's indulgence of his favourite – cottage pie.

'Roger, darling.' She greeted him warmly. 'You're later than usual. I nearly sent your father on a trek to the surgery to make sure you hadn't got lost coming from there to here.' She grinned but Roger only shrugged, too tired even to laugh at the well-worn family joke, the clinic where he worked most afternoons being attached to the other side of the house.

'You know how it is,' he said. 'There's always someone likes to arrive just as I'm about to close up for the night. It's as if they can't bear to let me go home.' Then he smiled. 'Though I must admit it has been busier than usual today. I think people are gearing themselves up to the fact that there really will be a war and they want to get any niggles sorted out while things are still running relatively normally. I suppose it won't do them any harm to be in as good a condition as possible if we're going to be hit by rationing and food shortages.'

'You might be right. But you should be more assertive.'

Freda playfully wagged her finger at him. 'Meanwhile, your dinner awaits. Julie's already had her tea but your father and I haven't eaten yet; we thought we'd wait for you, though we had almost given up on you.'

'But I want you to read me a story first!' Julie tugged at his arm. 'I've been waiting soooo long.' She sighed in such a grown-up way that it made Roger smile.

'All right, I'll read you a story.' He bent down and kissed her forehead. 'Though only one. No nagging for another one.'

'I promise.' Julie momentarily put her thumb in her mouth and quickly turned away before she could be admonished.

'But while I take off my things why don't you tell me all about your day at school,' Roger said.

Julie let go of his hand and ran through the short corridor that led into the kitchen while he hung up his coat on the hall stand and took off his jacket. She skipped back into the hall waving a piece of sugar paper that had been carefully folded so that it looked as if it had wings, and he could see it had been decorated with patches of pastel-coloured tissue paper that had been stuck all over it.

'Miss Pegg said it was really good and she pinned it up on the achievements board for the afternoon.' She made the word 'achievements' sound more like a sneeze and the doctor laughed. '*And* I got a star on my work chart,' Julie said, refusing to be put off.

'That's very clever of you,' her grandmother intervened. 'And now I think you should go up to bed and Daddy will come and read to you shortly.'

'Oh, can't I stay up a little bit longer?' Julie begged.

'You heard what Grandma said,' Roger said. 'I'm very tired and I need to have something to eat, but I'll put you to bed first with one story, as I said. And if you're really good and go to sleep then, like you promised, then we can go fishing in the park, maybe even this weekend so long as it doesn't rain.

'Ooh, goodee!' Julie clapped her hands with delight as she started up the stairs.

'But haven't you forgotten something?'

'Oops!' Julie said and she ran quickly back into the kitchen where Roger heard the sound of a sloppy kiss.

'Night-night, Grandad,' she called and within seconds she was back in the hall where the sound of the kiss was repeated. 'Night-night, Grandma,' she said. 'Come on, Daddy.' She pulled on his hand. 'Come and read *Mr Galliano's Circus* to me.' She put on an imitation of an adult voice, 'The sooner we start, the sooner you can eat. Isn't that what you always say?'

Roger couldn't help laughing at that. 'It is indeed.' He ruffled her hair. 'Now come on, my precocious little child, or Grandma will be chasing after the both of us.'

He didn't even get to the end of the chapter before he heard Julie breathing deeply and he crept downstairs so as not to disturb her. His father poured two fingers of whisky into a crystal glass and pushed it towards him almost the moment he appeared, and his mother began serving up the appetising dish of well-seasoned meat topped with creamy potatoes as if she had been standing, ladle poised, waiting for him to appear. But on cue, as they were ready to begin eating, they were assailed by a loud wail from upstairs followed by, 'Where's my water? I want a glass of water.'

Roger half rose but his mother patted his arm. 'You stay and eat; I'll see to her.' And Roger didn't protest.

'I'll be back in a moment, Cyril,' she said to her husband as she poured a tumbler full of water ready to take upstairs.

'Long day?' his father said when Freda had left the room. Roger nodded. 'I remember them well,' Cyril said smiling. 'And I can tell you, long hours are not something I miss.'

Roger took a sip from his whisky glass then sat back. 'Oh dear,' he said. 'That sounds ominous.'

'Oh dear? What's that supposed to mean?' Cyril said.

'It means I was hoping you were going to say something else. Does a tiny part of you really not sometimes hanker to come out of retirement and go back to work for a little while? Just to keep your hand in?'

The older man exploded into a blustering laugh. 'Good heavens, no! Why should I want to do that?' He picked up his whisky glass but he put it down again before it reached his lips and he gave Roger a quizzical look. 'You're serious? Come on, spit it out, old chap.'

'Unfortunate choice of phrase, Dad.' Roger gave a humourless laugh.

'Are you really saying what I think you're saying?' Cyril said, his brow creasing with a frown.

'Yes, I think I am,' Roger admitted. 'You must have seen the recruitment posters? They're all over the place.'

'And you're thinking . . . what, exactly?'

'I'm thinking that, as a medic, I could make a damned useful contribution.'

Cyril frowned, looking worried for a moment, but then he sat back with a look of genuine relief. 'But they won't want you, Roger. You're too old.' He hesitated. 'Aren't you? You won't have to go into the forces, surely?'

'Not immediately, no. But once this thing gets going, how long do you think it will be before they widen the parameters?'

'What? Do you mean extend the age groups?'

'That and the fact that they'll want trained doctors, not just medics or nurses.'

'You really think it's going to happen?'

'Without a shadow of a doubt, I'm afraid. If you listen to the news it sounds inevitable.'

'Hmm.' The older man nodded. 'You're probably right. So you'd rather pre-empt a compulsory call-up and volunteer?'

'I thought that if I did it might give me the edge, a little leverage, a bit more choice about where I end up.'

'Who knows what's going to happen? Who knows?' Cyril looked pensive but didn't ask any more questions and nothing further was said about it when Freda came back to join them.

They finished their meal without further conversation, the only sounds in the room being the genteel tapping of the highly polished silver-plated cutlery on the fine china plates. Then Roger helped his mother pile the dirty dishes into the sink in the kitchen and left her to deal with them while he poured another splash of whisky for himself and Cyril. He sat at an angle next to his father so they both faced the hand-embroidered fireguard that hid the empty fireplace and he pulled a small table into place between them. He refused the offer of a cigar but leaned across the table to grasp hold of the table lighter to light one for Cyril.

Dr Buckley senior puffed on the cheroot and turned his gaze on his son. 'So, what have you in mind then? When are you planning on going?'

'I don't know yet. I've nothing specific in mind at the moment,' Roger said, 'because there are certain things I'll need to do. But first I wanted to check out your thinking on the subject, to find out where you might stand in all of this.'

'Well, I'm essentially anti-war – as far as one can be

– as you know, but I'm also cognisant of the fact that one does have a moral duty when push comes to shove.'

'So, I suppose what I'm really asking is . . . would you be willing to?' Roger stopped and fiddled for a few moments with the lighter, flicking the blue flame on and off several times.

'Willing to what?'

'To come out of retirement and keep things afloat here if I did sign up? In other words, would you be willing to hold the fort and keep the practice going?'

Cyril cleared his throat. 'I would have to ask your mother before I could commit to anything definite, for it would affect her too, of course.'

'Of course,' Roger agreed.

'It would mean her looking after Julie full time, for a start.'

'Yes, I'd already come to the same conclusion, but I can't see her objecting to that, can you?'

'No, but she's the kind of woman who does like to be asked about things that affect her. You can't just take her goodwill for granted.'

'No, I understand that,' Roger said, quietly sighing with relief in the knowledge that this particular battle was already as good as won. 'But I know she loves Julie and that the feelings are mutual, so that would make things easier all round.'

'And what about you?' his father asked. 'I know you've never tried to replace Anna, and I don't usually pry into your private life but isn't there some . . .' He hesitated. 'Some sweetheart, some ladylove or potential amour whose feelings would need to be considered before you took such a step? In my experience, the womenfolk do like to be consulted.'

Roger felt his face flame and for a moment, without thinking, almost blurted out his guilty secret. But then he realised that that was all it was still, a secret, and unless he chose to give it away, that was how it would remain. No one knew of the woman he admired, the woman he wished he could get closer to, the woman he really didn't want to leave behind. At this moment there were no such complications for only he knew. No one else. Not even Pretty Polly herself.

# Chapter 3

Violet Pegg found the airletter at the bottom of the capacious bag she took to school each morning when she was clearing it out at home at the end of the day. She always had to make sure no one had dropped their rubbish into it as some of the cheekier little ones were prone to do. The almost transparent blue paper was badly crumpled and she tried to smooth it out on the kitchen table. She wasn't sure why she had bought it. She and her Canadian penfriend, Danny, didn't exchange letters as often as they used to, not like when they had first started writing while they were both still at school. Then they had sent a reply almost immediately they received new post. In fact, she'd only just sent off a letter to him that morning so who knew when she'd be writing to him again? She sighed. And what would happen if the war came, as everyone was predicting? Would she still be able to send letters abroad?

'Looks like you should be taking an iron to that,' her mother Eileen said, coming into the living room and loading a large knitting bag onto the table. 'What is it anyway?'

Violet explained. 'Knowing me, I'd scorch it if I tried to put the iron anywhere near it, so it would be no use anyway,' she said and giggled.

'Well, you can't afford to throw it away. It's the price of a good stamp that is,' Eileen said. 'And talking of throwing away, I need you to get round to Mrs Barker's and fetch me the rest of that knitting wool she's set aside for me, before she gets rid of it.'

'She wouldn't do that!'

'Oh yes she would if she thought I hadn't fetched it fast enough. Like as not she'd sell it to someone else.'

'She never would? Not once she's put it aside with your name on it?' Violet insisted.

'According to her that's all she does, puts it aside and it's not mine by right until I've paid for it.'

'Hmm. That's not very neighbourly, is it?'

'I'm learning that neighbourly doesn't count for much in her book. Believe me, she's done it to me before. Sold off my wool without any warning. Said I was too slow in claiming it. She can be a right misery, that Sylvia Barker, I can tell you – and her daughter can be even worse.' She stopped for a moment. 'I'm sorry if I'm speaking out of turn because she's your best friend,' she went on after a moment, her voice firm, 'but I'm saying it as it is. I'm not surprised they don't work well together in the shop.'

'Maybe Mrs Barker's got things to be miserable about.' Violet always tried to see the best in everybody. 'I've been hearing all sorts about her husband and if only half of it's true it's enough to make anyone feel downright miserable.'

Eileen looked at her sharply. 'Have you been listening to gossip again? Where did you pick that up from?'

'The usual place.'

'Oh, Violet.' Eileen looked disappointed. 'You do know you can't believe everything you hear, don't you? Particularly not if you hear it in the Post Office. That's the last place.' She shook her head. 'People do love a good gossip.'

'I know, Mam, and I promise I won't spread it any further than this room. But whether you want to believe it or not, when you hear such things coming from several different quarters, you can't help wondering whether there might be some fire to go with all that smoke.'

# Chapter 4

Rosie Barker didn't get home from work until late that evening, the third time in a week she'd been expected to do overtime without warning. She threw her bag down and slumped into the armchair, though only briefly, for she sat stiffly upright as soon as she heard her mother's footsteps. She had no intention of admitting that she might have made a mistake leaving the family business as abruptly as she had, even though at the time it had seemed like a smart move. When the local mill had closed down and reopened as a government-funded munitions factory, it had offered better-paid jobs to local women than they could get elsewhere. It had seemed like the perfect opportunity for Rosie to get away from Sylvia's small-time haberdashery shop, which she loathed. She was keen to take on what she called 'real work' and was soon boasting to her mother about the new job she was about to begin, for rumours had quickly spread that the factory would be manufacturing some ammunition as well as small but significantly important armoury parts. These would then be taken away to be assembled elsewhere into actual, formidable-looking weapons. On the face of it the work had seemed ideal. It sounded as though it would not be too heavy and should be reasonably manageable, and Rosie was happy to think that, without having to exert herself too much, she would be making a significant contribution to the country's needs should the threatened war actually materialise.

She had no time for the kind of frippery, as she saw it, that her mother stocked, no matter how hard Sylvia tried to convince her of its importance within their local community.

'I don't understand what you've got against haberdashery. It fills an important need,' Sylvia argued. 'Things like knitting wools and sewing stuff are essential, particularly at times like these. You should think of them as raw materials. This county's fortunes were founded on them, you know. Women make as important a contribution to looking after their families as men. What would they do if they couldn't make their own clothes, knit their own jumpers, and run up something for the kiddies? Many's the time what you call "fancy nonsense" has put bread on this table, let me tell you. When your dad's been having a hard time selling any shoes, we've been glad of my shop then.'

Rosie stopped listening. She had heard it all before. She had learned to knit and sew while she was still at school – she'd had no choice – but regardless of her mother's arguments, she still considered them to be hobbies rather than important skills to flaunt, much less encourage, in the workplace. Even the word haberdashery sent a shiver down her spine.

Sylvia shook her head. 'I make no apologies for what I sell, Rosemarie, these things are just as important as your armoury and munitions.' Rosie smiled. Her mother always used her full name when she slipped into lecturing mode. 'You don't have to be involved with heavy metals or gunpowder to prove your worth.' Sylvia's voice was scathing now. 'I'm proud to be able to say that I earn a living by helping women to help themselves.'

At first, Rosie had been delighted when she left her mother's business, convinced that she had made the right move. However, it hadn't taken long for her to find out the true meaning of 'real work' and it wasn't anything like the ideal she had dreamed of.

'Hard labour' was how Rosie usually described it to anyone who would listen, although she took care not to say such a thing in front of her mother. She didn't dare to complain about her work when she was at home. She wouldn't give Sylvia the satisfaction of gloating that that was exactly what she had predicted. And it wasn't as though there was much opportunity for social contact on the benches, for the place was far too noisy for that. There had been a din when it had been a mill, enough to prevent anyone from talking, even those working within a few feet of each other on the same work bench, but the racket in the munitions factory was even worse. If you made the mistake of looking away from the machines for a moment to try to lip-read what someone was saying, there was the chance that the shift of focus of attention could result in an accident occurring or something going badly wrong with the machine. Not only was the work relentless and physically hard, it was also boring, and the structure of the shifts meant that the girls had to work much longer hours than in any shop.

There was only one saving grace in favour of the factory over the wool shop as far as Rosie was concerned – apart from the extra wages she found in her pay packet at the end of the week – and that took the form of a certain Trevor Jones, a young mechanic she'd discovered on her first day. But that was something else she wouldn't admit in front of her mother.

'Fancy a cuppa? The kettle's not long since boiled,' Sylvia called out from the kitchen.

'No, thanks, you're all right,' Rosie said. 'We'll be having tea soon, won't we? I'll wait till then.'

Sylvia brought in her own cup of tea together with an oversized knitting bag stuffed full of skeins of wool yet to be unwound and several half-finished garments, and came to sit down at the table. She pulled out the jumper she was making for Rosie from an old cardigan of her husband Archie that she had unpicked. She checked where she was up to in the complex Aran pattern and began to knit.

'Could be a while yet before we eat,' Sylvia said. 'Your dad phoned to say he'll be joining us tonight, so I reckon it would be best if we waited.'

Rosie tensed involuntarily at the mention of her father's name and looked across anxiously at Sylvia to see what she made of his impending visit. He was away so much these days that the occasional trip home felt like a special occasion to Rosie, though not a particularly joyous one. But Sylvia's face gave nothing away and she refused to meet her daughter's gaze.

'It seems he's had a busy couple of weeks selling off the old lines of shoes to make room for the new stock.' Sylvia's voice was chatty and her brow crinkled as she concentrated on crossing the small open-ended cable needles back and forth to maintain the flow of the complicated knitting sequence. 'He's taken lots of orders this week, particularly for the new line he had in men's Oxfords and those lovely women's high-heeled sling-backs that he had in several different colours,' she said. 'I wouldn't have minded a pair of those myself and that's always a good sign. I believe he's sold all the old samples too. So he'll have to load up the van with a whole new lot to take down to Derbyshire.'

Rosie was about to ask if that meant he might actually have some money to contribute to the household kitty for once, but then she thought better of it. She was having trouble working out how to formulate the question so her mother wouldn't dismiss it as 'Rosie being disrespectful' or some such thing. There was hardly a beat before Sylvia changed the subject as she always did when they got on to the topic of Archie Barker. 'You missed your friend Violet this afternoon,' Sylvia said. 'She came in after school to collect the last of her mother's wool.'

Rosie recognised Sylvia's opening gambit as one that she used when she was trying to interest her daughter in the affairs of the shop. She was going to put her hand over her mouth in a mock yawn, but then changed her mind; there was no need to antagonise her mother unnecessarily.

'Violet finishes work early so she was able to slip in before I closed up for the night,' Sylvia said. 'It must be such a comfort to Mrs Pegg that her daughter always helps her out with things like that.'

Rosie refused to rise to the bait so several moments of silence elapsed before Sylvia asked, 'Are you planning on going out with your friend Penny this week?'

Rosie shook her head. 'I don't think so. Why?'

'I noticed there's a good film on at the Plaza, though I'm afraid I can't remember the name of it,' Sylvia said.

Rosie bit back the retort that had sprung to her lips that if she did decide to go to the Plaza it wouldn't be with Penny but, 'I don't know if I'll have the time,' was all she said out loud.

It was still daylight when Rosie came out of work a few days later, even though she'd had to work the couple of hours overtime that was becoming the norm.

'One of the delights of summer,' her friend Penny Downs said as they cleared the factory gates together arm in arm and set off down the towpath, the klaxon that had signalled the end of the shift still ringing in their ears. Penny and her younger sister Stella lived with their widowed father who ran the cobbler's shop at the end of the High Street. Penny, Violet Pegg, and Rosie had gone to school together before Violet went off to train as a teacher and now Penny had taken Violet's place as she and Rosie were mates at the factory, working as colleagues on the same bench.

Rosie stopped for a moment and whisked off her headscarf. The roll that she had so carefully pinned in that morning collapsed immediately and she shook out her golden curls, revelling in the fact that the breeze off the river immediately whipped them back from her forehead as she tilted her face towards what was left of the afternoon sun.

'I love it when you can actually feel the days getting longer, don't you?' Rosie grinned. 'And you can see people properly, too, not like when we're all lurking in the gloom in there.' She threw a disparaging look over her shoulder as she jerked her thumb in the direction of the old mill.

Penny chuckled at that. 'Oh, and who can you see? Have you anyone in particular in mind that you're looking for?' She raised her brows.

'No, of course not,' Rosie retorted, though she tried discreetly to peer around her friend as she spoke, in an attempt to catch a second glimpse of the young man she thought she recognised by the factory wall. He was sheltering a match in his cupped hands as he tried to light a cigarette and he had been standing with one leg pushing back against the wall behind him. Suddenly he lowered it and started walking towards her. She hoped that the fluttering she felt in her chest didn't show on her face but she couldn't help smiling when she realised he had clocked her too.

'Aye, aye, look out! Here comes trouble,' Penny said. 'I hope that's not one of the people you've been trying to see?'

Rosie looked at her sharply. 'Why do you say that? What's wrong with him?'

'Can't explain now.' Penny lowered her voice as he came nearer, his intended target obvious. 'All I can say is, you'd better watch your step with that one.'

There was no time to say any more as the lad approached. Rosie watched him take a long draw from his cigarette and when he reached her he proffered it in her direction. Rosie shook her head.

'No thanks, I don't smoke,' she said, wondering from the look on his face if she should perhaps have taken it. His fingers were none too clean but he rubbed his hands up and down his drill dungarees that fitted over his regular trousers in an effort to clear the worst, though it made no difference to the ingrained yellow nicotine stains on his fingers. His mousey-coloured hair had been blown into something resembling a haystack but she found the wild look extremely appealing. She thought of her father, always immaculately turned out, with razor-sharp creases and turn-ups on his trousers, his hair slicked back with Brylcreem and she wanted to giggle. Whatever would he make of Trevor Jones?

Trevor shrugged. 'Suit yourself.'

A cheeky smile played around Trevor's lips and his almost jet-black eyes seemed to be enjoying the joke too, so that Rosie had to look way, but she couldn't deny that in those few seconds he had made her feel as if she was the only girl on the street. Her hand fluttered to adjust the buttons of her cotton blouse, even though they didn't need adjusting as they were tucked securely into the band of her skirt. She fingered the belt that she knew flattered her trim waist and smoothed the folds of the flared skirt over her generous hips, grinning up at him as if challenging him to ask for a twirl. He gave her the benefit of a full smile then and this time she braved meeting his gaze. He was close enough that she could see one of his front teeth protruded slightly and crossed over to cover half of its neighbour, something she hadn't noticed before, but as far as she was concerned it somehow added to his appeal.

'Where do you live? I'll walk you home.' He said the words casually but Rosie could feel the intensity of his gaze. At the same time, she was aware that Penny had stopped and was standing stiffly beside her with her fists clenched.

'She'll be coming home with me,' Penny said pointedly. 'We was walking home together, wasn't we, Rosie?'

'Oh, yes, well . . . we were . . . but you know you don't have to worry about me.' Rosie turned to Penny, trying to sound offhand. She didn't want to appear too forward but she didn't appreciate her friend's interference.

Penny looked shocked. 'You don't have to mind me,' she said somewhat petulantly. 'I've some errands to do for my dad before I go home.' Then her face softened for a moment and she hesitated long enough to allow Rosie time to change her mind. 'If you're sure . . .?' Penny began.

'Yes, really, I'm fine,' Rosie said.

'Then I'll see you on the bench tomorrow, Rosie.' And without looking at Trevor, Penny flounced off, leaving the two of them alone.

Rosie stood for a moment, not sure what she should say next. For all her nineteen years she wasn't used to chatting up boys she didn't know, and she didn't find it easy to suddenly be flirtatious. She'd only stepped out with boys she'd grown up with from the neighbourhood, boys she'd known at school. Flirting with someone she didn't know anything about was a new experience. But she didn't have to worry for Trevor waited till Penny was out of earshot before he said, 'You can change your mind now your friend's gone, but you do know who I am. It's not as though we're strangers or anything.'

Rosie looked down at her heavy work shoes. One of the laces seemed to be coming undone, but she merely stared at it and didn't try to fix it. 'I'm sorry,' she said, 'I suppose that did sound rather rude, but I don't think Penny meant anything by it; she didn't mean to be awkward, but you know how it is.'

Trevor laughed. 'No, I don't really. It beats me sometimes what you girls think is going to happen when you're left alone with a lad. I'm hardly Jack the Ripper!'

Rosie felt her cheeks burn. 'I'm sure she didn't mean to offend you,' she said.

'I wouldn't bet money on that, but don't fret. I'm used to it, particularly from the likes of her,' Trevor said. 'Perhaps I should wear a suit tomorrow, to stop the scaredy cats being so afraid.' He chuckled. 'She might even change her mind if she'd see me in my Sunday best.'

He strutted in front of Rosie for a moment with his fingers under the shoulder straps of his dungarees, flicking them as if they were lapels. She could see now that Penny had hurt his feelings and she felt sorry. She wanted to make it up to him, though she wasn't quite sure how. She was glad when he said, 'I tell you what, why don't we have a fag together in the canteen, dinnertime tomorrow, then you can get to know me better? That would thumb your nose to your stuck-up so-called friend.'

'Nice thought, but I've told you, I don't smoke,' Rosie said.

'No, so you said, but we can soon change that.' A smirk replaced his easy smile and he suddenly grasped hold of her shoulders and turned her to face him. For a moment Rosie thought he was going to kiss her and she knew she ought to protest, but to her surprise she was disappointed when he didn't.

Instead he said, 'Which way?' and he jerked each of his thumbs in different directions.

Rosie hesitated, suddenly remembering Penny's warning. Did she really want him to know exactly where she lived? 'You can walk me as far as the High Street, if you like,' Rosie offered.

Trevor let go of her and pulled away. 'OK, best get going then.' And he strode off in the direction of the shops. They didn't talk as they walked and when they reached the parade Rosie was out of breath and glad to stop.

'This do you?' Trevor turned towards her.

'That's great, thanks,' she said. He put his hand up to cup her chin. Rosie felt her cheeks flame and something churn in the pit of her stomach.

'Then I'll see you in the canteen tomorrow,' he said. 'I'll find us a table at the back near the tray trolleys. Then you won't have to worry cos no one can see us there.' And without another word he turned away and began to walk briskly back the way they'd just come.

Rosie stared after him, a puzzled look on her face. She was trying to work out what had just happened between her and a factory mechanic called Trevor that her friend Penny had cautioned her to avoid. His tall figure, topped by the unruly thatch of hair, was lost in the crowds straggling on the pavements and in no time at all he had disappeared into the distance. What had Penny got against him, she wondered? And as she walked up the parade as far as the wool shop, she speculated about what her mother would have made of the situation if Rosie had let him see her to the door.

# Chapter 5

Roger Buckley was exhausted, so he was relieved when his bike finally crunched over the loose gravel path of the large detached house like a pianola playing a familiar signature tune. He was trying not to use the car on the days he didn't have far to travel because he needed to save it for emergencies. Petrol was becoming scarcer and there were rumours circulating about rationing it.

It had been a long day – even longer than usual as he had begun his rounds very early in the morning. He tried to confine his visits to the mornings though he accepted that as the majority of his patients were not covered by any health insurance schemes and had to pay for their own treatment they felt entitled to call on him at any time. The afternoons were usually designated to the drop-in clinic he had set up in his father's house and wherever possible he tried to keep the evenings free to put his feet up and spend precious time with his own family. However, he never liked to turn patients away if they needed his services, particularly if there was a genuine emergency. Tonight, this last outing had been in response to an emergency call from the Post Office, long after it had closed, and it was not one he felt he could ignore. He trusted Vicky's good sense that she would not request an out-of-hours visit unnecessarily. And his instincts had been right for he'd found poor Arthur Parrott lying prostrate on the couch having more difficulty than usual breathing. He had been unable to make it upstairs to his own bedroom, and was looking very unwell as he fought for every breath. He had seemed so bad at first that Roger had been inclined to suggest hospitalisation and was considering calling for an ambulance. But there was something about Vicky's calming manner that held him back once he had administered an injection that relieved the most alarming of Arthur's immediate symptoms and enabled him to breathe more easily. She hadn't panicked but had listened to reason while he had debated the best course of action, just as she had done when he had first known her, but then the debate had been about her own difficulties. She really was a remarkable woman. She had the knack of bowing to the inevitable where she had no choice, while at the same time changing that which could be changed. It was a trait he had long since admired.

Roger thought back to the beginnings of their friendship. Was it only three years ago that their paths had crossed so dramatically? He was transported back to another time when the three of them had been closeted in the same small room as they had been tonight, locking horns over life and death issues. But what they had discussed then had never been referred to since, not by any of them. And when Roger saw Vicky in the Post Office as he so often endeavoured to do, she showed no signs of wanting to rekindle any of the personal connection he felt they had forged on that day. She treated him no differently to any other customer, no matter how hard he tried to engage her in more personal conversation and he wondered if she knowingly misinterpreted his advances.

Was she really not aware of how he felt? He had often asked himself that question. Or had life changed for her so radically at that time that she wanted to shut out all memories of her former connections and the decisions she had made? There was no question that she had changed in the few years he had known her. She no longer had the youthful bluster, the almost cocky self-confidence she'd had when he had first known her. A layer of sadness now lurked behind her gentle grey eyes but he put that down to life experience and the maturity of her twenty-five years. Her dark hair was no longer cut short the way it had been when he had first set eyes on her, but when she swept it back off her face he could clearly see the fine lines of her delicate features. She was still a beautiful woman. And as he watched her stroke her father's hand, he wondered how much the inner Vicky had changed. But that was a question she had never allowed him to ask.

He watched her face and couldn't help his lips spreading into a smile. Despite her determined efforts to appear so capable, so completely in charge, she was unable to mask the compassion that she obviously felt for her father, and in that moment Roger knew that on the inside she was the same kind, empathic Vicky he had first known. He wished he could tell her how much he admired her, had always admired her, but he wasn't sure she would believe him. Yet he couldn't help but respect how she had handled this difficult situation, just like she had once before when she herself had been the subject of his ministrations. That was one of the things that he— He stopped, afraid to shape the word 'love' even in his own head, knowing how futile it was to dwell on the past. He looked over to where she was gently stroking her father's hand and he knew that it was important for him to refocus his thoughts on the present.

'Did you have any warning that that was what Henry was intending to do?' It was Roger who broke the silence. Arthur seemed to be sleeping.

'Yes, we both did. Henry told us last week that he was going to sign up,'

'And what was your father's reaction?'

'Dad seemed genuinely proud – even pleased. It can't be that that's triggered this attack, can it?' Vicky said.

Roger shrugged. 'It's impossible to say but I doubt it. With damage such as your father suffered to his lungs, it doesn't have to be anything you can put your finger on. There's any number of things that could bring on such an attack.'

'So we can expect something like this to happen again? At any time?' Vicky asked. She turned to look at Roger and though she was dry-eyed there was a sore-looking redness round the rims.

'It's possible,' Roger said, 'if I'm brutally honest.'

'I don't understand my brother,' Vicky said. 'I'd have thought after he'd seen what two wars had already done to this family, volunteering for a third would never have been on his agenda.' She put her head in her hands. 'He knows what could happen.' Her voice was muffled. 'But he doesn't seem to care. That, I suppose, is typical Henry.'

'And did you try to dissuade him from going?' Roger asked. 'Did you point out your position regarding . . .?' He nodded towards Arthur who was now breathing deeply and steadily with only a slight wheezing sound as he exhaled. 'He must know how difficult things are for you trying to cope with it all.'

Vicky gave a sardonic laugh. 'It seems that when you're the prodigal son you don't have to care; you can get away with anything.'

'I suppose in a strange way you should be flattered,' Roger said. 'Henry sees you as his big, capable sister who doesn't need help.'

'Yes,' she said, 'the sister who picks up after him and who deals with everything he leaves behind.'

Roger smiled. She was being so brave, taking on whatever life threw at her, he thought.

'I'm sure you must worry about not being able to cope in an emergency and I know things could change very quickly, but I think you're a lot stronger than you give yourself credit for.'

'You mean I shouldn't have called you tonight?' she interrupted. 'I'm really sorry; it won't happen again.'

'No, no, I'm not saying that it wasn't appropriate to call me out tonight.' Roger was regretting what he had said now. 'Really, you mustn't hesitate to call me day or night if you're worried. I totally trust your judgement on that one.'

They sat in awkward silence for a few moments before Roger asked, 'Will you be seeing Henry again or has he already been sent away for training? I don't suppose there's any possibility of making him change his mind?'

'There's still a few days before he says his final goodbyes, though Dad could find that upsetting, don't you think? But I believe he's actually signed up now so there's no going back.'

Roger looked at Vicky, not wanting to ask what Henry's reappearance might do to her. Vicky sighed and stood up. 'But you don't want to be spending what should be your evening off hearing about our family nonsense. I do appreciate you coming out, especially when you're having to use your bike, and I'm sure Dad will want to say thank you too when he wakes up to what's happened.' She moved towards the door and Roger moved with her.

'Vicky,' he said, 'I want you to know that you're not completely alone with this, although I can see how it might feel like that sometimes. I am here for you.' Without thinking, he clasped her arms and was pleased when she didn't shy away. 'I want you to look at me,' he said, and she looked up, startled. He removed his hands. 'I'm here for you, always,' he said again.

Vicky looked away and nodded.

'I'm hoping things will settle down for a while now. I honestly think your dad will be all right for now at least, but you mustn't hesitate to call me if he does have another episode.' Roger looked around the tiny room. For him, this was often an awkward moment with patients, and in this instance he was glad Arthur was part of the GPO's Health Insurance scheme which would cover his bill. He always felt uncomfortable charging patients when he knew they were having to pay the bills for his visits from their own pockets.

Roger felt confident that Vicky had everything under control and he made a move to open the door before the two of them stood together for a moment. It took some willpower on his part not to put his arms around her completely and offer a more concrete form of support. Instead, he clenched his fists, holding his arms stiffly by his sides, and then settled for parting with a firm handshake.

All the way home, as he pedalled through the deserted streets to the outskirts of the town, Roger worried about Vicky and tried unsuccessfully to erase the vision of her sad eyes from his mind. She was a grand lass, as local people were always reminding him – still young enough to look pretty, and interested enough in things going on around her to be good company. But right now there was no doubt she was facing an almost impossible situation as she juggled her various roles and he had no easy solution to offer. When would Arthur wake up to the fact that he was undervaluing her contribution and that without her the whole household, including the Post Office business, could fall apart?

When he finally reached home he rode up the path and dismounted, then wheeled his bike to the gable end of the house where he parked it with the rest of the family's bikes under the tarpaulin that protected them from the elements. His mother must have been watching out for him for he could see that she had opened the side door before he'd even had time to unhook his bicycle clips.

'You must be worn out,' she said as he wiped his feet vigorously on the coconut matting. 'Julie was sure she would still be awake when you came in because she wanted to make sure you hadn't forgotten your promise to take her to the park fishing tomorrow. She made a valiant effort to keep her eyes open, I must say, kept insisting I read her one more story, but in the end she gave in.'

'Is she awake now?' Roger asked.

'No, she fell asleep in the middle of one of her favourites second time around – or maybe it was the third – and thank goodness she's stayed that way. I've just looked in on her now.'

'I hate to say it but I'm glad to hear that, for I'm afraid I'd have had little patience for reading stories tonight,' Roger said. 'And I must admit, I had forgotten it was tomorrow I said we might go fishing. I've had a lot of other things on my mind.'

'A difficult visit?' Freda said.

Roger paused to think for a moment as the events of the evening replayed in his head, leaving him with a clear image of Vicky's face. 'You could say that,' he said. He patted his mother's hand. 'But it will all still be there tomorrow – and right now I could murder a cup of tea.'

# Chapter 6

Sylvia Barker whipped off her apron and ran into the shop when she heard the ping of the doorbell. It had been a slow day. In fact, it was already mid-morning and this was her first customer, so she was disappointed to find it was only the postman delivering the second post of the day. By the time she came through he had deposited several envelopes on the counter and turned to leave.

'Sorry to disappoint you that I'm not a customer, Mrs B,' he said, as she appeared behind the counter, 'though I'll be back later to buy something when I've finished my rounds. I promised the wife I'd pick up some darning wool.' He leaned over the counter confidentially and Sylvia was frightened for a moment that all the letters and small packages from his heavily laden sack would spill out and upset her carefully balanced displays of wools and knitting needles. 'You might not believe it, but I'm wearing through the toes in my socks like there's no tomorrow and my missus says I'll have to go without socks if I don't bring home some darning wool today as she certainly can't afford to keep replacing them.'

At that Sylvia laughed. 'Don't worry, if all else fails *I'll* darn them for you. I don't charge much.'

'Let's hope it doesn't come to that,' he said, and with a mock salute he left the shop.

Sylvia picked up the post, mostly large brown envelopes addressed to Archie that she knew must be bills, and she tossed them to one side. She was more interested in the one smaller white envelope that looked more personal, though from the thickness of the contents it seemed to enclose an unusually long letter. She wasn't used to seeing such good quality paper and she rubbed the thick vellum between her finger and thumb.

'This is nice, I must say, much better than I ever use. I wonder who it could be from?' She spoke the words out loud, something she often did when she was on her own though she never owned up to it. The occasional letters she sent were usually written on the flimsy onionskin paper stenographers used for copying. Archie brought piles of it and packets of brown envelopes home with him every time he visited his company's main office. Sylvia weighed the letter in her hand, noticing the London postmark, then turned the envelope over but there was no return address on the back. She took it into the room behind the shop where her cup of tea had grown cold and searched out the slim dagger of a letter opener that Rosie had bought her for Christmas one year while she was still at school.

Sylvia wasn't sure she recognised the handwriting, but as soon as the pages tumbled out from the torn envelope she realised who it was from. She felt her hands turn cold as she was clutched by a sudden fear, though she knew it was silly. How could she be affected by someone she hadn't been in touch with for years? Not that Sylvia didn't think of her sister often, but they hadn't exchanged letters for such a long time that she couldn't imagine why Hannah would be writing to her now – unless it was to tell her some bad news.

She stood for a few moments staring at the familiar scrawl that filled the small pages. If it was bad news she wasn't sure she wanted to know. Her hands shook as she tried unsuccessfully to refold the papers and put them back into the envelope. She brewed a fresh pot of tea and sat down to sip it slowly as she pulled the envelope towards her and settled her half-moon reading glasses halfway down her nose.

She had only got as far as, *Dear Miriam, I hope this finds you as well as it leaves me here . . .* when a mist clouded her vision. If she had needed confirmation regarding the letter's sender, her sister Hannah was the only person apart from her mother who had ever called her Miriam and the shock of seeing it written like that brought a lump to Sylvia's throat. Certainly no one in Greenhill knew that was her real name. She rubbed her eyes and tried to read on, but she was interrupted by the ping of the doorbell and she went scurrying once more into the shop.

There were several more interruptions after that – mostly for the collection of items that had already been put aside to be paid for each week on the never-never – and Sylvia only just managed to finish reading the letter through to the end before Rosie came home from work. When Sylvia heard the thud of her daughter's heavy work boots and the click of the back-door latch announcing Rosie's arrival, she quickly wiped away the watery accumulation that had pooled in the corners of her eyes and stuffed the sheets of paper back into the envelope. She looked round urgently then slipped the bundle into the table drawer. She took several deep breaths as she heard Rosie's voice ring out, 'It's only me!'

For a few moments she stared down at the drawer, unsure what to do next. Archie would be home soon as well. He had telephoned from the warehouse where he had gone to collect a van full of new shoe samples and she expected him back shortly. She would have to tell both him and Rosie about the letter as decisions would have to be made, though she didn't want either of them to actually read it because there would be too much to explain. She didn't want to tell her daughter the whole story right now, or to fill in for Archie the details about her family that he didn't yet know. She decided to leave the letter where it was for now and to tell both her husband and her daughter about the main thrust of its contents while they were having their tea, then she hesitated, but the shop doorbell tinkled and she knew it was too late to change her mind.

It was Archie, for once returning home in time to join them to eat, though Sylvia had to admit he was such a stranger at the dinner table these days that his presence felt like that of a visitor. Unfortunately, like an uncomfortably fidgety visitor who had already been to the local pub and downed several pints. She could smell it on his breath almost as soon as he set foot in the room – and when she recognised the unsteadiness of his gait, she suddenly felt fearful.

'And how are my lovely girls tonight?' Archie slurred his words slightly as he slid his arm round Sylvia and planted a wet kiss on her cheek. Rosie managed to duck out of his grasp and slipped into the kitchen to wash her hands.

'Your tea's up if you want to sit down,' Sylvia said, following Rosie as quickly as she could. She returned with a plate in each hand and put one of them down in front of Archie. It was piled high with beans surrounded by thick chunks of toast smothered in margarine.

Archie frowned as he glared down at it. 'What's this muck supposed to be?' he said. Despite the crudity of his words, for a moment his voice sounded reasonable, although from the way he screwed up his nose as he bent to sniff the beans, Sylvia realised with trepidation that what would follow would be anything but reasonable.

'I'm sorry, but I've had no time to do any serious shopping.' She flapped her hands uselessly in the air. 'You didn't give me much warning that you'd be coming home today and the local shops don't have very much choice anymore. There's very little meat or fish and hardly any eggs or cheese on the shelves, not now that it looks as if there really will be a war. I don't know if it will be easier or harder if they actually do start rationing things.' She punctuated her comments with a nervous laugh but even to her own ears it sounded more like a whimper.

Archie acted as if he hadn't heard her at all. 'You mean you expect me to eat that rubbish after a hard day's work? Are you kidding me, woman? When I've been stocking up the van, then driving to Derbyshire and back, and God knows what else today?' His voice was getting gradually louder and Sylvia felt cold shivers throughout her body, as if her blood was turning to ice. She wasn't sure whether to sit down and try to brave it out by eating her own portion or to disappear into the kitchen and wait till he went out again as she knew he was bound to do. In the event she did neither, for he was too quick for her. His response was to pick up his plate and throw it hard against the wall, narrowly missing Rosie who was about to sit down. 'That's what I think of your so-called bloody tea!' he yelled.

Shards of china flew in all directions and Sylvia watched helplessly as clumps of beans and globs of tomato sauce were glided slowly down the loose flaps of faded sunflowers – all that was left of the wallpaper. Sylvia could see Rosie's knuckles turn white as she gripped the table; her jaw was clenched too and she uttered no sound. She never did intervene when her father was in one of his moods and Sylvia didn't blame her, for they both knew what he was capable of, particularly when he had had a few like he had now.

As if reading her thoughts, Archie stood up. He pulled himself to his full six feet and, grabbing hold of Sylvia's blouse, lifted her off the ground, at the same time pulling her towards him so that their faces were almost touching. She felt the buttons pop and heard the silky material rip.

'I'm going to a place where they serve proper food!' He spat out the words. 'And where there are women who appreciate a proper man,' he added with a snarl. Before letting go he suddenly brought up his fist and aimed a punch at the side of her head. Sylvia's instinct was to turn her head sideways and her gasp turned into a sob while her head was spinning as she crumpled to a heap on the floor. She seemed to take the full force of the blow to her eye and cheekbone but she was thankful that he had narrowly missed making contact with her nose. Black eyes healed much faster than broken noses.

Archie didn't wait to find out the extent of the damage. To Sylvia's relief, he grabbed his jacket from the bannister and slammed shut the door that led into the shop. She heard the ping of the till and knew she could say goodbye to the day's takings. They would no doubt soon be on their way into the pockets of Fred Worral, the landlord at the Stoat and Weasel, the pub across the road from the Presbyterian church which Archie had once pretended he belonged to. He often joked that he was going to visit Richard Laycock the vicar, a widower who lived in the adjoining manse with his seventeen-year-old son, Geoffrey. But Sylvia knew from experience where he would really be and that Archie would not be back until closing time.

At the sound of the front door banging shut, Rosie went into the kitchen and came back with two well-soaked tea towels. They didn't have an ice box like some of their neighbours so she made do with cold water from the tap. She handed one to Sylvia to put over her rapidly swelling eye while she began attacking the wallpaper with the other, trying to gather together the glutinous mess that was still dripping onto the carpet. She knew from past experience that it was best for everyone if she removed the evidence as swiftly as possible, for if her father followed his usual form, by the morning he'd be full of apologies and it would be as if the entire episode had never happened.

Sylvia sobbed quietly as Rosie handed her the cold compress. She knew that she, too, would have to blot out the incident as soon as the swelling was under control. She was already trying to distract her thoughts from the pain of her cheekbone and the puffiness she could feel developing underneath her eye by thinking about the letter that was still in the drawer and what she might want to say about it now. She couldn't put it off, and it was essential she responded to her sister as though nothing was amiss. Indeed, she was already thinking about how she might frame the conversation she would now have to have with her daughter, going over in her mind the actual words that would best describe the long-kept secrets she imagined she would be forced to reveal.

Rosie had put on the radio to fill the edgy silence as soon as her father had slammed out of the house, but once the news had finished Sylvia got up and turned it off.

'Aw, I was listening to that,' Rosie complained as she wiped the last of the sauce from the wall and swept as many of the smaller chips of china that she could onto the dustpan.

'Oh, were you? Sorry, but there's something I need to talk to you about,' Sylvia said, her mind elsewhere.

'I was going to tell your father at the same time but . . .' she shrugged, 'under the circumstances I think I'll save that for another time.'

'What's that then? What's so important that you've got to talk about it now?' Rosie had thrown the last of the rubbish into the bin under the kitchen sink and was now busy attacking a broken fingernail with a well-worn metal nail file. She took a chair by the table while she inspected the nail and waited for her mother to sit down. Rosie stared at her intently, her brow wrinkled.

'I received a letter today,' Sylvia said softly, followed by a pause while she tentatively dabbed the compress on her eyelid.

'Yes? And? Congratulations?' Rosie said. 'What am I supposed to say? Should I be excited?'

'I don't know about excited, but the contents of the letter do affect you,' Sylvia said. This was followed by another pause and Rosie looked exasperated.

'Do you know, if you're trying to get me interested in your stupid post I'm not sure this is the best time to be doing it,' she said crossly. 'We've just had a major incident here, in case you haven't noticed. Maybe we should talk about that?' She carried on filing her nails as if she expected that to be the end of the conversation.

Sylvia ignored her. She turned the cold compress over, pressing the cooler side to her inflamed eye. 'How would you feel about having someone come to stay with us?' she said eventually.

Rosie frowned. 'What, with stuff like *this* going on?' She indicated her mother's face.

Sylvia didn't want to admit that that had been her first thought when she had read the letter. 'I'm sure things like this would stop if there was someone else in the house,' she said instead. 'You know how charming he can be around strangers.'

'What? You think it might put an end to it once and for all if there was someone else here living with us full time? Then maybe we should have taken on a lodger years ago.'

'You never know,' Sylvia said with a sigh. 'After all, it doesn't happen very often that he loses his temper like that – and there's usually good reason when it does happen.'

'What, like tonight?' Rosie said with heavy sarcasm. 'Then I'd rather you tell him about this amazing person who's going to change his behaviour than me.' Rosie gave a wry laugh.

'I will. If I can catch him at the right moment.' Sylvia spoke with more confidence than she felt. 'But I want to know how you'd feel about it first.'

'It would depend on who it was and how long they wanted to stay,' Rosie said. 'But hang on a minute, where would they sleep?' She went over to the couch and picked up one of the cushions, showing Sylvia where the flattened stuffing was beginning to push its way out through several places with torn stitching. 'This old thing has seen better days. They wouldn't last long, kipping out on this.'

'No, of course not.' Sylvia gave a little laugh. 'She'd have to double up with y—'

'Are you kidding?' Rosie exploded before Sylvia had finished the sentence. 'Me, share my bed with a complete stranger?'

'It's not really much different from you sharing with Violet when she stops over,' Sylvia said defensively.

'It's very different! She's my friend.' Rosie frowned at Sylvia. 'We grew up together.'

'Do you know it's not that long ago that stagecoach travellers on long journeys had to share a bed with folk they'd never set eyes on before, when they stopped at coaching inns,' Sylvia said.

'Then all I can say is thank goodness we're living in the twentieth century,' Rosie said. 'But why would anyone want to come voluntarily to somewhere like Greenhill? There's nothing much goes on here. And once the war starts there'll probably be even less.'

'Oh, but that's the point,' Sylvia replied. 'That's exactly why people would count themselves lucky if they were evacuated to a place like this. Compared to the large towns and cities they'd be coming from, this place would be so quiet.' She hesitated before deciding to go on. 'It's not likely to be a target for German bombs,' she said at last.

Rosie gasped. 'Do you really think that's what's

going to happen if there's a war? They'll be dropping bombs on us?'

'That's what most folk round here reckon will happen. Otherwise why else would the likes of you need to be working in a munitions factory?'

Rosie looked stunned, as if she had never considered such a thing.

'I wouldn't be a bit surprised if Greenhill wasn't on the list as a place to try and evacuate children to, particularly if the authorities want to get them out of London. I mean, it's surrounded by countryside where they could run around freely but it's near enough to a big city like Manchester so they wouldn't feel totally cut off. I bet there's lots of families round here would be willing to open their homes to city kids if the council or whoever asked them. Particularly if there's money involved.'

'Is that where this mystery person comes from? London?'

Sylvia nodded.

'But this isn't an official request, from the authorities or anyone?' Rosie was puzzled.

'No. Nothing like that. This is personal.'

'When are you going to tell me who it is? It can't be a complete stranger or else how would they know to write to you? Is it someone we know?'

'It is someone I know, well . . . partly. You don't know them at all.'

Rosie put aside her nail file. 'This is beginning to sound more and more strange. Do you mind telling me what's going on here? Who are we talking about?'

'We're actually talking about your cousin Claire.'

'My cousin? I didn't know I had any cousins. Claire who? And where's she suddenly sprung from?'

'I'm not sure of her surname; there was talk of them changing it.'

'And she lives in London?'

Sylvia nodded. 'At the moment.' She looked away; she was finding it hard to meet Rosie's astonished gaze.

'And how old is this Claire?' Rosie asked.

'You were born round about the same time, so around twenty, though I've never actually met her.'

Now Rosie's mouth opened wide in surprise. 'But you've known about her all this while? How come you've never mentioned her before?'

Sylvia pursed her lips and didn't respond, but that didn't stop Rosie asking more questions. 'So that means you've got a sister or a brother somewhere that I don't know about? I'm guessing in London?'

Sylvia nodded again. 'Yes, I've got a sister.'

'Are there any other relatives lurking about that you've kept from me?' Rosie asked.

'No. And I've not kept them from you, it's just that it's never come up, that's all,' Sylvia said. She was stung by what Rosie might be implying but she knew she could never let her read the entire letter.

'Then tell me more about your sister and this Claire. Where do they live in London? Not that I'll know the place, never having been allowed to go there.'

'No, it's unlikely you would have heard of it. It's a village on the outskirts of the city called Cricklewood. As I remember it, it's quite posh – or at least it used to be. They've got quite a fancy house. Much posher than this.' Sylvia found it hard to suppress the feelings of inadequacy that suddenly overwhelmed her, even after all these years. They were the same feelings she always felt when she thought of her older sister's life compared with her own and they lodged deep in the heart of her very being.

'Let me get this straight: your sister suddenly wrote to you out of the blue asking if her daughter could come here to stay?' Rosie still looked puzzled.

'That's about it,' Sylvia said, relieved that the worst of that particular conversation was over.

'Blimey!' Rosie said. 'She's got a bit of a nerve after all this time. Don't you think?'

'I can understand how she feels,' Sylvia said. She felt the need to defend her sister. 'She sounds genuinely worried that London is going to be bombed.'

'When was the last time you heard from her?' Rosie wouldn't let it go.

Sylvia shrugged.

'Does she know about me?'

'Yes, she knows about you. We both—' She stopped

suddenly, angry that she felt she had to justify herself to her daughter.

'And how long does this Claire want to stay for?' Rosie asked.

'I don't know,' Sylvia admitted. 'I suppose it depends how long a war would last. A couple of months?'

'That long? So who's going to pay for her? We can't afford another mouth to feed, not on the old man's wages.'

'Don't be so disrespectful of your father!' Sylvia snapped, though she hated to admit Rosie was right. 'But I can't see that being a problem. Hannah said she would cover Claire's expenses and I'm sure she'll be good for the money. I don't think she's expecting to put any financial burden onto us.'

'I still think it's a bloody cheek, to drop it on us like that, out of nowhere.'

'Oh Rosie, I do wish you wouldn't swear like that,' Sylvia complained. 'It's so unladylike.'

Rosie rolled her eyes heavenwards.

'But whichever way, I don't think you should dismiss this idea out of hand. I think Claire could be doing you a favour if she came,' Sylvia said.

'How do you work that out?' Rosie said. 'She'd be doing *you* the favour if he learned to keep his hands to himself while she was here.' She jerked her thumb in the direction of the door.

'I wasn't thinking of that; I was thinking more that

I could get her to help out in the shop, now that you've got your job at the factory. I'm sure that would be a very satisfactory solution that would suit everybody.'

'I still don't like it, the idea of having a stranger in my bed,' Rosie grumbled.

'Suppose it was the other way around?' Sylvia countered. 'How would you feel if the boot was on the other foot?'

'What? Would you really expect an aunt I've never set eyes on to take me in?'

'Why not? It's family. Where else should she go?' Sylvia challenged Rosie.

Rosie shrugged. 'Now all you've got to do is convince my father,' she said quietly under her breath.

Sylvia caught her words but didn't respond. She knew she still had one more enormous hurdle to jump because Archie had never met Claire. But that would have to wait for another day. And who knew how he would take the news. She was hopeful that it could all work out in her favour. Archie might choose to spend more time than usual down at the pub but she was certain he wouldn't want to be shown up by behaving badly in front of a stranger. For now, she considered it a success to have convinced Rosie. She stood up slowly, relieved that her head had stopped spinning and went into the scullery to wash what was left of the dirty dishes.

Rosie waited until Sylvia came back into the living

room. 'So?' she said after a few minutes. 'Are you going to tell me more about my long-lost relatives? Are there any more surprises in store?'

Sylvia could feel both her cheeks burning now as she thought about the letter once more. It was a good job Archie was out, she thought, for even he didn't know the whole story and she didn't know how much she would end up telling Rosie now. 'Depends how you look at it,' she said.

'Why did this aunt – what did you say her name was? – why did she go to London in the first place?'

'Hannah didn't go to London from here,' Sylvia began, 'it was the other way round. I came here from London after I met your dad.'

'How long did you live in London?' Rosie sounded really curious now and Sylvia didn't know whether to be glad or worried that she had finally piqued her interest.

'I grew up in London. I went to school there.'

Rosie looked surprised. 'I always assumed you came from Manchester.'

Sylvia didn't respond for a moment, then she shook her head and instantly regretted it. She steadied it in both hands until the pain stopped. 'We lived in London,' she said, though she realised that she still couldn't tell Rosie the whole story.

'Do you remember much about London?'

'Of course I remember it. I lived there till I met your dad.'

'Does Dad come from London, then?' Rosie sounded incredulous, as though she could never imagine such a thing. 'He doesn't sound like he does.'

'No, your dad's from round here. But he was working down south for a while. That's where he began selling shoes. He was working for the same company he does now. He was just starting out but then his mother got sick and he had to come back. The company carved out an area in Derbyshire for him.'

'How did you two meet, then?'

'We met at a dance hall. There was one in Shoreditch – I forget what it was called. They used to have special dances with one of the jazz bands playing every Wednesday and Saturday night.' Sylvia's eyes unexpectedly misted over as she recalled the early days of their courtship and the lead-up to their marriage. 'He was a good dancer, was your dad, and everyone used to say what a handsome couple we made. I spent ages practising the steps on my own so's he'd think I was better than I was.' Sylvia couldn't help smiling at the memory. 'I must admit I enjoyed showing off a bit.' She sighed. 'We hadn't been courting that long when he asked me to marry him. Times were hard; it was soon after the Great War so we were well-placed with him having a job. It seemed like a good idea to come to live up here though, because property was so much cheaper up north. I'd been living in digs on my own; I had one room in an old Victorian house that had been split up so I was glad to leave it. And he had no one down south to stay for. Besides, his plan was for me to take over his mother's shop at the time. She'd been poorly and she was getting to be quite frail by then so it did seem to make sense.'

'And didn't you mind leaving your family?'

'My mother had died already. She got TB. Consumption, they used to call it. But Hannah and me . . . well, we didn't see eye to eye. She was already married and we didn't see that much of each other. To come up to Manchester . . . for me was like a big, exciting adventure.' She sat back on the couch and closed her eyes while she lifted one of the loose cushions and rested her head. Instantly, images of Archie Barker swam into focus. She'd been totally smitten by him but that wasn't something she felt she could say to her daughter. It was hard to believe now, but back then he had been a really good-looking man, before the beer had over-reddened his cheeks and bulged out his belly well beyond the constraints of his belt. She was the envy of most of the girls at the dance hall as any one of them would have loved to hang up her hat with him and they were green at the gills when he came to pick her up at the sweatshop where most of them worked. Hadn't they been jealous when he'd asked her to get wed?

Sylvia blew her nose cautiously into a tiny cotton handkerchief with an embroidered motif in one corner and thought about the young Archie. She almost wanted to laugh when she thought of Archie then and Archie now. When she had first known him, he'd had a fine physique and he'd done his best to keep fit. Not like now, when he found the walk home from the pub up a slight incline something to moan about. She sighed as she thought back. How could anyone change that much? From the loving husband she had truly loved to the beast of terror who used her like a punchbag to the point where she had even thought seriously of leaving him. The odd thing was that, if she was honest, she still found him attractive. He had a certain something that could make her stomach flip somersaults. One glance and an electricity bolt could catch her unawares and rip through her with a hidden magnetism that she could never explain to her daughter. And on the odd occasion they'd been out for a drink together, even recently, she'd seen proof of how he continued to turn other women's heads and beguile them with his glib, if unoriginal, lines of patter. Wasn't that why she accepted his apologies every time he begged for her forgiveness for all his misdemeanours and forgave him when he swore he wouldn't do it again? But she could no longer say that she actually loved him. He'd disappointed her far too many times for that.

'I don't suppose you ever saw his . . .' Rosie hesitated. 'His darker side?' she said.

'Not while we were in London, and once I'd moved

up here I doubt anyone would have believed me if I'd told them. He was always so charming as far as they were concerned – you know how he can be. That's why I never told anyone about . . .' She stopped. 'Nah, but it doesn't matter.'

Rosie sat up suddenly alert. 'Yes it does,' she said. 'What were you going to say?'

'I was thinking of a funny story, that's all. Well, it's funny now, though it wasn't so funny at the time.'

'Go on, you must tell me now; you can't leave it dangling like that now you've mentioned it,' Rosie urged.

'Hannah always called it the pawning tale and I think she was even more upset than I was at the time,' Sylvia said, thinking back. She was not sure whether it was a story she should be telling her daughter, although she would have found it difficult to stop now that she'd begun. 'It happened soon after we got married,' she said. 'We were having a difficult time making ends meet, like most young couples then. Jobs were scarce and money was even scarcer so your dad had to take my engagement ring and a few other little gold pieces I'd been given by his mother to a pawnbroker near our flat in Manchester. The ring was platinum with a very small diamond and none of the other items were worth a large amount, according to my mother-in-law, but the stone in the ring had an unusual cut so I suppose he got a bit more for that. Anyway, we were able to eat well for some time from the proceeds. It kept us going for a bit. Then, thank goodness, he landed his first job after the Great War and there was great excitement, as you may imagine.' She paused and sighed. 'The trouble was, he was so pleased to be earning money that he forgot about the jewellery and he left it in hock. By the time he remembered it was too late to claim the items back. His pawn ticket had expired and it seems the man had already sold the pieces.'

She gave a resigned smile.

'So that's why I've never seen you wear an engagement ring?' Rosie said. Sylvia was about to nod but held her head still just in time. She didn't want to add that that had possibly heralded the beginning of their problems, for she had never forgiven her husband for losing the ring in that way. And she didn't believe him when he subsequently claimed that he couldn't afford to replace it.

'What did his mother say? I never knew either of my grannies but I presume she was still alive while all this was going on?' Rosie asked.

'Oh yes, though she was getting quite frail by then so we never dared tell her the full story.

'Would you ever think to ask him now for another ring?' Rosie wanted to know. 'It would be a good way of getting some money out of him.'

Sylvia laughed, though she instantly regretted the painful movement which felt as if it engaged all the muscles of her face. 'I did in the beginning but then

I stopped. Somehow it doesn't seem to be important anymore.'

'What happened with you and Hannah?' Rosie asked. 'Did you fall out?'

'Sort of,' Sylvia admitted, though it was not connected to the pawning tale. 'After our mum died we more or less went our separate ways. She never wanted me to marry Archie . . .' She hesitated. She had no intention of trying to explain why Hannah had disapproved of Sylvia's boyfriend, even though she'd never actually met him. There were things about Archie that had come between her and Hannah that Sylvia wasn't yet ready to discuss.

Rosie looked surprised. 'What about Hannah's husband? How did you get on with him? Did you like him?'

'Yes, we got on all right though we had very little in common.' She remembered Ivan – harmless but dull were the words she'd always used to describe him and she wondered what he was like now. Archie had been so different from Ivan. Much more exciting. He had always been fun, though that was not a word she'd use to describe him anymore.

'Who knows what he's like now,' Sylvia said out loud with a sigh. 'People change.'

'When you moved up here, did you and your sister write then?'

'At first we did, though we were never great correspondents even in the early days, and it became even more difficult as time went on. Our lives were very different.' *I only have to look in the mirror to see how different*, she thought. *I can't believe I was so madly in love with Archie. I wouldn't hear a word against him and certainly not from Hannah or Ivan.* To Rosie she said, 'After our mother had died and we were on our own for the first time, I suppose we felt at first that we had to keep in touch, for her sake. But once the babies arrived it was more difficult for both of us and we had less time.'

'Those babies being me and this . . . Claire?'

Sylvia nodded.

'When we first got a telephone we tried to talk occasionally, but we were on a party line so we couldn't always get through. And then it was a trunk call and even though evenings and weekends were cheaper it was still very expensive. You can imagine your father didn't like me making long-distance calls, so it wasn't long before we stopped communicating at all.' Sylvia got up painfully, and slowly went over to the drawer in the table where she pulled out the envelope. 'That's why this letter felt like a bolt from the blue,' she said. She stared at it as though she was seeing it for the first time. She had tried to sound blasé about what she had related to her daughter and it had been a huge relief after all the years of silence telling Rosie even part of the story, but she was still no clearer about how she was going to tell Archie of its contents. She could only hope he would accept her niece and not give her cause to have to explain his behaviour while Claire was there.

But it was too late to worry about that now, for at that moment she heard a noise coming from the shop that she guessed was Archie coming home. She moved as quickly as she dared to return the letter to the drawer and, grasping Rosie's hand, whispered urgently, 'We still haven't resolved the question of Claire coming to stay. We'll have to talk again tomorrow, for I'll have to get back to Hannah as soon as possible. In the meantime, I think we'd better get off to bed.'

'And what about Dad? When will you tell him about the letter? After it's all been agreed and settled?' Rosie whispered back. 'How do you think he'll react to that?'

'I'm not sure. I'll have to think about it', Sylvia said the urgency sounding in her voice. 'But enough for now. I've talked a lot more than I intended. Now let's get going upstairs.'

Rosie needed no second bidding; she flew up the stairs and out of sight. She had no wish to meet her father again tonight. Sylvia, however, was still in pain and moved too slowly. She put her foot onto the bottom step and screamed as she felt someone tugging at her hair and yanking her back into the sitting room.

The following morning, Sylvia opened the shop at the usual time. She wasn't surprised when Archie didn't appear for breakfast. Rosie was on the early shift so had already left the house, leaving Sylvia alone with her husband. But for once she didn't feel afraid, not if the state he'd been in when he returned home the previous night was anything to go by. It would no doubt take him some time to sleep off all the effects of what appeared to have been a steady night of drinking and she felt sure that he would be in no state to attack her again. She rarely felt afraid the morning after, firstly because Archie was usually the worse for wear and secondly because he was always so contrite. This morning what she felt was anger. Anger when she looked in the mirror to see what her husband had inflicted on her. Anger when she checked the till and confirmed her suspicions that Archie had helped himself to the whole day's takings the night before. Anger at herself for never having had the courage to leave him.

'I hope you don't have too many customers today questioning where you got that shiner.' Sylvia swung around at the sound of his voice, surprised to see he had come up quietly behind her without her knowing. But what she saw reassured her that he didn't appear to pose any kind of threat. His hair was tousled and the dark shadow of growth on his face picked out his hollow cheekbones so he looked like he hadn't slept for a week. His dressing gown was tied ineffectually across his oversized belly, the two sides straining to meet. Overall, he looked as though he had been thrown the loser's gown after having gone twelve gruelling rounds with one of the world's boxing champions.

'Shall I tell them the truth?' Sylvia turned to face him as she spoke so he could see the full effects of his handiwork. 'Or should I be blaming the cupboard door again?' she said, feeling emboldened by Archie's obviously weakened state.

'Are you saying it was me?' For a moment Archie sounded incredulous and Sylvia felt another flare of anger, but before she could say anything he rushed on. 'Look, if it was me, then I'm sorry. You know I didn't mean it. It was the drink, not really me. You know how things can get when I've had one too many.'

Sylvia bit back the instant retort that sprang to her lips. It was always the same, but maybe this time she could manipulate the situation so it worked in her favour. He seemed sufficiently repentant, as he so often did, that she decided to take a chance and use his moment of contrition for her own purposes. She would tell him about the letter.

'It was you well enough, as you no doubt know. But let me assure you, you won't be able to do any such thing ever again.'

'Oh? What does that mean?'

'It means that in the future there will be someone else here,' she said, to test his mood, 'and I'm sure you won't want to show yourself up.'

'Someone else? Like who?'

'Like the guest we're soon having to stay. A guest who's likely to be here for quite some time to come.' Then she briefly outlined the contents of Hannah's letter.

'What? The daughter of your snooty sister in London wants to come here?' he began defiantly. 'The same sister who was too posh to even meet me, despite the fact that we lived only a simple tube ride away? Why would I want to entertain her kid?'

'You wouldn't have to entertain her at all; that's the point,' Sylvia said, determined to press home her advantage. 'You would hardly need to see her, come to that, for she'll sleep in Rosie's room and work in the shop with me during the day.' She took a deep breath and crossed her fingers for luck behind her back. 'Besides, I'm only telling you as a matter of courtesy because I think you owe me at least one small favour.' She put her hand up to her eye, wincing as it came into contact with her swollen cheek. He turned away and Sylvia smiled. She seemed to have made her point successfully enough, but she couldn't help wondering if she had only given him another excuse to stay away from home.

It was two weeks later that Claire stood on the concourse at Manchester's London Road station and hoped she was in the right place. She had never been out of London before. She was used to the local underground trains and managing all the interchanges, but to travel on a steam train on her own to another big city was both exciting and scary at the same time. She kept reminding herself that at almost twenty years of age she was not a child and she was perfectly capable of finding her way around the country, yet she had to admit that the journey had been fraught. Trying to keep one eye on her luggage while travelling in a confined space with a compartment full of strangers had been unnerving and the younger travellers had been mostly boisterous and noisy so she'd not been able to relax. And now, having arrived at what she trusted was the correct meeting point on the station concourse, she felt no less unsure and as she looked about her she could only hope that even if she wasn't immediately able to identify her cousin, her cousin would at least be able to find her.

Under the clock, her aunt's letter had said, and that was where she was standing. Directly underneath the enormous overhead clock face, looking about her for someone who answered to the description of her cousin Rosie. She trusted Rosie was looking for her although there was no one holding up a sign that said *Claire Gold*. No one with a blue fedora-style hat with a prominent feather in it like the letter had indicated. Claire had not wanted to sound boastful when she described the fashionable suit with the flared skirt and pinch-waisted jacket that she intended to wear, though she realised now that because the fine wool worsted was grey it could easily be overlooked in a dismal station. But she had emphasised the fact that the crimson lining opened into reveres that sat on the lapels – a feature too striking to miss. She had also described the matching crimson beret she had decided to wear at a jaunty angle, and that it would be pinned to her shoulder-length fair hair with an unmissable Charles Horner pearl-ended hatpin. It had all sounded so straightforward, down to the black patent-leather clutch bag that matched her black patent-leather slingback high heels, but what her aunt's instructions had not accounted for were the hundreds of other people who would be milling about on the concourse at the same time. There was no sign yet of cousin Rosie.

Claire took a deep breath and tried to keep calm as she searched for someone in an official uniform so that she might ask for some kind of help, but even as she approached them they seemed to be more concerned with other matters and ignored her. She was on the verge of tears and tempted to walk away from the designated spot and widen her search for Rosie when she finally spied someone sporting a feather in a saucy blue hat running across the forecourt, her eyes wildly searching as she shouted blindly into the melee, 'Claire!'

Claire saw the young woman pause to catch her breath and gave a wave with her gloved hand to indicate that she had seen her, and when she saw the young woman give a tentative wave back with a sigh of relief she began to move towards the running figure.

'My mother will kill me!' was the first thing Rosie said when she finally reached Claire. 'You've got to promise not to tell her I was late.'

'N-no of course not,' Claire said. 'You're here now and that's all that matters.' She gave a nervous laugh.

They stood for a moment while Rosie caught her breath, 'Thank you so much for letting me come to your home,' Claire said, the words rushing out. 'Mummy was getting really anxious every time she turned the radio on and it seemed like the war and bombs were more and more likely to happen.' She hung her head. 'And I must admit I was getting worried too.'

'You'd better grab your suitcase and make sure you haven't left anything,' was all Rosie said in reply and she began to lead the way out of the station, indicating by her hand signals the direction they were heading to catch their bus.

'Mummy said you live in the country,' Claire said after several minutes of silence. She was a little breathless as she hurried to keep up with Rosie. Her suitcase was heavier than she'd thought.

'Well, it's not exactly the country,' Rosie said, 'though you can see the moors from the bedroom window.'

'How very exciting,' Claire said.

'I don't know if your mother told you, but you'll be sleeping in my room,' Rosie responded immediately. 'We'll be sharing a bed.'

There was something about the resentful way she

said it that made Claire feel uncomfortable and she made a mental note to make sure to take up as little space as possible. Suddenly she felt awkward and she looked down at her suitcase which looked unnecessarily large. Had she brought too many clothes? She began to worry. Was Rosie trying to warn her about the situation she would find? She thought she had been careful about what she'd chosen to bring but what if there was nowhere for her to put everything? She tried to sneak a glance at Rosie whose mouth had set into a hard line and worried that she might be starting out on the wrong foot. She had hoped so much to be able to blend in and had promised her mother she wouldn't be any trouble.

'Is Greenhill far from here?' Claire asked as they left the concourse and headed down the station approach towards what looked like a main road.

Rosie shrugged. 'We've to catch a trolley bus and then a local bus. It'll take about an hour – longer if we have to wait for a connection.'

Claire tried not to register her surprise. She was used to travelling distances to get across London but she had imagined Manchester to be so much smaller that bus journeys would take no time at all. She suddenly realised she was hungry, though she didn't want to admit that to Rosie. But thinking back to the station clock it must be well past five o'clock by now. It seemed like a long time ago that she had eaten the sandwich her mother had made for her.

'I always think that trolley buses look more like trams, only without the road tracks, don't you?' Claire commented, when the overhead wires of their bus flashed and sparked as they connected to the electricity source. 'And of course we have lots of local railway lines in Cricklewood. There's a whole network of them which go underground near where we live and Cricklewood has its own station which is only about a ten-minute walk from our house. Where's your nearest station? I wonder if I could have come out on it and saved you the trouble of coming all the way into town?'

Claire was about to say more, not feeling comfortable with the silence that kept lapsing between them, but she was aware of Rosie rolling her eyes heavenwards so she tried not to comment on everything she saw. But that didn't stop her asking questions.

'Are there any other villages like Greenhill near here? Have you got your own cinema or do you have to go into Manchester? Where are the nearest smart dress shops?' she asked in quick succession, though from the look on Rosie's face she worried that she was bombarding her cousin with too many questions without Rosie showing any curiosity in return. After a while, though, Claire sat back in silence, taking in the changing scenery as it shifted from the predominantly red-brick structures of the city centre to varying degrees of the slate greyness of buildings and sky. They seemed to be riding over endless mud-covered cobblestones but she'd seen nothing yet in the way of the promised greenery.

The bus trundled through the sprawling suburbs where the majority of houses seemed to be lined up in rows of back-to-back terraces with the occasional relief of a large stone house with its own garden. In some ways the villages didn't look all that different from Cricklewood in layout, although Cricklewood boasted more signs of industry and several streets of grander brick-built Victorian and Edwardian houses. It wasn't until they eventually transferred to a small single-decker local bus that she was finally rewarded by expanses of green grass punctuated by the occasional tree against a backdrop of hills, which she had definitely never seen in Cricklewood. A street sign announced that they had arrived in Greenhill and, as the bus chugged its way up and down the hilly terrain, Claire was surprised how small the place was. It had narrow streets, many of them boasting a variety of shops selling fresh produce or providing local services. It might be styled as a town, Claire thought, but in reality it was no bigger than a village and it was certainly not as big as Cricklewood.

The bus stopped halfway up a hill by a small parade of shops and they alighted. Claire dragged her suitcase off the bus and thanked the driver, then she struggled to follow Rosie into the end shop called Knit and Sew. They went in through the shop entrance, the doorbell pinging as Rosie pushed it open. An older woman, looking not unlike Claire's own mother, though wearing a far thicker pancake of make-up than Hannah ever wore, instantly stepped out from behind the counter, holding out her arms.

'Claire, my love,' she cooed, embracing Claire in a huge hug. 'I'm so glad Rosie found you – or should I say you found each other? Come in, anyways, you made it. Welcome to our home.' She reached out to take Claire's suitcase but made no attempt to move it. 'Your Uncle Archie was really sorry to be missing you, but he had to go away on business today and he'll probably be gone for some time. He does go away quite a lot, I'm afraid,' she said, taking on a confidential tone, 'though that shouldn't affect us.' She gave a little laugh. 'In any case, if the war does go ahead, chances are that you'll still be here when he gets back. So why don't you take your suitcase up to your room for now. Rosie will show you where to go, won't you, my love? I hope you've left Claire plenty of space in the cupboards.'

Rosie gave her mother a cross look and made a noise that sounded as though she was clearing her throat as she led the way up the stairs.

'I've made a whole shelf ready for you,' Rosie mumbled as she opened one side of the tall cupboard that fitted tightly into the alcove beside the fireplace. The plain wood had once been painted but it looked as if it was ready for a fresh coat. She indicated the highest shelf that Claire could just reach at a stretch.

'And if you've anything to hang up I suppose . . .' She grudgingly opened the door on the other side of the cupboard. 'You'll find some room in here . . .' Her voice trailed off because the rail was already overflowing with dresses and skirts that she pushed as close together as possible.

'That's what you get when your mother's a dress-maker,' Rosie said with a giggle, obviously discomfited at having to reveal the full extent of her wardrobe.

'Is she the knitter as well?' Claire asked, trying to keep her voice light as she pointed to the jumpers that filled most of the lower shelves.

'Well, it's not me, I can assure you,' Rosie said.

'Do you think she'd show me how to knit properly?' Claire sounded tentative. 'Only, these fancy patterns are all the rage and I can only do plain knit and purl so I wouldn't know where to start.'

For the first time, Rosie smiled broadly. 'I'm sure she'll be delighted,' she said.

*And so will I if it gets her off my back,* she added silently.

# Chapter 7

Vicky was woken by much banging and knocking and she hurried downstairs to find out what was wrong. To her surprise, she found Henry noisily opening and closing the doors of the food cupboards. He had thrown packets of biscuits and dry goods onto the table and he was now piling them into a large duffle bag.

'What on earth are you doing?' she asked.

He spun round and glared at her. 'What does it look like I'm doing? I'm off today so I'm taking as much stuff as I can with me. Emergency supplies.'

'But I thought you weren't going for several days yet?' She had still hoped it wasn't too late and that she might have one last chance at persuading him to stay; surely the army would understand if he changed his mind?

'I've got things to do before I actually need to report for training, so I'm leaving Greenhill today,' Henry said.

'You mean you were going to sneak out without saying a word to anyone?' Vicky challenged him.

'You're here, aren't you? What more is there to say? I told you I was going and that's an end to it.' He bent down and peered into the cupboard to make sure he hadn't left anything behind.

'I can't believe what a selfish blighter you've turned out to be,' Vicky said in despair, for once not trying to hide the anger that was constricting her throat.

'Oh, bugger off,' Henry said. 'You always were all about you.'

'Me?' Vicky was stung into responding and she couldn't prevent the tears that sprang to her eyes from tippling down her cheeks. 'Well, go then if that's all you think of me and your dad.'

'You know darned well I'm going with Dad's blessing,' Henry said. 'You're just jealous that you can't do something heroic.'

'Heroic? Is that what you think you're doing? Empty gestures, more like,' Vicky said with disdain.

'Ha,' Henry scoffed. 'You heard Dad. He'd go out there himself if he could. At least I'm not hiding behind a stupid Post Office counter. Why don't you get yourself a proper job?'

'What on earth—?' Vicky began.

'I'd have thought you'd be much more use in the

munitions factory, and you don't even have to walk far to get there,' he said, a jeering note in his voice.

Vicky usually tried not to lose her temper, particularly at home where she knew it disturbed her father, but she could feel her anger beginning to boil and in the heat of the moment she looked round for something to throw. 'Ugh, I hate you Henry Parrott! I want you to know that. And you certainly don't go with my blessing,' she screamed.

Henry stopped what he had been doing and looked into her face. Vicky saw the thing she hated most, for there was pity in his eyes. 'Do you know, you've turned into a right bitter old cow,' he said. 'No wonder your so-called boyfriend left the country. Even fighting in Spain was better than staying here. He probably couldn't bear having to look at the likes of you, day after day.'

Vicky glared at him, horrified. 'How dare you!' She lowered her voice and all but spat out the words, 'You aren't fit to polish the boots of my Stan – or me, for that matter.' She shook her head as if in sadness and disbelief. 'And after all I did for you, even though you ruined my life.'

Henry looked puzzled. 'How do you work that one out?'

'It was because of you that I had to leave school early, you know. Dad said he wasn't prepared to keep shelling out money for Dot to take care of the pair of us when I was old enough to look after you on my own. I should have refused. I should have let him send you away to one of those homes. That's all you're fit for. You're certainly not fit to be my brother and I don't want you around here a moment longer. You can't get out of here soon enough for my liking!' And she grabbed one of the packets of biscuits from his hand and threw it back into the cupboard. 'Go on, get out of here.'

'Don't worry, I'm going,' he snapped back, zipping up his bag. 'The sooner I can stop looking at your ugly mug the better. The war can't come soon enough for me.'

'Well, if that's all you've got to say then you needn't bother coming back!' Vicky shouted, but even as she banged shut the door of the top cupboard, narrowly missing Henry's head, she knew she didn't mean what she had said. He had goaded her beyond endurance until she had uttered those vile words and she immediately wished she could take them back. Knowing she couldn't, she ran up the stairs, where she slammed her bedroom door – momentarily forgetting that her father was still sleeping – and threw herself down onto the bed. It was only when she heard her father's reedy voice calling out, 'Victoria, what on earth's going on?' that she remembered where she was.

'Nothing, Dad,' she shouted back. 'It was just our Henry coming to say goodbye. You can go back to sleep now. He's gone.' And she balled the end of the sheet into her mouth to stifle her sobs.

# Chapter 8

In the High Street haberdashery store, Rosie Barker's thoughts were filled with Trevor – and as she stared blindly at the colourful skeins of knitting wools, she realised they were the kind of thoughts she had no wish to share with anyone. Rosie had been smitten by Trevor at their first meeting on the factory floor and since then had been excited and flattered that he'd paid her so much attention. This was a new experience for her. She had never been particularly popular at school and she'd always had to fight for attention from the lads she'd played with on the street. But with Trevor it was different. He didn't seem to look at any of the other girls and was always hanging around her at break time and at dinner. When their shifts coincided, she would often find him waiting by the entrance ready to walk her home, or as near to home as she would allow him to get.

So she was surprised one afternoon when she stepped up to the gates as the metallic clang of the klaxon horn marked the end of the early shift's working day to find a group of her bench colleagues waiting for her . . . and Trevor nowhere in sight. They were led by her High Street neighbour, Penny Downs.

'We checked the rosters and he's been swapped to lates,' Penny said as Rosie gazed about her, trying to spot Trevor in the crowd.

'That is, if you're looking for who we think you're looking for,' a second girl said.

'We've been wanting to have a private word with you for a while since,' Penny said, 'and as you know it's well-nigh impossible in that place.' She jerked her thumb in the direction of the factory.

'Oh, but I . . .' Rosie floundered, taken by surprise, but the group seemed to close in on her until she was uncomfortably surrounded. She tried to step forwards, then sideways, but the girls stood firm and showed no signs of giving any ground.

For a moment Rosie felt intimidated and she took a deep breath, hoping her voice wouldn't give her away while her eyes appealed to Penny. 'What are you doing? I thought you were my friends,' she said, trying to laugh.

'We *are* your friends, and that's why we want to talk

to you. It's for your own good. Honest,' Penny said. 'I'm sure you remember that I've mentioned it before, but it seems you've took no notice.'

'Notice about what? What is it you want?' Rosie asked.

'We want to talk to you about him. You know . . . what's his name? The one you're always with,' the third girl, who was now standing behind her, said. Rosie couldn't see her face but she could hear a nasty snarl in the girl's voice.

'Trevor Jones,' Penny supplied.

'Ah yes,' the second girl said. '*The* Mister Trevor Jones. How could I have forgotten that?'

'What about him?' Rosie shifted her weight uncomfortably from foot to foot, uncertain about where to look first.

'Are you sure you want to be associated with the likes of him?' It was the third girl who asked the question so Rosie had to spin at an awkward angle to face her. 'We're all wondering if you know what you're doing? Because it seems to us you could end up making one hell of a fist of things if you don't,' she said, indicating the rest of the group.

'Don't forget, you're the new girl here,' Penny said, 'so we're only trying to help. We thought we'd better set you straight before you do something you might regret.'

Rosie focussed on Penny for a moment and tried to stare her out as she was finding it almost impossible to pay attention to the whole group at once. 'What do you mean?' she said, then she deliberately looked from one face to the other, trying not to sound anxious. 'Are you saying I shouldn't be friends with him?'

Now the girls looked at each other. 'At last!' the second girl said.

'You do know he's got a reputation . . .' Penny said and Rosie wasn't sure if it was a question or a statement.

'And that none of us would ever give him the time of day,' the second added and she poked Rosie in the shoulder in a pointed and provocative way.

Rosie recoiled, looking puzzled. 'And just what kind of a reputation would that be?' she said.

'The thing is . . .' It was Penny who spoke again. 'We've seen the way he's always making sheep's eyes at you, giving you smokes, fetching you cups of tea at dinner. And it doesn't seem very healthy to us . . .'

'Cos he's not doing it out of the goodness of his heart.'

'You must know what it is that he's after . . .'

'It can only be one thing with Trevor Jones,' Penny had the final say as each took a turn to pass the warning around the group.

Rosie sighed with relief and she glared at Penny. 'I get it now. Jealous, are you?' she retorted, relieved to feel that she finally understood. But she was disconcerted when the whole group laughed.

'No, it's not that at all. You've got the wrong end of that stick,' Penny said. 'Do you not get it?'

'You must understand . . .' the others chipped in. They still managed to sound threatening but they did begin to pull away. 'What you don't seem to realise is that—'

But Rosie didn't let Penny finish. 'If that's all you have to say I'll thank you to butt out of my business and keep your comments to yourself. No one's going to tell me who I can and can't be friends with,' Rosie said and, with as haughty an air as she could manage, she pushed through the ring of girls and marched away with her head held high.

She didn't want to admit even to herself that she felt rattled by the encounter. Of course she had heard of Trevor's reputation – who hadn't in the factory? And she well remembered Penny warning her before. But she had refused to listen then – and she still didn't want to hear such things, convinced that the 'Casanova' label they tried to brand Trevor with wasn't warranted. 'I take folk as I find them,' Rosie had said whenever anyone challenged her, for it was her honest opinion that no one could be as nice as Trevor had been and not mean it. Wasn't it only yesterday that he'd told her he loved her and she had no reason not to believe him, though it was a secret she would keep tight to her chest for the time being. Behaving badly was what he did with others, she'd decided, not with her, and she knew that for a fact. With her he might have tried to push his luck, asked her to go further than she wanted to, but what boy didn't? But he had never forced her into going too far. He always treated her with the respect her mother had taught her was her due. He was polite and attentive, listening with interest to everything she had to say and as far as she was concerned she couldn't ask for more. Well, not unless she considered the small matter of a ring. She looked down and stroked the third finger of her left hand. Without that she would never let him overstep the mark.

Things remained unsettled at work for Rosie, though she refused to give up seeing Trevor, choosing to ignore Penny and her friends instead. And they weren't much better at home. Rosie had known it wouldn't be easy sharing her bedroom, especially with someone her own age who was used to having lots of space around her, though she had to admit Claire was doing everything she could not to get in her way.

'I think you're getting used to sharing your room, aren't you, darling,' Sylvia said one morning when Rosie added one of Claire's newly washed blouses onto the pile for ironing. 'I told you that would happen, didn't I?'

'You can get used to anything if you have to,' Rosie grumbled, 'but it doesn't mean I like it. I still feel hemmed in and claustrophobic most of the time.'

'Thank goodness she doesn't have as many clothes as you do, is all I can say.' Sylvia tried to laugh it off when Rosie complained and she patted her daughter's arm. 'Or if she has, she hasn't brought them with her.

But you've not been very fair, now have you? I don't know how she's managed to squeeze all her clothes into that wardrobe of yours. Some of her things are really lovely but they're getting very badly creased. You really haven't given her much space.'

'How do you know? You shouldn't have been looking,' was Rosie's immediate and heated response. 'But if you want to know, that wretched suitcase she brought was bigger than it looked; the amount of stuff that came out of it was astonishing.'

At that Sylvia grinned. 'I know what you mean,' she said. 'When she first arrived I made the mistake of trying to pick it up!'

'It's one thing sharing a bed and even a wardrobe,' Rosie said, not wanting to give too much ground regarding her cousin's stay, 'but I didn't realise I'd have to share every aspect of my life with her. 'Rosie would you like to take Claire here, Rosie would you like to show Claire that, Rosie would you like to introduce Claire to— You never stop nagging at me! And if you must know, the real answer is no! No, I wouldn't like to do any of those things, but you won't let me get away from her.'

'You must understand,' Sylvia began, 'you need to make allowances—'

But Rosie swept her arguments aside. 'I understood at the beginning because she didn't know her way around and everything was new, but you seem to expect me to let her trot along beside me wherever I'm going and I'm getting sick of it!'

'But she doesn't know anyone here,' Sylvia said. 'You can't leave her on her own all the time.'

'I know and I've introduced her to some of my friends but she's going to have to make some friends of her own now; she can't expect to be tagging along with me all the time.' *Especially not when I've got a chance to meet up with Trevor*, she added silently, but she had no wish to bring him into the conversation yet.

'Well, you might be lucky with that one,' Sylvia said. 'Your friend Penny came into the shop one day last week for some ribbon and buttons. She thought she'd bring a new lease of life to one of her old dresses and I got Claire to serve her; the next thing I could hear Claire offering to do some major alterations for her. When Penny came in for a trying-on session she seemed to be very pleased with what Claire had done. She really is good with a needle. And then I heard Penny asking Claire to go to the pictures with her and her sister Stella.'

'That's funny, Penny never said anything, and neither did Claire,' Rosie said, feeling yet another barb of resentment against her cousin. She knew Claire was a far better needlewoman than she would ever be but she hated the thought that her mother might be comparing her with her cousin, and she couldn't help feeling an initial stab of jealousy at what she thought was another of Claire's attempts to work her way into Sylvia's good books, like when she was the first at the table for meals or the first to offer to wash up when they had finished eating. Rosie had felt like her cousin was throwing down the gauntlet and it took some time before she gradually began to accept that there really was no need for her to be jealous and that she would be better off stepping back and letting her long-lost cousin do whatever she needed to do to make herself feel that she was part of the family.

Thankfully, Rosie's fears that Claire would be a witness to Archie's beastly behaviour towards Sylvia came to nothing for he had been away selling shoes almost from the first day Claire had arrived, and gradually she began to see that Claire made a much more useful ally than foe and that, in fact, there were some definite advantages to having her cousin live with them.

'Aunty Sylvia,' Claire said one day when the three of them were sitting down to tea, 'I know you don't know me very well yet, so I'm really glad you feel you can trust me to serve in the shop.'

Rosie looked at her in surprise, wondering what this could be leading to.

'You're family; of course I trust you.' Rosie frowned at Sylvia's predictable reply.

'Well, I want you to know I never came here with the intention of sitting about the place all day, so I'm glad I've been able to help.' Claire said.

Rosie's first reaction was to make some disparaging remark to discredit Claire, comparing the work her cousin did in the shop with the important work she was doing in the munitions factory. But when she saw that her mother was actually sitting up and paying attention to her niece, for once Rosie held back and listened to what Claire had to say.

'It's easy enough to ring a few sales into the till and to sell a few items over the counter,' Claire said, 'but I've been wondering if there might be something more that I could do?'

'Such as what?' Sylvia asked, obviously taking Claire seriously.

'I told you when I came that I don't know a lot about knitting, but after all your help I hope you'll agree that I'm a fast learner,'

Sylvia nodded. 'Most definitely. You've mastered the Aran patterns, for example, extremely quickly.'

'Well, I wondered if I could learn a few more skills? If you don't mind taking the time to show me a few more things, then I could do some serious knitting. You know, turn out some items that you could sell in the shop, or even take specific prepaid orders from people who can't or don't want to do it for themselves.'

'Now that sounds like an interesting idea, don't you think so, Rosie?' Sylvia was sounding enthusiastic.

Claire beamed. 'I was looking through some of the patterns only the other day,' she said earnestly, 'and I thought maybe I could knit something for you, Rosie,' Claire offered, 'as a sort of trial piece, if you don't mind being my guinea pig, that is.' She giggled. 'In a manner of speaking.'

Rosie was thoughtful as she felt the familiar wave of resentment and she wondered for a brief moment if she'd done the right thing by dismissing out of hand the idea of working in her mother's shop. Maybe she should have persisted.

'How about if I try to make you one of those new styles with the wide shoulders and the tapering ribbed waist? I could put shoulder pads in to make it really stylish.' Rosie raised her eyebrows at the suggestions. It did actually sound interesting. Sylvia looked interested too. Claire paused and looked from Sylvia to Rosie and back again. 'I don't know how you would feel about that?' she said, with sudden diffidence.

'Hmm.'

'They're all the very latest.' Sylvia looked impressed. 'You'll be like a top-line fashion mannequin on this street if you turn out with one of those, Rosie,' Sylvia said, then she turned to Claire. 'I'm sure I could help you work out the pattern in the first instance if that's where you would like to start. I think it sounds like a great idea.'

'And what about those new Fair Isle patterns?' Claire asked. 'Could you show me how to do that kind of fancy knitting too? I've always wanted to have a go at turning out one of those.'

'I don't see why not,' Sylvia agreed. 'Once you can read a pattern, I always say the rest is easy.'

Rosie managed to swallow the familiar antipathy that she felt towards her cousin when she realised she might be able to turn this situation to her advantage, but before she could say anything she heard Claire bubbling enthusiastically.

'Of course, the one thing I do know how to do is to sew and I did wonder what you would think of this.' She got up from the table and pulled something from underneath one of the cushions on the couch where she had hidden it. 'I thought you could display this in the shop window,' she said, and she lifted a notice she had drawn up earlier.

*NEW DRESSMAKING SERVICE*
*PERSONALISED ALTERATIONS, FINISHING, REPAIRS AND INVISIBLE MENDING, NEW GARMENTS MADE TO ORDER*

*FOR DETAILS ENQUIRE WITHIN*

'I know you already do some dressmaking and I thought we could perhaps combine our skills by offering a sort of repairs and advisory service. Of course, they'd have to pay a fee for each different service and you could have a list of prices for the various jobs up in the shop.'

At that Sylvia chuckled. 'I know where you've got

all those business ideas from, not to mention your actual sewing skills,' she said, thinking of the hours her own mother had spent training her and her sister. 'But it's not something I could think of doing when I was on my own. I've run up the odd dress or a pair of curtains for someone but that was more like a favour. I definitely think that something like this,' she said, waving the poster in the air, 'might draw in new customers and maybe some from further afield.'

This time Rosie didn't know what to say. She had to sit back and admire her cousin's initiative; she was certainly enterprising. Rosie had to accept that she couldn't match it and she looked at Claire in a new light. Maybe, with a few extra pounds coming in, Sylvia wouldn't have to worry so much about Archie's wage packet occasionally going missing.

The main advantage of having her cousin to stay, as far as Rosie was concerned, however, was that Claire deflected the spotlight away from her so that Sylvia was no longer constantly interrogating her about her comings and goings or asking awkward questions like why had she taken up smoking?

'I haven't,' Rosie had snapped when her mother tackled her about it one evening. 'But why would you care anyway? Just because you don't smoke. There's nothing wrong in it.' She felt irritated and hoped Sylvia would drop the subject but she had a hard time dodging the barrage of questions that followed. She had reached the stage when she was about to admit the truth that it was Trevor who had introduced her to cigarettes, but somehow she knew instinctively not to bring his name into the conversation. She had not yet told her mother about him and had no intention of telling her now, so she couldn't admit that she smoked purely in order to please him so that they could slope off together to share a smoke during their breaks. If truth be told, she didn't enjoy smoking, though she loved the sensation of actually holding the cigarettes like she'd seen film stars do. It made her feel grown-up and as so many of the girls in the factory smoked, it made her feel like she belonged.

One Sunday afternoon Rosie lay stretched across her bed, taking advantage of the fact that Claire was out, when her attention was drawn to a small lacquered box that Claire kept on top of the nightstand on her side of the bed. It was pretty, with delicate birds painted on all sides, and Rosie rolled across the counterpane to have a closer look. She ran her hand over it, admiring the smooth satin finish of the wood and she took the lid off to sneak a peek at the contents. Inside, the blue velvet lining was covered with jewellery trinkets that she was surprised to find looked like real gold.

Rosie had never possessed jewellery of any value and she laid out the dainty pieces on the bedcover, gazing at them in fascination. She only possessed some brightly coloured bead and paste necklaces which she kept in an old cigar box in her bedside drawer. She had never before handled the real thing and was surprised at how small and delicate the pieces seemed. Her mother didn't possess any proper jewellery either, and she was frowning, remembering the pawning story, when she heard Claire's footsteps on the stairs and she hurriedly put the pieces back into the box. She replaced the lid and put the box back on Claire's nightstand. Then she rolled back to her side of the bed, lying flat on her back while she tried to compose the expression on her face.

'Everything all right?' Claire addressed Rosie's prostrate figure.

'Everything's fine. Why shouldn't it be?' Rosie said, yawning and stretching. She hoped her face wasn't registering the guilt she felt for rummaging through her cousin's jewellery.

'No reason. I've come up to change my earrings,' Claire said. 'I don't know why, but one of my ears is feeling very sore today.'

'Oh dear.' Rosie sat up and swung her legs off the bed. 'I've often wondered how you manage to wear those things all day.' She came round to Claire's side and peered at her ears. 'Have you really had holes punched into them?

Claire laughed. 'I don't know about punched but yes, I had them pierced years ago when I was a little girl.'

'Wasn't it painful?'

Claire shrugged. 'I don't remember much about it. Why? Are you thinking of getting yours done?'

Rosie shook her head and pulled a face.

'You should,' Claire urged. 'I'll come with you if you want, or we can ask Aunty Sylvia, if you'd rather. Is there a jeweller's near here?'

'Not on this parade of shops,' Rosie said. 'Besides, I'm not sure my mum would approve.'

'Why not? I bet her ears are pierced,' Claire said. 'I know my mum's are.'

'Hmm. My mum doesn't really have any jewellery and I've never seen her wearing earrings, or a ring for that matter,' Rosie said, and she shared with Claire the pawnbroker's tale.

Claire laughed. 'Oh dear, though I don't know why I'm laughing because it's really quite sad. I bet she was upset.'

'Angry is probably more accurate. And she still sounded angry when she talked about it,' Rosie laughed. 'But Dad never did replace it.'

'I don't really have much jewellery,' Claire said, 'and the bits I do have I tend to wear most of the time.'

'I know,' Rosie said. 'I've never seen you take your necklace off.' As Rosie spoke, Claire's hand went instinctively to her throat where her fingers twirled the small flat disc that hung from a dainty gold chain.

'My father gave me this for my last birthday,' Claire said.

'That's really nice,' Rosie said grudgingly. 'I couldn't see my father ever giving me anything like that, not if he thought it might be worth a bob or two.'

'I don't think this can be worth much,' Claire protested. 'It's only small, though it is nine-carat gold and I am rather fond of it, I must admit.'

'I can see why,' Rosie conceded. 'It's got such a pretty pattern on the pendant; I've never seen it close to before.' Rosie reached out to touch the charm at Claire's neck.

'Oh, that's not a pretty pattern. It's a Hebrew word,' Claire said.

'Really?' Rosie was surprised.

'Yes, didn't you recognise it? It says "mazel". It means luck.'

Rosie looked at her quizzically. 'How would I know that?'

Claire's face flushed. 'Sorry, but I thought you might have . . .'

'How do *you* know what it says, for that matter?'

'I . . . I used to go to Sunday Hebrew classes when I was a kid,' Claire said.

'You mean like Sunday school?' Rosie was puzzled.

'Well, yes, I suppose it was, though the Bible we learned was only the old testament and it was written in classical Hebrew. Not that I remember much of it now.'

Rosie stared at her, not sure what to make of what she was hearing.

'I . . . I don't suppose you ever did any kind of Hebrew studies, then?' Claire's words were tentative and she gave an awkward laugh. 'No, of course you didn't.' She answered her own question. 'I don't imagine there were any on offer round here.' She hesitated. 'I don't suppose there are any synagogues nearby . . .' her voice trailed off.

'Certainly none that I've ever heard of,' Rosie said in astonishment. 'Why, are there synagogues in Cricklewood?' As she asked this her face changed and a strange thought struck her. She stared at her cousin for a moment, allowing the information to sink in. 'Are you trying to tell me that your family's Jewish?' she said eventually.

Claire looked down into her lap and nodded. 'Yes, we are. I'm surprised you didn't know.'

Rosie shook her head. 'Does my mother know?'

'Of course, she—'

'Then how come she's never said?' Rosie said defiantly, making it sound like an accusation.

'I don't know. It's not my fault.' Claire was suddenly on the verge of tears.

'I really can't believe it. I never would have guessed,' Rosie persisted. She was struggling to make sense of Claire's words.

Claire shrugged. 'How could you? What is there to guess? Jews don't really have horns that set them apart, you know!' she said testily. "We don't really look different from anyone else.'

'I never thought they did.' Rosie was affronted. 'But . . . I just . . . well, I assumed . . .'

She got up and stood staring out of the window into the street, though all she could see was the shop's awning below, flapping helplessly in the stiff breeze. 'I've never met anyone Jewish before,' she said after a long pause.

At that Claire gave a sudden hoot of laughter. She put her hand to her mouth and pointed her finger at Rosie. 'How can you say that?'

Rosie frowned and turned back to face her cousin. 'Why are you laughing? What are you trying to say?' Rosie sounded incredulous. She was aware that Claire was staring at her and she gave a little laugh. 'No,' she said, 'That can't be!'

Now Claire smiled patiently. 'I'm afraid it is. Think about it. Our mothers are sisters, don't forget. They both had the same mother and they grew up together, even if they haven't seen each other for years.'

'No, something's wrong here. This can't be right,' Rosie said, still trying to make sense of what her brain was telling her. 'My . . . my mother can't be Jewish.'

'Why not? Mine is,' Claire said.

'But she's never said.'

'Have you ever asked her?'

'No, of course not,' Rosie blustered, 'it's not exactly something we would talk about over the tea table, now is it?'

'Then might I suggest that you do?'

'But if what you're saying's true . . .' Rosie's mouth opened wide as she finally processed Claire's words. 'Then *I'm* . . .'

Claire nodded. 'I thought you understood that,' she said.

'And what about my father? Are you going to tell me he's Jewish as well?' Rosie said derisively after a brief pause.

'No, not according to my mother. And Barker's not a very Jewish name. But he doesn't have to be in order for you to be Jewish. In Judaism, the religion passes down the maternal line.'

'What about *your* father? Gold isn't a very Jewish name, either.'

'It used to be Goldberg,' Claire said, as if that explained everything. 'My dad only recently changed it to Gold after his parents died. He thought it sounded more English. But names don't really tell you the whole story. My mum's name is Hannah and I believe your mother's real name is Miriam, which might say that they come from Eastern Europe where our grandmother came from, but doesn't necessarily make them Jewish.'

'Claire Gold. Fancy that. Well, you might be Jewish but you are English first and foremost, just like me,' Rosie announced defiantly.

Claire met her gaze for a moment but soon had to lower her eyes. 'Oh dear,' she said. 'I do seem to have upset you, haven't I? And I'm sorry. I went to a school where everyone was Jewish so I suppose I've never really thought much about it.'

'But no one needs to know that that word on your necklace is Hebrew,' Rosie said.

'Would if matter if they did?' Claire replied.

Rosie stared her out. 'Yes, Claire, I'm afraid it might if we really do end up going to war.'

# Chapter 9

Roger waited until he'd finished his morning visits before taking his letters to the Post Office and he managed to slip inside before Vicky flipped over the notice that warned she was closed for her dinner hour. He was out of his usual morning routine but today he was on a special mission and he had planned his visit carefully. He glanced quickly around, pleased to see he was the only customer in the shop.

'Not like you to be so late, Dr Buckley,' Vicky said. 'You're usually first in.'

'It's been a busy morning. But don't worry, I won't keep you from your dinner. I've not that much to be posted today.' He beamed at her as he handed over the correspondence he had written the previous night.

Vicky weighed and stamped the envelopes as usual and slipped them into the despatch sack, ready to be collected by the Post Office van later but she didn't reciprocate his bonhomie. She actually looked away as she pushed the change from his ten shilling note back towards him; but he had made his mind up and was not to be deterred.

'You're looking tired,' he said, his voice sympathetic. 'I've not seen you since Henry left. Don't you think you might be working too hard?'

'Probably,' she replied with a sigh, still not looking at him directly. 'That, and not sleeping too well. You know how it is, what with the shop, my father, and a home to look after.' Her shoulders slumped. 'And as you say, Henry's gone.'

'What you need is a rest, a break,' Roger said trying to keep his voice bright. 'Maybe even a night out?' He tried to make it sound as if the idea had suddenly come to him rather than something he had been cautiously planning for a while.

'Now where would I find one of those?' she responded automatically with a disparaging laugh as she stared down at the counter.

'You never know. You might be surprised,' he said. 'It would do you good to get out once in a while.' He gave her a moment to consider then said, 'There's a new film on at the Plaza that everyone's talking about. I think it's called *Gone with the Wind*. It's based on an American book. How would you like to go and see it? I know I would.'

She jerked her head up. 'With me?' She looked at him, suddenly flustered, as if unsure what to make of what he had just said.

'Don't you fancy it? I mean, a night out with me?' he said. The words jumped out spontaneously before he could stop them. He hadn't meant to crowd her like this, knowing from bitter experience that she didn't respond well to that sort of pressure. He hoped he hadn't offended her, but it was impossible to tell from her face. He put his fingers on his lips by way of apology. Then he smiled and tried to make eye contact but she refused to meet his gaze.

'Do I take it you don't think that's a good idea?' he asked. 'Even though it's a doctor who's prescribing it?'

'It's a very kind thought,' Vicky said quickly. 'I've heard about that film too, but at the moment I don't feel that I can leave my father alone for a whole evening, not when he's spends so much time on his own most days.'

'Then what we need to do is to find someone to keep him company for a few hours,' Roger said. He did his best to keep his voice light and was encouraged by a moment of hope and the flicker of a smile that flashed across Vicky's face. 'How is he, by the way, your father?' Roger asked, determined to press home his advantage.

'Complaining as usual,' Vicky said.

'That must be a good sign at least,' Roger said, grinning, and to his surprise she responded with a diffident smile.

'I suppose it is. When he moans that he's bored at least it proves his mind's active. The problem is that he doesn't like to go out much, complains that it's either too cold or too hot, both of which make his breathing difficult, but that means that he's stuck in here with no one to talk to all day. So when I come in after I've closed up the shop, all he wants to do is talk, but of course, I find it hard to make the time for him. So he blames me and calls me all sorts of names which, quite frankly, I've learned to ignore. But it's not as if I don't understand. I want to help him and believe me I do my best . . .'

Roger stood perfectly still as the words poured out without stopping. It was as if the dam had burst and she wasn't even conscious of what she was saying.

'He doesn't consider that I've all the chores to catch up with. He thinks now that Henry's gone life should be easier. But it isn't.' She shook her head.

On the surface she looked as though she was in control of her emotions but Roger could see that she was close to tears, closer than he had seen her in a long time and he understood what those tears were really about, because he was one of the few people who knew about her past. When he had first known her, her future had seemed so bright. He had known her fiancé, heard about their wedding plans. But then he'd been there when the letter had arrived with the dreadful news that Stan wouldn't be returning from the Spanish Civil War. He had seen what the news had done to her and how she had suffered from the consequences. Sadly, he knew what it was like to have someone you loved virtually ripped out of your arms and to watch your future crumble, and all he wanted to do now was reach out to Vicky and tell her he understood. He wanted to tell her that she mustn't let go, and that she still had the possibility of a future for there was always hope.

Roger blinked hard and forced himself back into the present. When he was sure Vicky had got a grip on herself once more he said, 'If we're to make it to the pictures, I think we need to get my father on the job.' He tried to sound as casual and offhand as possible.

'How do you mean?' Vicky asked.

'I was thinking that maybe the two of them could spend the evening together, your father and mine. They must have a lot in common; they were both in the Great War and I'm sure they must both have lots of stories to tell. They could look after each other! My dad would love that, I know. He gets a bit lonely sometimes for male company of his own age and it would give my mum a break too.' He ended with a hearty laugh but that didn't stop him scanning her face anxiously for he could see that she was wavering.

He was surprised when Vicky asked, 'Does your dad

play cards? Only, my dad likes a game of gin rummy now and then and I know he's not played for ages.'

'I think Dad can play most games, including a spot of blackjack when the occasion arises,' Roger said and was gratified when Vicky gave him a full smile.

'As you know, he was a GP too,' Roger said, 'though he's retired now. He ran the practice before me, so if there are any problems with your dad's breathing . . . I don't know why I hadn't thought of it before.' He didn't want to tell her he'd been thinking of it for some time but hadn't worked out how to broach it. 'So, what do you think?' he asked.

It was not easy to read her face and for several minutes she seemed undecided, but then, to his amazement, she seemed to relax.

'I remember seeing your dad when I was a little'un and got taken to the surgery. He was very nice to me. Gave me a boiled sweet when I had a cough.' They both smiled at the memory, and Vicky relented. 'I suppose it's not such a bad idea. It would give Dad something to look forward to,' she said, 'though I'll have to be careful how I put it to him; he's quite capable of playing silly beggars if he thinks I'm trying to organise his life.'

'I know what you mean, but I'm sure you can do that well enough; you've had several years of practice.' Roger said, delighted by her response. 'And I'll have a chat with my father,' he said. 'If I play my cards right, he'll enjoy feeling that he's being useful.' Roger chuckled. 'Pun very much intended.'

Vicky thought for a moment then she said, 'The only thing is, your father would have to come round here. I can't have my dad going out at night when he could catch a chill, cos that would be bound to go straight to his chest. I'm sure you understand.'

'I don't think that should be a problem,' Roger said, determined to meet all her objections. 'I could bring him when I come to pick you up and pick him up on my way back.

'Right, then,' she said, 'is there anything else I can get you or is that it?' Vicky was suddenly all business-like again as Roger pocketed his change.

'No, that's all, thanks. I take it you'll come?' Roger looked at his watch. He felt hopeful when Vicky hesitated, then without another word came round from the other side of the counter to turn the sign over to read 'closed'.

'So what have you heard about this film that makes you want to see it, if we can manage to arrange things?' Vicky asked.

'I've heard that Vivian Leigh is very good in it. Reason enough?'

'Ah, but have you heard that it's very romantic?' she asked. 'Clark Gable is quite the heartthrob you know, and makes all the ladies swoon. I could get overcome. Are you sure you're ready for that?'

Roger laughed. 'Is that so?' he said. He was standing so close to her now that their faces were only inches apart and, to his surprise, she made no attempt to pull away.

'There's still time to change your mind,' she said. Her voice took on a teasing tone. For once she was looking at him directly and that made Roger want to smile.

'But it's a story about war and people's reactions to it,' he said, 'so it will be pretty topical if nothing else.' He looked serious for a moment. 'You can change your mind too,' he offered, while crossing the fingers of both hands behind his back.

'Hmm,' she said, 'maybe I should,' and he couldn't be certain whether or not she was serious.

'You can always hide your face in my coat when we get to the scary bits,' he said. He stared at her intently for a moment and was surprised when she continued to meet his gaze, though he couldn't help noticing that her lower lip was trembling slightly. But her voice was strong as she said, 'And where will you look when we get to the bits you don't like?' and that made him laugh out loud.

'I'll find somewhere,' he said. He squeezed her hand and to his amazement she squeezed back.

'OK, the Plaza it is then,' Roger said with a smile. 'That should work out well for everyone.'

'You'd better clear it with your father first,' Vicky

said. 'Make sure he's happy to come here as I'd hate to disappoint my dad if he'd already got his hopes up.'

'I'll let you know in the morning,' Roger said, 'and if all goes well we can go at the weekend. See you tomorrow.' He stepped outside, but as he turned to bid her farewell, he found the door had already been closed.

Vicky didn't mention Roger's suggestion to her father until the following night, by which time she knew that Cyril Buckley had told his son he would be delighted to challenge Arthur to a game of cards.

'What's brought that on, I wonder?' Arthur said. 'I know the old man used to look out for me when I first came back from the war,' he gave a rather artificial cough, 'but that was years ago. Why's he suddenly worrying about me now?'

'Actually, it was Roger who suggested that you might appreciate a bit of distraction now that Henry's gone away,' Vicky said. 'And I suppose Cyril's at a bit of a loose end too.'

'So, what will you be doing while Cyril's here?' Arthur wanted to know.

'I shall be going out.' Vicky did her best not to look at him.

'Where to?'

'To the pictures.' She hesitated. 'With Roger, as a matter of fact.'

'Oh, I see!' Arthur slapped his thigh. 'I knew there

must be some method behind your madness. But I didn't think you were bothered about him, so how come he's suddenly asked you to step out with him?'

'We're not stepping out,' Vicky protested. 'He wants to see the film that's at the Plaza and he doesn't want to go on his own,' she lied.

'Oh, I see. It's nothing to do with the fact that you've only just woken up to the idea of him being sweet on you after all these years?'

'Don't be so daft!' Vicky chastised him. 'What are you blethering on about now?' She pulled him upright then pushed him more roughly out of the way while she finished dusting the arms and legs of the chair he'd been sitting in.

'Never mind you thinking I'm blethering about that Doctor Roger, or however the young pup styles himself, you should be listening to what your father is telling you. He's a good man, is that one. You could do far worse than hang your hat up there, you know. He's been carrying a torch for you ever since—'

'Will you stop being so soft,' Vicky cut off his words before he could finish. 'He never has been sweet on me and he never will be. He's kind because, to my shame, he happens to know most of our family secrets, that's all. And because he's a kind man.'

'Aye well, I still say you're reading this all wrong, only you can't see it. I'm telling you, he's a force to be reckoned with. I believe there's a reason he's kept his word all these years and never spread any tales about this family to a living soul, and that's the truth of it.' He wagged his finger in Vicky's face and she had to step back to avoid him poking her in the eye.

Vicky sighed. It was not the time to be raking up the past now. 'I can leave you a tray ready so's you can make some tea,' she said, making no excuse for changing the subject. And to her relief her father let it rest.

'So, what's on at the Plaza that's so special?' Arthur asked.

'It's a film called *Gone with the Wind*,' Vicky said. 'It seems to have made quite a sensation wherever it's been shown and it's got a British actress in it, Vivian Leigh. Everyone's talking about it.'

'That's the trouble with being in the shop all the time,' Arthur said. 'You're hearing all the local gossip all day long until you begin to think it's important. I suppose you can't help but get caught up in it.'

Vicky shrugged. 'I would hardly say that – and don't worry, it won't make me feel anything more or less about the good doctor, but it will make a nice change to get out of here.'

Vicky trawled in disgust through the deep drawer in her wardrobe where she stored her jumpers. Roger would be here soon and she still hadn't found anything decent to wear. She so rarely thought about clothes these days that everything she pulled out as a possible looked older and shabbier than she remembered. There were one or two that looked as if the moths had been feasting and the rest mostly had large, faded patches under the arms so that almost immediately she stuffed them back into the drawer. It was time she went to the local market; she deserved some new clothes, and she'd best hurry before the rationing that was being threatened took effect. She could go one Saturday afternoon when the Post Office was shut, she decided. On the other hand, she could more easily go to Barkers' Knit and Sew shop a few doors down in her lunch hour, for they never seemed to close. She could treat herself to some fresh wool and a modern stylish pattern and knit something new. Sylvia Barker or that new young girl, her niece or something, who was serving in the shop, might be able to make something up for her. She slammed the drawer shut. But none of that helped with her immediate problem.

Eventually, Vicky pulled her best navy skirt off the hanger in the wardrobe and decided to brush it down thoroughly so that it would at least look respectable, and she matched it up with a pale blue sweater. She stuffed a shoulder pad under each shoulder so that somehow it didn't look as old as it was and she glanced in the mirror before she started down the stairs. Halfway down she changed her mind and went back up again.

'What are you faffing about for?' Arthur sounded irritated when she appeared on the stairs for the third time in yet a different jumper where the only hole she could see was under the cuff in a place that could easily be disguised. 'What's the matter with you? You're up and down like a bloomin' kiddie's yo-yo.'

'I can't decide what to wear tonight,' Vicky moaned.

Arthur tutted. 'It's not as though he's going to see it, whatever you wear.' He sounded scornful. 'It'll be dark inside the cinema and it'll be dark in the street outside by the time you come home.'

'That's not the point. It's to make me feel good,' Vicky protested.

Arthur laughed at that. 'Since when have you cared about things like that? Besides, he's a doctor so he doesn't see real people; he only sees patients or potential patients who are probably all like slabs of meat to him. He'll be more interested in your mind.'

Arthur slapped his thigh and guffawed but tears rose to Vicky's eyes. She liked it better when he said nice things to her like he had earlier. Henry had been just as bad but maybe that was her fault, because she expected too much from them. All she wanted was to enjoy, for once, the sensation of dressing up, of feeling smart. But when her father knocked her down like that he only succeeded in knocking what little self-confidence she had. It wasn't often these days that she had an excuse to wear something different from what she wore day in and day out behind the counter. Why couldn't he see that? But she had to accept some of the blame:

maybe she was being unreasonable in expecting them to understand. How could her father – or Henry, for that matter – know what she needed when she never bothered to tell them? She flopped down onto the couch, deflated, no longer caring that she might be crushing creases into her skirt. If nobody else cared, she might as well not bother . . . but maybe that wasn't quite true. Maybe they did care but had different ways of showing it. She got up and stood for a few moments in front of the mirror over the fireplace. Then she smeared a light coating of bright red lipstick across her pale lips and rubbed a dab of bright pink rouge onto her cheeks the same instant she heard the beep of a car horn. At the same time, the doorbell rang and she let Roger's father into the kitchen.

Vicky hoped none of the neighbours had heard the horn or were watching her as she ran out to the waiting car. All the shops on the parade were closed now and most of her neighbours were already in their living quarters at the back. Vicky felt grateful that she didn't live in an ordinary terraced street because the net curtains would have been twitching wildly by now, she thought. Although there was someone watching. She thought she saw Mrs Boardman from the newsagent's next door standing at the upstairs bedroom window. She glanced up and realised she was right; it must be Caroline Boardman because she waved. Vicky didn't wave back. She strode across the pavement and ducked her head into the car as Roger opened the passenger door for her.

'I thought it was going to rain,' he said as he jumped into the driver's seat beside her. 'I've brought my coat in case it does.'

'Me too,' Vicky said and she gave a nervous laugh, amused that they had begun the evening talking about the weather.

Roger had bought the more expensive tickets in the rear seats of the cinema but Vicky was relieved to see as he led the way that he chose to sit in the first row of the best seats rather than in the back row itself. There, courting couples were already entwined even though the lights had not yet been dimmed in the auditorium. Vicky looked round before she sat down, wondering if there was anyone in the theatre that she knew. When she thought she caught a glimpse of one of the Post Office regulars, she pulled the brim of her fedora-style hat low over her forehead and took her place quickly next to Roger who stood up to help her off with her coat. He had bought a small box of Dairy Milk chocolates and he handed them to her as she sat down. 'A little something to keep us going,' he said, stripping the cellophane cover off the box so as not to make a noise once the film started. Almost immediately, the lights went down and Vicky clasped her hands together tightly underneath her coat that lay folded in her lap.

Vicky was surprised how engrossed she was by the film and had to blow her nose hard into her handkerchief several times. She quickly swiped away the few remaining tears as the lights came up on the magnificent shots of the sacking of Atlanta that signalled the interval. Roger went off almost immediately in search of ice creams and by the time they had finished them, the second half was about to begin.

They talked about the film all the way home, Roger seemingly delighted that Vicky had enjoyed it so much.

'I can certainly see why there has been so much fuss about it,' Vicky said. 'I couldn't help feeling sorry for Scarlett in the end, even though she was so nasty to Rhett, taking him for granted like that.'

'The acting was superb – and I agree, you couldn't help being won over by her in the end, and at least it wasn't too sentimental,' Roger said. 'I would say it was a pretty fair summary of what the ravages of war can do to society.'

'It does make you think,' Vicky said.

Roger nodded. 'And I think we should do this more often,' Roger said as he pulled up outside the Post Office.

Vicky gave him a shy smile. She was surprised how much she had enjoyed the evening. 'It's always great to see a good film,' she said.

Roger was about to get out of the car to open the

passenger door but he stopped. 'Feeling hungry?' he asked. 'I see the fish and chip van's still open for business.' He pointed to the stall that stood in front of the fresh fish shop where Barry and Wendy Hargreaves sold hot battered fish and chips with mushy peas every Saturday night. But Vicky refused automatically.

'No, thanks all the same. I'd better get in and see how Dad is,' she said and she tried to make a hasty exit out of the car.

Roger laughed. 'I'm sure you don't have to worry about him; he's in good hands, you know. It's not as if you left him on his own.'

'I know but . . .' Vicky felt embarrassed, because it was true and it wasn't as if she was really worried; she hoped she hadn't offended him.

'My father might have retired a few years since but he knows how to handle sticky situations should Arthur not feel well. But I bet everything's been fine. There's not too much to get worked up about over a hand of gin rummy,' he said and chuckled.

'No, I suppose not,' Vicky conceded. 'Things have calmed down generally now that Henry's gone, even though I know Dad does miss him.'

'And what about you?' Roger asked. 'I bet you miss him too?'

Vicky shook her head. 'Henry's a pain, to be honest with you. We were always arguing so he's no loss as far as I'm concerned. Quite the opposite, actually; it's nice to have some peace in the house,' she said, her jaw set firm. 'Will you be taking your daughter fishing tomorrow?' She changed the subject.

'It's unlikely to be tomorrow, but I've promised I will take her soon. Didn't you say you used to enjoy fishing in the park when you were young?'

'Yes, I did,' she said

'You should come with us sometime, then.'

Without replying, Vicky hurried out of the car and down the side passage to the back door and Roger followed several steps behind.

The two older men were supping tea and the playing cards were stacked to one side of the table.

'Good film?' Cyril Buckley asked.

'Excellent.' It was Roger who answered. 'We had a lovely evening, didn't we?' He turned to Vicky but she'd slipped up the stairs to remove her hat and coat.

'So who won?' Roger asked.

'He beat me hollow.' Arthur pointed to Cyril. 'But he's promised me a rematch, to give me a chance to win my money back.'

Roger heard the crackle of gravel under the tyres as he drew the car into the driveway and smiled as Cyril got out. A satisfactory evening all round. He certainly hoped he'd be able to persuade Vicky to do it again. There were several films he had heard about that might tempt her out of an evening and he knew he would have no problem persuading his father to have a round or two of cards with Arthur Parrott. He watched Cyril cross the path and almost immediately his substantial figure was silhouetted as the front door opened and light flooded out from the hallway. He could hear his mother's voice calling him to hurry.

'It's for you, Roger,' he realised she was saying. 'It's Mr Bowdon, the greengrocer from the Greenhill parade. He wants to speak to you urgently about his daughter Ruby. I was just going to take a message.'

She held out the telephone receiver from the phone that stood on the hall table by the front door and Roger quickly grabbed it from her hand. He had only recently seen Ruby after she'd been discharged from the hospital. She was recovering well from polio and he was pleased that she'd been making excellent progress.

'Dr Buckley,' he said, anxiously checking the time on the grandfather clock that said it was close to eleven. He sat down hard on the hall chair and listened carefully to what Ruby's anxious father, Billy, had to say.

'All right, Mr Bowdon,' he said. 'But firstly let me assure you that that is highly unlikely. She— You—' he unsuccessfully tried to butt in. 'Yes, you're quite right to let me know and I promise you I will come around to the house so that I can check her out. The thing is not to panic. Keep doing what you're doing. Cold compresses and a cooling sponge bath, they're just the thing, and make sure she doesn't have too many blankets. Give her a chance to cool down and I'll be there as soon as I can.' He stood up and hung the receiver back onto the base. 'I have to go out again, I'm afraid, as you've probably gathered,' he said to his parents who were regarding him anxiously. 'You probably remember hearing about Ruby; she was the young girl who had polio not so long ago.'

'I thought I'd heard she was recovering well?' Freda Buckley said.

'She was . . . she is, but it seems she's developed some kind of fever and, not unnaturally, the parents are extremely anxious, as you can imagine. I'd better go and check.' He went into the first room off the hallway and came out with the leather Gladstone bag that he always carried when he was working. It had been a present from his parents when he'd graduated from medical school. 'I think it's best if I go now to find out what's going on. I can't afford to leave it until the morning in case . . .' He didn't complete the sentence. He'd learned the hard way that you never could be one hundred per cent certain. 'That way, if necessary, I could take them to the hospital. They'd have no easy way of getting there at this hour of night.'

'Sounds like a sensible precaution. 'I'll drive you over,' Cyril offered immediately, and Roger didn't refuse. He saw his mother's mouth open as she seemed about to protest, but she hastily closed it again as Cyril picked up his hat.

# Chapter 10

Rosie was surprised her mother had said nothing more to her about Claire or her relatives and had never actually shown her the contents of Hannah's letter. She began to wonder how much her father knew about her mother's background and what he thought about having an apparently Jewish wife and daughter. But she decided she would not be the one to broach the subject at home. She didn't feel the need to share the secret of her recent discovery with anyone else as she had indicated to Claire when she had sworn her to secrecy.

'I'll say you're a friend of friends from London if I have to introduce you to any of our friends and neighbours,' Rosie said firmly. 'People will understand that I'm sure, as lots of people are heading out of London in case of war for safety. I don't have to say you're my cousin. Least said, soonest mended, I always say,' she added.

If Claire felt hurt by Rosie's reluctance to acknowledge her heritage, she tried not to show it and didn't raise any objections. Everyone knew about the first Kindertransport which had arrived in Britain the previous December and there had been major debates in Parliament about it. The stories circulating about people who were fleeing Europe and were now seeking a safe haven in Britain were very disturbing and she knew Rosie had heard them too. But Rosie seemed to be convinced that so long as she avoided any discussion about the ugly situation that was developing on the continent then she could deny that it was actually happening and Claire realised there was little she could do to change Rosie's mind.

Rosie certainly had no wish to discuss the topic with any of her colleagues at work either. In the past she had heard several disparaging remarks about the perceived power of the Jews who were usually all branded as being rich and greedy, even those whose desperate poverty was clearly catalogued, and she had no wish to become the centre of such misconceived attention. She had declared a tentative truce with Penny and her friends who worked on the same bench in order to make the time they spent together more tolerable, though she made it clear by her actions that she had no intentions of heeding their warnings regarding

Trevor Jones. She refused to talk about any such personal matters and reduced the opportunities for social chit-chat by keeping out of their way as much as possible. She usually shared breaktimes and dinner-times with Trevor alone, when the two of them chose to eat their sandwiches together in a quiet corner of the canteen, followed by a cigarette in the courtyard.

Neither did she deem it necessary to reveal anything about her Jewish family to Trevor. The thought did occur to her to tell him but she suddenly felt afraid as she had no idea how he might respond. They never discussed any serious matters beyond the daily happenings on the shop floor and she realised that she didn't know anything about his political or religious leanings, if indeed he had any. They had been getting along well together, at least superficially, and she had no wish to test out his reactions regarding important political matters now. She was enjoying the idea of having a boyfriend – her first of any significance – and wanted to continue basking in his unadulterated attention for as long as possible. She had begun to relax and to feel almost carefree when she was with him, which was most evenings now that the days were longer and lighter.

Rosie was flattered that Trevor almost seemed to take for granted that they would spend time together outside of work as part of their regular routine. They would usually meet in the park after tea to go for a walk. And as he didn't seem to mind where they went, she would find different paths to follow that steered them well away from her mother's shop and the other shops on the parade. She had no wish to be seen by anyone she knew. However, she couldn't resist his offer of a trip to the funfair that had been set up in the local park prior to the Whitsuntide holidays and would stay there for a few weeks. By that time, she had begun to feel as though they were 'stepping out' as her mother might have put it, although so far she had not actually told Sylvia about her new boyfriend, always claiming that she was going out with unnamed friends from work.

'Well, that was fun,' Rosie said, trying to catch her breath as she and Trevor climbed down from the swing boats. 'Even if it did make me feel a bit sick.'

They had met as usual in their own special place down by the river then Trevor had suggested they head off in a different direction to see what the funfair had to offer.

'I don't feel so much sick as thirsty, all that flying about,' Trevor said. 'What do you say to us going down to the pub?'

Rosie held back for a moment, thinking that the nearest pub was the Stoat and Weasel where her father usually drank. Not that he was home at the present time, so there was no danger of bumping into him by accident. He was in Derbyshire, where he seemed to be spending most of his time these days. But she didn't really want to meet any of her neighbours who would most likely be only too eager to report back to her mother that they'd seen her.

'I'm hardly dressed right,' she said evasively, but that made Trevor laugh.

'You don't have to dress up or owt like that to go to your local. Have you never been to the Stoat? It's nowt posh.'

Rosie shook her head. 'What do people wear then, in pubs? I've not been before. I don't want to show you up,' she said, though she knew it sounded like a feeble excuse.

'You could never do that, darlin',' Trevor said with a grin. 'You always look perfect to me.' To her surprise he brushed her cheek affectionately with his hand.

'Really?' she asked, feeling as if she had been lit up from inside by a warm glow.

Trevor didn't reply but there was a flirtatious glint in his eye.

'I haven't told my mum I might be late . . .' she began.

'Then the earlier we go the earlier we can get you home. Come on, let's go,' he said and she could think of no other objections.

Rosie didn't know what she expected of a pub with a name that was evocative of the countryside, but she was disappointed the moment she stepped over the threshold, for the first thing she was greeted by was what felt like a wall of smoke. The air was so thick and hazy she could hardly see to the other side of the room.

'Gosh! Does it always smell like this?' she couldn't help exclaiming.

'Like what?' Trevor looked puzzled. 'All pubs smell the same to me. Here, have a fag.'

Before she could say anything further he lit two cigarettes at once, Humphrey Bogart style, and handed one to her. The gesture made her want to giggle but she didn't want to embarrass him by making any comment. She took hold of the cigarette and inhaled. It suddenly felt like a very grown-up thing to be doing and she hoped that she looked as sophisticated as she felt. Trevor found two free stools with a small table between them and indicated she should sit down.

'What are you having?' he asked.

'I don't know. What do ladies usually drink in a pub?'

'You mean you were serious that you've really never been in one before? I thought you were kidding and it was just this pub you were talking about.' His look was incredulous and she felt her cheeks redden.

'No, I honestly haven't been in any pub before,' she said, wondering if she had made a mistake admitting that, not wanting to let him down.

'You could have a beer, say a half of bitter or a lager and lime, or a port and lemon. I dunno, what do you fancy?' He sounded slightly irritated.

Rosie looked at the women sitting close by and

noticed several of them seemed to be nursing a long dark drink in a tall glass with slivers of lemon floating on top.

'How's about one like that?' she asked. Trevor nodded and went straight off to the bar.

It seemed like an age before he came back and put two drinks down on the table. Then he began to search in his pockets.

'Well, that was embarrassing,' he said. 'I seem to have spent every last penny at the funfair. Can you lend us a couple of bob? I owe the landlord.' He held his hand out and didn't look in the least embarrassed.

'Two bob? Were they that much?' Rosie was shocked.

'No, but it saves me having to ask you every time I need to get a round in,' he said and he nodded towards the bar where someone she recognised from the factory raised his glass to her.

Rosie felt her cheeks flame but she scavenged in her handbag and eventually handed him a florin, ashamed lest any of the people nearby had heard their exchange.

Trevor went back to the bar several times after that though she continued to sip slowly on her first drink. 'Do you always drink this much?' she said when he came back with yet another fresh glass.

'Who's counting?' He shrugged his shoulders and grinned. 'In fact, next time I'll get you another one, it won't do for you to be so far behind.'

Rosie took a long sip from her glass and shifted

uncomfortably on the stool. She wasn't sure she wanted another one. After a few minutes he went once more to the bar and this time he didn't come back. She could see him chatting to the young man from the factory and several drinks passed between them. He occasionally glanced in her direction and smiled but he didn't make a move. Rosie felt dreadfully exposed sitting alone at the little table because she seemed to be the only woman who was on her own. She wished she was sitting on one of the velvet banquettes at that moment, then she could have slid back into the high-sided upholstery and been hidden from view. She was surprised when, a short time later, one of the young barmaids swung the clapper of a heavy-looking bronze bell behind the bar back and forth and gave a shout for last orders. She hadn't realised it was so late; what would her mother say? It was time they were heading home. There was a general flurry as people hurriedly got in their final round for the night and she was anxious for Trevor to come back. She could see him by the counter but she couldn't catch his eye and she wondered if she should go without him. Then to her relief he looked in her direction.

'I must go home, it's late,' she mouthed the words and pointed up at the clock. He nodded and gave a little wave. What seemed like only seconds later he was back with two small shot glasses of a yellowish-looking liquid that he set down on the little table.

'What's that?' she said.

'It's what's known as a chaser,' he said. 'I got us one each.'

Rosie frowned. She had only just managed to finish her long drink.

'You're supposed to down it in one go, like this,' Trevor said and he put the small glass to his lips and drank the contents in one gulp.

He lifted the other glass and pushed it into Rosie's hand. He was looking at her encouragingly. 'Go on,' he said.

'I'm not sure I can,' she protested.

'Of course you can, it's only tiny,' he insisted and he raised the glass to her lips, making encouraging noises as she sampled a mouthful of its contents.

Trevor laughed as Rosie spluttered and began to cough, but he tilted the glass so that she had to finish it. 'See, it's not hard,' he said. 'I told you you'd enjoy it.'

Rosie heard calls of, 'That's it now, folks! Time, gentlemen, please,' in firm tones from the man she presumed to be the landlord and people began reluctantly putting on their coats and gathering their belongings.

It took several minutes for her to stop coughing, but by that time Trevor had helped her into her coat and they were exiting, albeit a little unsteadily, through the swing doors. When Rosie stepped outside, the clarity and freshness of the air struck her even more forcibly than the coolness of the late spring night and she took in a deep breath, glad to be free at last of the smoke and haze. The sky was pitch black and she could see clearly how it was speckled with myriad stars, backlit only by the soft glow of a small crescent moon. But, poetic as it might have looked, she wasn't feeling in a romantic mood. If anything, she was feeling light-headed and she wondered what had been in the small glass. She took Trevor's arm to steady herself and they hadn't taken more than a few steps before she realised that she must actually be feeling a little tipsy. Trevor, on the other hand, was surprisingly sure-footed and she clung to his arm as they set off in the direction of her home.

They hadn't gone very far when Trevor stopped abruptly. He clasped her hands and gently pulled her so that she was facing him.

Then, without a word he pressed his mouth over her lips, his tongue seeking hers. Rosie, taken by surprise, was overwhelmed by an excited stirring that began deep in the pit of her stomach and rippled through her body. She knew she should say 'stop!' but she couldn't put a voice to the word, and she couldn't prevent her body from responding instinctively. She felt his tongue rough against hers and flashes of an electric-like current continued to spark their way out to the tips of her fingers and toes. It was a kiss that took her breath away, leaving her helpless and exposed.

'It's . . . it's really late; I've got to get back or my

mother will come looking for me,' she stammered, struggling to break the spell.

Trevor let go of her hands and her arms fell limply by her sides. He brought his hands up to her face, stroking her cheeks, drawing her towards him until his lips formed a seal once more. But this time she pulled away. She could feel his hot breath on her cheek and a warm nuzzling in her ear. Then she heard him whisper, 'Do you know something? I think I love you . . .' not in the flippant way he'd said it before but sounding as though he meant it and she felt as if her whole body was melting.

'Oh! Do you really?' She gasped. 'I don't know what to say.'

'You could say that you love me too.'

'But of course I do. I thought you'd have realised that by now. Why else would I have let you kiss me like this?'

'Well, you obviously liked it,' he said, taking her hands in his once more. 'So how about . . .?'

She felt his hands fumbling with her coat buttons but this time she pulled away sharply. 'No! No! You mustn't. We can't!' she cried and to her relief he withdrew his hands.

'Nah, you're probably right,' he said. 'Come on, let's be getting you home.'

# Chapter 11

Roger was exhausted after sitting up half the night with the Bowdons.

'I know it looks like a relapse,' he'd told her father as soon as he saw Ruby, 'and at the moment it's impossible to diagnose exactly what's wrong as I can't be sure what's brought it on. But I don't want to waste valuable time trying to get her to the hospital, not at this stage, not while there's still quite a lot that we can do to help her here.'

He did know that the difficulties she had in breathing and her high temperature meant that the possibility of it developing into pneumonia was a very real threat but he preferred not to go into such details with her distraught parents right from the start. What was more important was to watch Ruby closely in the hope that the fever would break. He could only admire the way Billy and Marie Bowdon responded to his orders and he'd been grateful that they'd carried them out calmly and conscientiously though he could see they were trying hard not to panic.

'The boys were woken up by the commotion when she first felt unwell. She was shouting out and crying. She seemed to be seeing creatures and figures and it was frightening the boys but we've sent them back to bed, hopefully to sleep,' Marie had told him.

'We're ready to take our turn tending Ruby now,' Billy added. 'Just tell us what we need to do.'

'Exactly what you've been doing already,' Roger said. 'The most important thing is to cool her down.'

It wasn't easy, as he well knew, to watch someone you loved hang on to their life by a tenuous thread but neither Billy nor Marie wanted to leave their daughter's side. Her breathing was painful to listen to and all the while her temperature was spiking but thankfully Ruby had hung on, while her watchers muttered their silent prayers and willed her to pull through.

It was approximately three in the morning when Roger became aware that the fever had broken; her temperature steadied and her breathing was no longer laboured. 'The worst is over,' he cautiously announced as he wiped her forehead and took her temperature once more. Billy exhaled noisily as if he had been holding his breath for the longest time while spontaneous tears burst forth from Marie.

'I-is she really going to be all right?' Marie hardly dared to ask.

'I certainly hope so,' Roger said. 'I think she's finally won the battle,' and he turned away using the moment to wipe his own cheeks and eyes.

He waited until he was assured that Ruby was comfortable and sleeping naturally before he left the family alone and he went home to grab what sleep he could before the breaking of the dawn.

'Come on, Daddy!' He heard someone calling and he felt someone tugging at his arm that was at odds with the vivid dream that was swirling in his head. 'Don't be such a lazybones,' the same little voice said, 'it's time to take me to Sunday school.'

Roger rolled over, barely able to see his little daughter Julie through his bloodshot eyes. They felt scratchy but that didn't stop him rubbing them awake. 'What time is it?' he muttered. He was trying to read the luminous dial of his bedside clock but his head was at an odd angle.

'The big hand is on the twelve and the little one is on the eight,' the young voice announced proudly. 'Does that mean it's eight o'clock?'

'It does, I'm afraid.'

'Then please can you get up and get dressed or I'm going to be late.'

It was then that Roger realised where he was and

he remembered why he'd had so little sleep. He slid his feet into his cracked leather slippers and he quickly tried to dismiss the dream as he jerked out of bed and ran down the stairs.

'Any messages for me?' he called out to his mother in the kitchen as the smell of bacon crisping up assailed his nostrils.

'Mr Bowdon rang to say there's been no change, and that Ruby was still peacefully asleep, thank goodness. He said not to wake you.'

'Thank goodness indeed.' Roger heaved a sigh of relief. 'That was some night, I can tell you. I'll drop in there after I've delivered Julie.'

Ruby was awake by the time he got there. She looked pale and, having lost much weight during her earlier battle with polio, her cheeks were hollow but he was delighted to see that she was breathing normally and her temperature was hovering close to normal. She smiled when he entered the bedroom and struggled to sit completely upright on the pillows that were already propping up her back.

'You gave us a bit of a scare last night, young lady, as your mum has no doubt told you,' Roger said as Marie Bowdon joined him in the room. 'I wonder what that was all about?'

'I know and I'm sorry, Mum.' Ruby reached out her hand and sounded contrite, 'but I honestly don't remember much about it.'

Marie laughed as she ruffled her daughter's hair. 'That's probably a blessing.'

'Do you think I'll be fit to take part in the Olympics in Helsinki next year, Dr Buckley?' Ruby asked, and there was a naïve eagerness in her eyes as they shared the joke that warmed his heart.

'No reason why not,' Roger said, grinning down at her. 'Unless they decide not to hold them, of course.'

'Could they really do that?' she asked.

'Maybe they would do it just to spite you,' he joked.

'That would hardly be fair when you've gone to so much trouble to make sure I'm ready.' Ruby did the perfect imitation of a pout.

'Well, maybe it wouldn't only be on your account,' Roger said his smile broadening. 'It may be that there are one or two other things going on in the world.'

Marie laughed. 'You might think you're joking, Dr Buckley, but I do believe if there was an Olympic competition in roller skating being held right at this minute, then this one might well be nagging to enter,' Marie said pointing her finger at Ruby.

'Yes, indeed I've heard that you're pretty nippy on those skates of yours,' Roger said without thinking as he turned to Ruby.

Ruby's eyes clouded over at that and she suddenly turned her face to the wall. 'Not anymore, I'm not.' There was a catch in her voice.

'Well, you'll have to think of something else that you

can polish up to Olympic standard instead,' Roger said with a smile, quickly trying to cover his error.

Ruby turned to look at him and tried to smile back but he could see, not surprisingly, that the spark of humour had gone.

'Actually, you'll have no time for the Olympics,' Roger said. 'I hear you're leaving school in a few weeks.'

'As soon as they break up for the summer,' Ruby said.

'It'll be far more fun to look for a good job and to be earning some money soon,' the doctor said.

'She's going to help her dad and me out in the shop, aren't you, Ruby,' Marie picked up his cue but Ruby frowned.

'Not if I can find something better to do,' she said and Roger was relieved to see her old impish grin.

'Well, you never can tell,' he said. 'I might hear about something while I'm on my travels and if I do I'll let you know,' he said. He put his thermometer back in his Gladstone bag and stood up to go. 'But maybe now's not the time to talk about such things. You gave us all quite a fright last night, so it might be an idea to build your strength up first and get fully mobile, before you start planning seriously for the future.'

Ruby heaved a sigh. 'I suppose so. As mobile as I'm ever going to be.' Roger could see her lower lip begin to tremble as she glanced in the direction of the calliper that lay on the floor at the end of her bed.

'That's up to you, Ruby,' Roger said brightly. 'If I know anything about you, you won't let something like that get in your way.'

Ruby looked at him uncertainly and he could see she was already blinking back tears. 'I don't know about that,' she whispered.

'But I do,' he said cheerily. 'Knowing you, you'll be running around in no time. And if you promise to work at that, then I promise to have a think about what other kind of work you might like to try. Something that your mum and dad would approve of as well, of course.'

Roger had no idea what had made him say that, for although he did have the kernel of an idea at the back of his mind, he hadn't given it much serious thought. However, he knew he had struck the right note with his patient when he was rewarded by a classic Ruby smile.

It was no surprise to those who knew him that Roger Buckley was the celebrity of the day in the Post Office on Monday morning, although for once the young doctor didn't actually appear. Not that that stopped the gossip machine, for it seemed everyone had something to say about the generosity of the doctor's actions that they all agreed marked the measure of the man they were proud to call their local GP. By dinnertime, Vicky had heard all the different opinions and theories about what had occurred after Roger had left her and her father on Saturday night, although few seemed to realise it was she who had been with him earlier in the evening. There was no doubt he was the hero of the hour, though there were so many differing versions of the story that it wasn't easy for Vicky to separate fact from fiction.

'Just fancy, he was prepared to take the Bowdons to the hospital in his own car,' she heard someone say.

'Even though he'd been out all evening.'

'That's Dr Buckley for you.'

'It was well after midnight.'

'I've always said I'd be happy for him to look after me if I ever got ill!' This was followed by giggles.

'He's such a lovely man.'

'Do anything for anyone.'

'He's a saint, never mind a man.' The speaker made the sign of the cross.

'It's the Bowdons's only daughter, you know . . .' A new wave buzzed.

'It would be such a shame if the polio's come back . . .'

A gasp. 'Do you really think . . .?

'And her only fourteen years old.'

'Aye up, don't write her off, she's not dead yet, you know.'

'Only thanks to the good doctor.

'Course they've got two lads besides, have the Bowdons, so it goes without saying they'll be desperate to make sure they've not caught owt.'

'But a lass is always kind of special.'

A deep sigh. 'Even if she recovers, you've got to wonder . . .'

'She'll never be the same.'

'Polio leaves its mark, you know.'

'I heard they called the priest.'

'I didn't know they were . . .'

'St Bernadette's.'

'Happen there'll be prayers, then.'

'Must have been already. I heard she's making good progress.'

Vicky knew Ruby Bowdon well, before her illness she'd been a pretty little girl with a naturally bright and cheerful disposition. But she had been overindulged by her parents and most of the neighbours complained she was mischievous. Much to the annoyance of the shopkeepers on the parade, she loved nothing better than to roller skate in and out of the shops though always with a bright smile, some cheeky chit-chat and her giggles were infectious. Vicky always found it hard to get cross with her.

That's why everyone had been stunned when she had caught polio and had become so poorly. Vicky had prayed for her, even without going to church, and she was sure that all of Greenhill had too. She had been delighted when the news spread that Ruby had been discharged from hospital. But then Vicky discovered that she had not made a complete recovery and that she might have to wear calliper on her leg and she did wonder what the future held for the young girl, so it was particularly upsetting to hear that there had been a further setback. Vicky thought of Ruby's parents, Billy and Marie, faced with the possibility of losing their precious child and although she couldn't speak of it, she could empathise with the depth of their despair. It was why she had been moved to hear of Roger's involvement last night for she knew that he understood it too.

Ruby was actually about to turn fourteen now and would be leaving school, having missed too many lessons because of her illness to warrant staying on for another year. Vicky was greatly relieved that the conversation ended on a note of hope.

It was a few days later before Roger was able to go to the Post Office. He was on his way home and he arrived as Vicky was beginning to lock up for the night. The closed sign was already showing through the glass pane though Vicky hadn't yet pulled down the blinds and he could see her still moving about the shop. He waved and she opened the door and peeped out.

'Anything urgent I can get you, Dr Buckley?' Vicky said. 'I'm a few minutes early closing up.'

Roger had intended to talk to her there and then and be on his way, but when he saw the resignation that seemed to be etched into her tired face, he had a better idea. 'It's such a lovely evening, I was wondering if I could persuade you to come out for a walk a little later, to take advantage of the extra hours of daylight?'

When he saw her draw a deep breath he thought she was going to refuse but then, to his surprise, she blushed and for a moment he even thought he saw her eyes sparkle. 'After tea, do you mean?'

Roger nodded. 'It needn't be for very long if you're worried about leaving your father . . .'

'No, that's not it; his cough's not been too bad of late. It's just that I've had a busy day.'

'Then a gentle walk might be exactly what you need. Besides, there's something I wanted to discuss with you,' Roger said.

Vicky looked startled. 'If it's that important then I'm sure I could manage half an hour,' she said.

'Great, then I'll come back to pick you up about eight.'

Roger hadn't realised how closely they were walking together, their hands almost touching, until he saw Vicky take a deliberate step away. She didn't say anything but continued walking.

'You must be wondering what I want to talk to you about?' Roger waited until they reached the towpath and were walking beside the river.

Vicky looked up at him expectantly and he suddenly felt uncertain.

'Is everything all right with Julie?' Vicky asked.

'Yes, thanks, she's fine,' he said, grateful that she had

unwittingly given him an opening. 'It's not Julie I wanted to talk to you about,' he said. 'It's Ruby Bowdon.'

Vicky frowned. 'Ruby? Is she all right? I heard she'd had a bit of a setback recently.' Vicky stopped walking and turned to face him, her eyes anxiously scanning his.

'She's better now. It seems to have been something and nothing, thank goodness. Tell me, how well do you know her?' They set off walking again.

'As well as I know any of the local kids. They're in and out of all the shops on the parade on weekends and after school, generally making a nuisance of themselves. They're high-spirited as Violet Pegg always says, and she should know. Why do you ask?'

'Because Ruby's leaving school very soon. Her parents seem to expect her to work with them selling greengroceries, but I get the impression she doesn't really want to.'

'What does she want to do?'

'That's the problem; I'm not sure she knows, but I promised I would scout around to see if there might be something better she might like to do.'

'And you thought of the Post Office?' Vicky said.

Roger grinned. 'Am I that obvious?'

'In this circumstance, yes.'

'I know you've been thinking of trying to get some extra help to take over from your father,' Roger said, 'and I wondered . . .'

'That's true, but would Ruby want to do that kind

of work? It can be pretty hard as there are so many different things to do and it's not always easy to keep switching, you know; there's such a lot to learn.'

'Her options are going to be somewhat restricted . . .' Roger began. 'Not that I'm trying to sell you a pig in a poke, because I sincerely believe she'll be a hard worker.'

'I take it her leg is not going to get much better?'

'Not significantly, no. She'll have to learn to work round it, as it were, and I thought the Post Office could be ideal. Not too far to stretch, no stairs to negotiate, and I presume she could probably sit down for large parts of the day?'

'Possibly some parcels to heave about ready for collection, but that's not insurmountable.' Vicky looked thoughtful. 'Any idea what she's been like in school?'

'I've no first-hand knowledge though she's always struck me as being quite bright. I'm sure you could get a reference from Mrs Diamond or whoever her last teacher is.'

They had reached the munitions factory where stragglers from the early evening shift were still drifting homeward.

'Thank you for thinking of me, that really is very kind and I'll certainly . . .'

'I'm glad to be able to help,' he said and for a moment took hold of both of her hands, hoping he could get her to meet his gaze. But she looked away and for a moment neither spoke.

'Do you want me to say anything to her?' Roger asked finally and he let her hands drop.

Vicky cleared her throat. 'I wonder if it might be more appropriate for me to approach her? Though I would tell her it was your idea.'

'That sounds good; after all, you know more about the job than I do.' He grinned. 'Let me know what happens when you've had a chat.'

# Chapter 12

The more Claire became embedded in the Barker household, the more she began to question whether she had done the right thing in coming all this way to be with people who were tantamount to strangers, even though her mother insisted on calling them 'her family'. There was no denying that she enjoyed working in Aunty Sylvia's shop and she was grateful to her aunt for giving her the opportunity to develop her own sewing and knitting initiatives. That was something she would never have been allowed to do at home and she appreciated Sylvia entrusting her with what she considered to be such grown-up responsibility. Aunty Sylvia had done her best to make Claire feel at home; Claire knew that. She was kind and generous and she always tried to be helpful, but somehow their association had not progressed beyond the superficial. Whenever she was alone with her aunt, or her cousin for that matter, she still worried that somehow they didn't feel like real family.

The main problem was Rosie, who never passed up a chance to remind Claire how much she resented having to share her bedroom, and try as she might, Claire never felt able to make a true connection with her cousin. In addition, it had come as a shock to discover that neither Sylvia nor Rosie shared her religious beliefs and she wondered why her mother had never seen fit to mention this before she came. Hannah must have known that Sylvia had renounced any religious affiliation when she had married outside of the Jewish faith, something that was frowned upon in the religious community Claire had grown up in. Indeed, it was the only explanation for why her mother had never met Sylvia's husband but it wasn't something Claire had ever been able to discuss with her aunt.

Uncle Archie was more distant – a shadowy figure even within his own household. Claire had met him briefly on only a few occasions and from the little she had seen of him he seemed to be a complete enigma. He was rarely at home, was referred to infrequently, and it seemed that neither Sylvia nor Claire saw much of him either. He stayed in rented digs in Derbyshire during the week when he was working and even some weekends when he was not. At first Clairc had thought it might be her fault and that he objected to having a stranger living under his roof, but as time went on she began to doubt if that were true, though she didn't feel it was something she could talk about with Rosie or Sylvia.

The only place Claire heard mention of Archie's name was when she'd overheard gossip about him – which she had on more than one occasion – when she had been out shopping locally. Most of it implied that he drank too much, that he was quick to lose his temper – and even worse, that he actually hit his wife. But mostly these were isolated whispers, fragments that she had not been able to string together into a coherent whole, because people usually stopped talking as soon as they realised she was there. Not that she'd ever seen any evidence of such behaviour when Archie was home, though she wasn't sure she would always know what signs to look for. She had never seen anyone who had drunk too much nor witnessed anyone being slapped about except by a teacher in school.

She tried to imagine what Archie might be like if he were totally inebriated and out of control, but she had no experience of what the consequences of such over-indulgence might be. She thought of her own father, a gentle man who never drank anything except a small ritual glass of sweet wine on a Friday night after the benediction of the Sabbath and occasionally a tot of whisky if he was invited to someone's special celebrations after the service in the synagogue on a Saturday morning; neither her mother or father had ever raised a hand in anger. Besides, if her mother had had any knowledge of such wild behaviour then surely she wouldn't have let her daughter come all this way to live with them, no matter how much she feared the bombs that were threatening London in the event of war? Claire felt trapped in a difficult situation and she didn't know what to do. She wrote letters home each week but was careful not to mention any of her concerns. She didn't want to be seen telling tales and there was no point in having her mother worry about something she couldn't change.

Now that the days were longer and the weather was fine, Claire sometimes took a walk after tea so that she could enjoy the country air. It smelled so much fresher and cleaner than the air in London. Rosie always seemed to find some excuse for not joining her but as Claire had made at least one new friend she tried not to be a nuisance to her cousin.

When Rosie came home one night, excited about the funfair that had opened recently in the local park and to which she'd been once already, Claire thought it sounded like fun and was pleased when Sylvia suggested that she and Rosie should go to it together as Claire had never been to one before.

'Yeah, she could probably come with me sometime,'

Rosie said, 'but not tonight as I've already promised to go with friends from work and they wouldn't take kindly to other people muscling in.'

'How long will the fair be here?' Claire asked.

Rosie gave a shrug of her shoulders. 'Dunno. But I'll let you know what night I'm free.' Then, 'Gosh, is that the time?' Rosie said. 'I've got to get going,' and she pulled out her coat from under a pile on the bannister. 'I'd better get off; I'm already late. See you later.' And she slipped out of the house and disappeared.

'Oh, the wretched girl, she can be so thoughtless.' Sylvia watched her go. 'Claire, why don't you go after her? If I know her she's probably meeting Penny and her sister and I'm sure they won't object to you joining in.'

'Oh, do you think that would be all right? I don't want to upset Rosie.'

'But you're friends with Penny; Rosie's probably forgotten,' Sylvia assured her. 'No, you go. If you go straightaway you can catch them up before they get to the park.

'If you really think I should?' Claire said, as she rescued her own coat from the pile on the bannister.

'Definitely, now shoo, and have a lovely time,' Sylvia said.

Claire walked briskly in the direction of the park and found the funfair easily enough but there was no sign of Rosie and she lost heart and gave up hope of finding her as she wandered up and down the aisles of dried mud that divided the field. She stopped each time she came across a group of young girls chattering and laughing but there was no sign of Rosie and Claire began to feel dejected. Although the stalls were exactly as Rosie had described them, she had omitted to mention the fact that everything cost money and she looked down miserably at the few pennies she had in her pocket. It would seem wasteful to throw them away on a slot machine, or to shoot at a row of mechanical ducks. The only thing that did attract her was the dodgem cars and she stood watching them wistfully, not wanting to try them on her own.

'Claire?' She turned round when she heard someone call her name and to her great relief found she had come face to face with Penny and her sister Stella. 'I thought it was you – but what are you doing here by yourself?' Penny asked.

Claire's gaze darted beyond the two girls, though she still couldn't see her cousin. 'I've been looking for Rosie, but it seems I've missed her, somehow.' She gave a self-conscious laugh. 'She came out before me and I thought she was meeting up with you.'

'No, she's not with us tonight,' Stella said. 'Which direction did she go?'

'I don't know, that's the problem,' Claire said.

'Oh well, never mind, you're with us now,' Penny said and the sisters linked arms with Claire.

'So come on, get some speed up. Are we going on

the dodgems or not?' Stella asked. 'At this rate they'll be closing up before we've had a chance to go on anything.'

'Of course we are, I wouldn't miss the dodgems for the world,' Penny said. 'What do you say, Claire?'

'I'd love to. I thought they looked like fun though I've never been on them before.'

'Then come with us, lass,' Penny said heartily. 'They really are great. Stella can go in one car because she much prefers to drive on her own and you and me can go together in another one. I'll show you what to do.' And before Claire could protest, Penny had persuaded her to part with one of her precious pennies and she was bumping and weaving and being swung from side to side as the cars violently collided. They were all laughing and trying to catch their breath by the time the bell sounded to signal the end of their ride and Claire couldn't remember when she had had such a good time. After that she was happy just to look at all the stalls, though she was persuaded to buy some candyfloss.

'I really enjoyed that,' Claire said, wiping the wisps of sugary cotton from her mouth. 'I'm so glad I bumped into you – quite literally.' They all laughed. 'Thanks very much for letting me join you.'

'It was our pleasure,' Penny said. 'We enjoyed it too. And we can do it again sometime because the fair will be here for a while. But I suppose for now it's time to go home, whether we want to or not.' She pointed to the stallholders who were beginning to close up their booths.

It was rapidly getting dark and the lights of the fair were winking out one by one.

'Why don't you come back home with us, Claire, for a cup of tea,' Penny said.

'Good idea,' Stella said. 'It'll give me a proper chance to get to know you at last.'

'That's very kind, but my aunt will worry if I stop out too late,' Claire said.

'You can drop in there first and tell her where you are, then she won't be concerned,' Penny suggested.

'Thanks, then I will,' Claire said, and she felt a warm glow with the excitement of meeting up with her two new friends.

It wasn't until they had exited the park through the double wooden gates that Claire realised that they were not the same gates she had entered and that she didn't actually know where she was. She stood for a moment staring at the brick wall that surrounded the entire park. It looked no different from the wall that enclosed her local Gladstone Park in Cricklewood, and for a moment she shivered with a sudden flash of homesickness. But she had no time for that; they needed to get home. The streets were deserted now and the girls used their torches that they pointed downwards, although the diffused beams were so weak in the crepuscular light that it wasn't easy to see where they were going and Claire was glad they hadn't left her on her own to find her way own way home.

It had been fun being with the Downs sisters, Claire decided, when it was time for her to go home. She knew that Rosie had had words with Penny in the past, although she didn't know what about, but she had enjoyed getting to know them and they had chatted together companionably for the rest of the evening. Perhaps it was fortunate that she hadn't found Rosie, though she did wonder what had happened to her cousin and she hoped she was all right.

'Do you need an escort or do you think you can find your own way home from here?' Penny joked when Claire finally got up to leave. 'It's all of four shops down. But take care and we'll see you soon. Perhaps we can go to the pictures together next time?' Stella called after her.

'Yes, please,' Claire agreed and she walked away smiling. Up ahead she could see a young couple, arms linked, weaving an unsteady path along the pavement and the thought crossed her mind that it might be the consequence of someone having had too much to drink. She could hear the couple's laughter as they kept stumbling into each other and then rolling apart. As she came closer, the light breeze that was coming off the water wafted the smoke from their cigarettes in her direction and, despite being outdoors, it made her splutter and cough. Claire walked slowly, not wanting to overtake them. But the young couple stopped suddenly when they almost bumped into a lamppost on the street corner and Claire stopped too. None of the lamps in the street had been lit for some reason and she peered into the darkness, hoping the scant moonlight would illuminate the Knit and Sew shop's banner. She could see that the couple had stopped outside the Post Office and, having extinguished their cigarettes they turned towards each other to kiss. As they did so, a small cloud flitted away from the narrow crescent of the moon and Claire could see quite clearly that she had finally found Rosie.

# Chapter 13

Ruby had fallen in love with Dr Buckley the first time he had attended her bedside, though she would never have had the courage to tell him that at the tender age of eleven. But now, as far as she was concerned, he was her hero. He had saved her life twice – and any man who did that deserved her undying love, particularly a doctor as handsome and as kind as Roger Buckley. The first time he had saved her was when he had personally rushed her into hospital with suspected polio. She hadn't been able to breathe and his prompt actions had ensured that she was hooked up to an iron lung as quickly as possible. And then he had saved her again the other night when he had sat up with her parents for most of the night until he was certain she was out of danger and didn't need to go to the hospital. Was there ever such a wonderful man on this earth?

And now Ruby was excited because he had promised to look out for a job for her and she knew that she would be forever in his debt.

Ruby had always hoped she might be able to stay on at school, maybe undertake a teacher's training course so that she could go to work in the village school as Violet Pegg had done. But she had missed so many classes in the years she had been ill that her teacher, Mrs Diamond, had advised her to leave because it would take her too long to catch up the months of schoolwork she had missed.

'You need to be considering other options and I'm sure there are lots of things you could do,' Mrs Diamond had counselled, and Ruby realised, with much reluctance, that she would have to be sensible and realistic and put aside her dreams. Her brothers were much younger and it would be some time before they were ready to take on the mantle of the family's greengrocery business; in the meantime, she knew that her parents were keen for her to work with them in the shop. It was a kind and well-meant offer and she knew they would spare her some of the more arduous tasks, such as having to go to the market to pick up fresh produce in the early hours of the morning. But it also meant that she would never be independent and free. Helpful as it seemed to be offered a job that she could begin immediately, she didn't want to be tied to them or committed to selling fruit and vegetables for the rest of her life without being able to consider any other options. The trouble was, she didn't know how to tell them.

'It will only be until you get married,' her mother said when Ruby finally tried to explain.

But that was not what Ruby wanted to hear.

'Get married?' she scoffed. 'Do you seriously think someone would want to marry me?' She had hoped to avoid such a scene and she began to cry. 'Who will want me with a thing like this attached to my leg all my life?' she sobbed, and she picked up her calliper that she had rested against the chair and threw it to the other side of the room. 'Maybe an old man who's a cripple himself from the Great War.'

The doorbell rang at that moment and, thinking it must be the doctor, Ruby quickly rubbed away her tears and insisted on opening the door herself. She was eager to show off that she could take some steps on her own thanks to his suggestions about undertaking daily exercises to prevent her leg wasting any further. 'See how I'm getting stronger every day.' The words bubbled forth and were on her lips as she opened the door but she was surprised, not to say disappointed, to find Vicky Parrott standing on the step.

'Is it the doctor?' Marie Bowdon shouted from the back room. 'Ask him to come in.'

Ruby invited Vicky in. 'Mum's in the back,' she said.

Vicky hesitated. 'Actually, Ruby, it's you I've come to see,' she said.

'Me?' Ruby laughed. 'No one ever comes to see me – except of course the doctor – so you'd better come in.'

Vicky had never been behind the greengrocer's shop-front before though she wasn't surprised to find the layout exactly the same as in her own home. Marie was getting up from the kitchen table and had started gathering the tea dishes, ready for washing.

'Not often we see you here, Vicky. Is everything all right?' Marie said.

Vicky pulled a chair up to the table and sat down without waiting to be asked. 'Everything's fine, thanks.'

'What can we do for you, then?' Marie said, putting the dishes down. 'Can I get you a cup of something?'

'Actually, it's more about what I might be able to do for you,' Vicky said, 'and a drink won't be necessary, thanks all the same.'

'I'm all ears,' Marie said, looking interested. 'But perhaps Ruby might want to go to—'

'No.' Vicky put a restraining hand on Ruby's arm. 'Ruby needs to hear this,' and she outlined the conversation she had had with Roger Buckley. She was gratified to see Ruby's eyes light up, even if Marie looked wary.

'I realise it might not be what you were planning for

Ruby,' Vicky said quickly when she saw the look on Marie's face.

'To be honest, we hadn't talked much about it,' Marie said. 'We only want whatever's best for her.' She turned to face Vicky. 'And if she doesn't want to work in our shop then that's fine,' she said, though the stiff smile on her face said something different. 'I'll have to discuss it with Billy, of course, as we were relying on her coming to give us a hand. But I'll get back to you by the end of the week. If that'll be all right?'

'That's fine,' Vicky said. 'Sorry to land it on you like this. But one quick question before I go because you've not had a chance to say anything, Ruby.' Vicky stood up and turned to Ruby. 'How would you feel about working in the Post Office with me?'

Ruby's whole face was filled with excitement. 'I would love it,' she said. 'I think it's a great idea. Please can I, Mum?'

But all Marie would say was, 'We'll see.'

# Chapter 14

Rosie twisted in Trevor's arms, straining to see in the moonlight, and it took several moments for her to register who it was that had stopped a few feet away. But she could see Claire quite clearly now that the moon had finally emerged. Claire was usually in bed by the time Rosie got home and she wondered where her cousin had been that she was still out.

'Is that you, Claire?' she called out.

Claire took a tentative step forwards and was facing the couple directly.

'Are you all right?' Rosie asked.

'I'm fine, thanks,' Claire said. 'I've been at Penny's. We went to the funfair.'

They stood awkwardly for a few moments. Rosie

wasn't sure if it was the effects of the alcohol she'd drunk earlier wearing off, but she suddenly felt foolish. 'I'd like you to meet Trevor,' she said, managing to smother the giggle that had risen into her throat. 'He works at the factory. Trevor, this is Claire.'

Trevor gave an embarrassed laugh and to Rosie's surprise he put out his hand to Claire. 'Pleased to meet you,' he said formally. Claire muttered something, though Rosie couldn't make out the words and before Rosie could say anything further Claire had hurried down the alley between the shops that led to the Barkers' back door.

'Who was that?' Trevor scratched his head when she'd gone.

'She's just someone from London who's living with us right now,' she said quickly, not wanting to explain the family connection.

'Was she spying on us?'

Now Rosie did laugh. 'No, you've no need to worry,' Rosie said. 'She's no trouble but I am surprised my mother's not got a search party out looking for her.'

'How come she's not got one out looking for you?'

'Because I told her I might be a bit late as I was going out with friends.'

'A friend? Is that what I am, then?' Trevor said and he nuzzled his face into her cheek.

'Well, you are, aren't you?' she said.

'But I want to be more than that. You do know that, don't you?' Trevor rubbed his body against hers and Rosie felt a mixture of alarm and excitement. She giggled but didn't answer.

'So will your mother not worry about you?' Trevor persisted.

'Of course she will. Now that Claire's home I expect she'll be out on the doorstep any minute.'

'Then you can introduce us and I promise to be charm itself,' he said, his voice suddenly smooth.

'I don't doubt that,' Rosie said, offering her lips to be kissed, but then his lips clamped down on hers.

'What would she say if she saw what her daughter was up to?'

He pressed himself against her again and put his hand inside her jacket, squeezing her nipple through her blouse.

'I don't know what she'd do . . .' Rosie's voice suddenly had a catch in it and her breathing was uneven. 'D-don't do that.' Rosie didn't sound as if she meant it. 'I'm telling you, my mum's going to appear any minute.'

'But there's no sign of your mum yet,' Trevor murmured. 'And what about your old man? He's not one of those keeps a shotgun under his bed, is he?'

Rosie laughed. 'Hardly. But you don't have to worry about him. I doubt he'll be home tonight. All the same, I think you'd better go now,' Rosie said, reluctantly pulling away. But it was too late, for at that moment there was a dainty pinging sound that seemed at odds with the force with which the front door was flung open and Sylvia appeared in the shop doorway.

'Rosie, is that you?' she shouted. 'Claire's home and I think it's high time you came in as well. I don't know how you can see a thing out there.'

'I'm coming,' Rosie answered. 'We were talking about work tomorrow.' And she had to smother another giggle as she felt Trevor's fingers prod her ribs. 'Can I introduce you to Trevor before he goes?' Rosie called after her mother as she saw her turn away. Sylvia stopped and looked surprised.

'This is Trevor from work,' Rosie said, emphasising the last word. 'Trev, this is my mum.'

# Chapter 15

Ruby was excited to be working in the Post Office and could hardly believe that her parents had finally agreed to let her try selling something other than fresh fruit and vegetables. It was all down to Dr Buckley, or so Vicky Parrott had said when she'd come round to discuss with the Bowdons the possibility of taking on Ruby as her assistant.

'He thought you would make a very good trainee Postmistress,' Vicky had told her. It was the main reason Ruby had jumped at the chance and begged her parents to let her do it, particularly when she realised it meant working behind the counter where no one could see her bad leg.

'Fortunately, there's no climbing of ladders required or running up and down stairs,' Vicky had said. 'And I would make sure my dad kept out of your hair; he can talk the hind leg off a donkey when he's a mind.'

'Oh, that's OK,' Ruby said, 'I'd love to hear his stories.' She added quickly, 'So long as there was no one waiting to be served in the shop, of course.'

That had made Vicky smile.

Ruby hadn't thought that she would enjoy the work as much as she did. Vicky had strict rules and made her work hard but she had been very patient while explaining all the different tasks the job entailed. More importantly, Vicky seemed to understand what it meant to Ruby that she had been forced to leave school earlier than she'd intended and hadn't been able to follow the career she had dreamed of.

'I wanted to be a teacher too,' Vicky admitted to Ruby with a sigh. 'Somehow, when I was at school it seemed like a very glamorous job to have.'

'That's how I felt,' Ruby said, 'although maybe it was Miss Pegg that made it seem that way. I always wanted to be like her.'

Vicky laughed. 'I know what you mean. She and I were at school at the same time.'

'Looking after people's post and parcels can be fun too,' Ruby said quickly.

'It can indeed,' Vicky agreed. 'You wait till it's the birthday of someone in the village and there are cards and mysterious-looking parcels, not to mention telegrams flying about. And it's the same at Christmas.'

Ruby couldn't wait to see the doctor again so that she could thank him in person for his helpful intervention and for putting in a good word with Vicky – or Miss Parrott as she had been told to call her at work. To Ruby's delight, she was rewarded at the end of the week when he appeared with his pile of letters and packages to be weighed and posted.

'Glad to see you settling in so well, Ruby,' the doctor said beaming, 'even serving on your own.'

'Miss Parrott's only behind that door if I need her,' Ruby confided, 'but she's shown me what to do and she thinks I'll learn best by doing it myself.'

'I thought you would get along with Vicky – pardon me, Miss Parrott,' he said. 'I trust everything's working out all right?' Vicky still hadn't made an appearance so he had lowered his voice and Ruby beamed at him with delight. 'I'm loving it,' she said softly, 'so thank you again for thinking of me. I really do appreciate it.'

'Then I think we should celebrate your first week at work,' he said. 'I don't suppose you've had much of a chance to get out in the fresh air this week.'

'Not really. I've only had to walk the few yards from our shop to this.' Ruby laughed.

'Then how about joining me and Julie for an outing to the park on Saturday?'

'What, to the funfair?' Ruby said without thinking, her face flushing with excitement.

Now it was Roger's turn to laugh. 'No, not the fair, I'm afraid. I've been promising for ages and now I'm finally taking my little daughter fishing for tiddlers in the big pond over by the bandstand and you'd be very welcome to come with us.'

Ruby's cheeks reddened. 'That sounds lovely,' she said, but then she frowned. 'Oh, but I'll be working, so I can't.'

'You only work in the morning on a Saturday, surely?' the doctor said. 'You'll be free by dinnertime, won't you? We won't be going till then so we can stop off to collect you at closing time. That's providing it doesn't rain, of course.'

'Yes, that would be fine,' Ruby said.

'You'd better check with your parents and if they say you can come, bring a sandwich and we'll have a little picnic. I think it would do you a lot of good to spend some time in the open air, get some pink back into your cheeks permanently.'

Now Ruby nodded with some enthusiasm. 'Thank you. That does sound like fun,' she said. 'Are you sure Julie won't mind?'

'She's very sociable, my daughter,' Dr Buckley said. 'I'm sure she'll be delighted. She likes having people join us.'

Roger paid the bill and Ruby gave him his change, proudly marking it up on the till roll. 'Is – is Miss

Parrott available?' he said as he prepared to leave. 'Perhaps I could have a word with her before I go.'

Ruby glanced behind her where the door to the living quarters remained firmly shut. 'She's actually busy at the moment and she said not to disturb her unless I had a problem,' she said hesitantly. 'But I can go and check if you like, in case she's finished.' She slid off the stool she had been perching on but Roger stopped her.

'No, don't bother,' he said. 'I'll get in touch later. It's not urgent. I'll see you tomorrow.' He tipped his felt trilby hat and left.

It took Roger some time to come to, on Saturday morning, even though Julie was bouncing on the end of his bed in an effort to wake him up.

'Come on, Daddy, or we'll be late,' she chanted over and over and though he tried to close his ears, Julie meant business and refused to let him go back to sleep.

'We don't need to be ready so early, you know,' he said struggling to sit up. He finally opened his eyes and was not surprised to see that Julie was already dressed, although her jumper was inside out and she had different coloured socks on each foot. 'Ruby's coming with us today, remember I told you?' he said. 'And she's working until dinnertime.'

Julie's face fell. 'I thought we were going to have a picnic,' she said.

'We are. I've asked Grandma if she could rustle up

some sandwiches for us and I've told Ruby to bring some too. Let's hope it doesn't rain, that's all.'

At that, Julie jumped off the bed and clapped her hands. Then she ran to the window.

'It's not raining!' she announced, 'but the sun's not shining.' She sounded disappointed.

'That's because it's too early,' Roger said, and he pulled the blankets up to his chin. Julie giggled and Roger took a deep breath. 'Is that coffee I can smell?' He gave an exaggerated sniff.

'Grandma's making breakfast,' Julie confirmed, 'so you'd better hurry up or you'll miss it and then you'll have to wait till dinner.'

Roger checked off his list as he packed up the car with the equipment that would be required for the gathering of frogspawn and whatever else might be swimming about in the pond. The small fishing nets were years old but somehow they'd survived and he tucked the long poles out of harm's way in the boot, wedging them in with jam jars that had string through their lids to carry home their catch.

It was funny, he reflected as he added a thermos flask, egg sandwiches, and slices of his mother's best parkin, that nothing much had changed since his own father had taken him fishing when he was not much older than Julie was now. But this was not the time to get lost under a heap of sentimental memories.

'I think you'll need a warmer jumper than that,' he said as Julie ran out into the yard. 'It's nice and sunny now but a bit cool still, I'm afraid. Why not put on that new one Grandma knitted for you? We can't afford for you to get a cold.'

'If I do, you can always make me better,' Julie said with an impish grin and she turned her face towards him for a kiss.

Roger caught his breath as he bent to oblige though he tried to smile. But such remarks would catch him unawares and stab him in the heart. He still suffered agonies of guilt over the fact that he couldn't always make people better, such as the time when he hadn't been able to save the life of his beloved wife . . .

Julie grabbed his hands and pulled him upright, trying to make him turn in a circle. When he didn't respond immediately, she ran up and down the yard, jumping into the puddles that had formed overnight, then complained that the water had dripped over the top of her shiny black wellington boots and had wet her socks. She ran back to take his hand again, trying to encourage him to jump with her.

'What are you thinking about Daddy?'

Roger shook his head. 'That's a very good question, my darling, to which I have no answer. I will have to give it some serious thought.'

'Oh, Daddy, you are so silly,' Julie chastised him. 'You must know what you were thinking about.'

'Not necessarily,' he said, frowning and looking down into his daughter's trusting face. Her dark brown eyes, not unlike his own, blinked back at him. Then he squeezed her hand and guided her into the back seat of the car.

'Now, let's go and pick up Ruby at the Post Office,' he said.

'Is Vicky coming too?' Julie asked innocently.

'Well, no,' Roger said. 'I thought it would just be Ruby, you and me.'

'But I want Vicky to come!' Julie bounced up and down and sounded so eager that Roger smiled at her.

'That sounds like a good idea, though it might be too late,' he said, 'but I suppose we could ask her.'

# Chapter 16

The machines in the munitions factory had been running all night as they always did but when Rosie clocked in for work she was surprised to find hers was idle and a girl she didn't know was standing by the bench, looking anxious. She was biting her nails which looked as if they were already down to the quick. A man in work overalls was lying on his back under all the heavy metal and she thought she recognised the boots that were sticking out from underneath.

'What's going on?' Penny came up to join her and was peering down at the mechanic. 'What's he doing here? Can't keep his hands off you for more than a minute, eh?' She turned to Rosie who clenched her jaw to prevent an angry retort. But she didn't have time to form a reasoned response before the stranger said, 'The machine just stopped and I'm waiting for it to be fixed so's I can go off my shift.'

A few minutes later, Trevor emerged from under the tangle of wires and pipes, his face shining with sweat, triumphantly brandishing what looked like a small key.

'God knows how it got wedged down there,' he said, 'but this is what was jamming up the works.' He brushed down his overalls as he stood up.

The young girl who'd been impatiently waiting grabbed the key. 'Ta very much, I need that. Sorry to have bothered you!' she said and rushed away to clock off.

'Without the likes of you, darling, I'm out of a job,' Trevor called after her, then he caught sight of Rosie and grinned. 'A quick squirt of oil and your machine should be as right as rain,' he said and he slid his hand across her back and pinched her bottom as if Penny wasn't there. Rosie couldn't prevent a yelp escaping and she glared at Trevor. He quickly flicked the switch on the side of the bench and the machine fired into life. When Rosie dared to look at him again he was earnestly gathering his tools. He looked up and winked. 'See you later,' he said and before she could respond he was gone.

'I do wish you wouldn't do things like that,' Rosie said to Trevor later when they were standing outside the factory gates, taking their final puff on their cigarettes as the bell sounded the end of their dinner break.

'Like what? I didn't do owt wrong.' Trevor looked surprised.

'You know what I mean.' Rosie was impatient.

'No, I don't. I don't know why you're so scared of that stuck-up little madam, Penny. I wouldn't believe a word she says.'

Rosie stiffened. She hated when he called the girls names.

'You always seem to be scared of somebody,' Trevor said. 'You didn't want me to meet your mum, did you? But there was nothing to it, in the end. What did she say when you went in?'

'Nothing, really,' Rosie had to admit. 'She didn't like me being out so late and particularly with a lad. You know what it's like, "what will the neighbours say" and all that. I had to promise to be in earlier next time, but I think she was glad to see that you looked reasonably respectable.' Rosie giggled.

'See! What did I tell you? I said you worry for nothing. I'll see you tonight, then? I can have another go at shooting them ducks.'

'What? To win me a cuddly teddy?' Rosie said not without sarcasm.

'If I win, the prize will be more than a cuddly teddy bear,' Trevor said and he gave her a long, suggestive look that made her stomach flip in the now-familiar somersault. She took a deep breath as she stamped out her cigarette and refused to look at him again. 'I'd better get back to the bench before Penny really has something to say,' she said.

When they met up after tea, Rosie had changed her mind; she didn't really want to go to the fair again

'Where do you want to go, then?' Trevor asked. He kicked at the grass on the verge that ran parallel to the Parade, and managed to dislodge a large divot.

'Why can't we just go for a walk?' she said. 'It's a nice enough night. Or we could go to the pictures,' she said. '*The Lady Vanishes* is on again at the Plaza; that's supposed to be good and I missed it when it came out at the beginning of the year.'

Trevor shrugged. 'You got any money on you? Cos I haven't.' He pulled his trouser pockets inside out to show that they were empty.

'How were you going to pay for us at the fair if you've no money?' Rosie wanted to know.

'I wasn't. You were,' he said without embarrassment. 'You seemed to have plenty of money last night.'

'But there wasn't enough for tonight as well.' Rosie felt cross. Where she came from, she expected a man to pay if he was taking her out.

Trevor suddenly grinned. 'We could always go down to the summer house in the park,' he said. 'That doesn't cost owt.'

'I didn't think anyone would be there at this time of night,' Rosie said.

'That's the idea,' Trevor said, and Rosie thought she caught an odd glint in his eye. But she didn't want to start an argument. 'Come on then,' Trevor said, his voice suddenly cajoling, 'let's go now.'

'I've never actually been there,' Rosie confessed. 'What's it like?'

'Come with me and I'll show you,' he said with a broad grin and he held out his hand to her.

Rosie thought calling it a summer house was rather too grand a way to describe the dilapidated structure they stopped in front of and she wondered if it had looked much different even when it had been at its best. Now, the once-white paint was peeling from the pillars – the only substantial part of the structure that remained. They looked as if they had been planted like trees, long ago, and they still stood in a circle, supporting the tiny dome of the roof. There was no glass between the wooden struts and a gentle breeze blew through the empty frames and across the interior, rustling the leaves that carpeted the tiled floor. Rosie stepped inside gingerly. Trevor had already sat down on the ledge that was attached to the inner circumference of the small building, without bothering to clear the debris that covered it. He didn't seem to notice that the dried leaves, twigs and thick, soil-like dust immediately clung to his khaki drill trousers. He beckoned to her, indicating that she should sit on his knee.

'Come and join me,' he said and pulled her onto his lap. Almost immediately, his lips were on hers and, as he sealed the kiss, one hand slipped inside her jacket while the other flashed under her skirt in one fluid movement. Heat flared between her legs, radiating in all directions and she kissed him back almost involuntarily. His response was to slowly push her backwards until she was lying directly on the seat and he was parting her legs with his knee. She felt small twigs and leaves tangling in her hair but she had been so overwhelmed by the rush of excitement that seemed to take over her body that she didn't protest. When his fingers stopped moving inside her blouse she realised it was because he was fumbling with his own buttons and she began to feel alarmed, as if it was only then that she understood the full import of what he was doing and she flailed to get free. She grunted with the effort as she tried her best to squirm out from underneath him and heaved a sigh of relief as one foot actually touched the floor. He was half-sitting, propped up on one elbow. His breathing was heavy and it took several moments before he could speak.

'What on earth were you doing?' he said eventually, his voice hoarse.

'I was trying to tell you to stop,' she said. 'You were going way too fast for me.'

She was close to tears.

'Don't tell me you didn't want it as much as I did!' he said testily.

Rosie didn't say anything and started to cry.

Trevor slid down off the ledge and put his arm round her. 'The trouble with you is that one minute you think you want to go all the way then the next you don't.' He ran his fingers through his hair, clutching handfuls in frustration. 'You don't know what you want. Do you know your problem? You're just a bloody great tease.'

'That's not true!' Rosie gasped. 'I told you from the start that I didn't want to go all the way,' she protested. 'I've never tried to pretend. And you kept saying you'd never try to push me further than I wanted to go. But that's just what you did a minute ago.'

Trevor stood up straight and shook his head.

He was still breathing hard but he moved away and she was relieved to see that he had fastened his buttons.

'It's obvious you don't love me,' Trevor said without looking at her.

'Of course I do,' Rosie responded immediately. 'Really, I do.'

Trevor's hand moved to his belt and for a moment the look on his face softened as he said, 'Then why won't you show me that you do?'

He was staring down at her and when she didn't move he leaned in towards her and put his hand between her legs, even higher than before. Rosie was caught unawares by the sensations that rippled through her but somehow managed to stay standing.

'I won't give that away. Not until I have a ring on my finger,' she said with as much dignity as she could muster. But as she turned and began to walk slowly out of the summer house, she couldn't help but wonder what it might have felt like if she had let him have his way.

# Chapter 17

When Roger stopped by to pick up Ruby, the Post Office was already closed and Vicky was in the middle of making a pile of sandwiches.

'I thought Ruby and I might have a bite together before she went home,' she explained. 'I didn't realise she was going to be joining you for a picnic. But it's no problem to wrap her sandwich up so she can take it with her.'

'That's very kind,' Roger said, 'but I think you should wrap up your sandwich and then you can come with us as well. It wouldn't be any extra work, would it?'

'No, of course not,' Vicky said, laughing. 'But I wasn't suggesting that I should—'

'Maybe you weren't, but I was,' Roger said with a

grin. 'Or, more accurately, Julie is. I know it's a bit last minute but she asked me to ask you, and you know how insistent little girls can get.'

A flush came to Vicky's cheeks and she didn't respond immediately.

'Do you have anything special on this afternoon? I trust your father's OK?' Roger said.

'He's fine, thanks, and no, I don't have anything special planned it's just that . . .'

'No excuses then,' Roger said. 'I'm sure Ruby won't mind, will you?' He turned to Ruby and Vicky was surprised by the look that flashed across her young assistant's face.

'Besides, you wouldn't want to let Julie down, now would you?' Roger said.

'Well no, you're right, I wouldn't, but . . .' she began, and she meant it, for she had grown very fond of Julie, and she wasn't able to think of any reason why she shouldn't go.

The weather stayed fine throughout the afternoon and despite the clouds gathering ominously, there was no actual rain. Ruby seemed to be in a strange mood and almost as soon as they found a suitable place on the grassy bank to unpack the car, she had taken one of the fishing nets and wandered off to sit on her own. Vicky had become uncomfortably aware of the adoring way the young girl kept glancing at the doctor and she felt a moment of concern as she watched Ruby go, but she didn't feel able to say anything. Things had been working out well between them at the Post Office – better than Vicky had imagined when Roger had first put forward his suggestion. It had crossed her mind, too late, that Ruby might have preferred to have had all of the doctor's attention and not have to share it with the person who was her boss. She hoped she hadn't jeopardised their good relationship by accepting his invitation.

But she had little time to worry about it for she was soon diverted by Julie who commandeered her from the moment they spread out the large tarpaulin sheet and opened up their greaseproof-wrapped sandwiches. Julie didn't leave her side all afternoon and together they filled several jam jars with what Roger pronounced to be frogspawn in varying stages of development. Julie was convinced she could see some tadpoles but it was not easy to see exactly what was swimming about in the murky water.

By the time Ruby had rejoined them, Vicky had already played hide-and-seek and several rounds of I spy. 'Let's play again,' Julie begged, tugging at Vicky's skirt.

Vicky gave an exaggerated sigh. 'I think it's time for you to have a round with Ruby, or maybe with Daddy,' she said with a grin.

'Has she worn you out?' Roger asked as he came to sit beside her on the sheet. 'She does have a habit of doing that.'

But Julie was already pulling on Ruby's arm. 'Come and look at our jars. Vicky and I are going to have loads and loads of baby frogs very soon.'

By the time Roger's A7 pulled up outside the Greenhill High Street parade of shops, Vicky was feeling more relaxed than she had for a long time. 'That was a really nice day, thank you so much for asking me,' she said sincerely as he switched off the engine. 'Did you enjoy it, Ruby?' she asked, turning to the girl sitting behind her.

'It was very nice. Thank you very much, Dr Buckley,' Ruby said, sounding rather formal.

'You're welcome,' Roger said. 'It's been lovely for both me and Julie to have company for a change.' He turned his head to get an endorsement from his daughter on the back seat but Julie was sound asleep and suddenly gave a loud snore which set them all laughing.

'Do you need any help getting out of the car?' Roger asked Ruby.

'No, thanks, I can do it myself,' Ruby said stiffly.

'Then I'll say goodbye,' he said. 'Maybe we can do this again some time but, in the meantime, make sure you keep up with the exercises.'

'Have a nice day tomorrow,' Vicky called to Ruby, 'and I'll see you on Monday.' But Ruby didn't reply as she limped away.

'I think I'd better get one very tired little girl home as soon as possible,' Roger said. 'Although I would like to have a word with you. But first things first.'

Vicky was trying to find the handle to open the door on her side but she stopped, aware that he'd turned to look at her. She looked away quickly.

'What do you want to talk to me about?' she asked.

'It'll keep for the moment. But, by the way, I don't know if you've seen the posters that there's a big dance being held in Manchester next week. I wondered if you'd like to go?' Roger said. 'It's at the Ritz ballroom.'

Vicky froze for a moment, thinking of the posters she'd carefully been trying to avoid and her relaxed mood was instantly destroyed.

When she didn't reply Roger said, 'You might want to think about it and let me know.'

'No, I can tell you now. I'm afraid I won't be able to go, I'm sorry,' Vicky said quickly, her hand grasping a tight hold on the door handle. She pulled it down hard and almost tumbled out on to the pavement as the door opened.

'Hold on a minute, don't go without—' Roger called after her. But she had already disappeared down the alley at the side of the terrace.

# Chapter 18

When Rosie arrived home from her evening with Trevor she was so busy rehearsing an explanation for her crumpled appearance that at first she didn't register that her mother wasn't there. Rosie had entered the kitchen by the back door and it took her a few minutes to realise that Sylvia was preoccupied with her own concerns in the front of the shop. She was standing by the open till, busily counting out the ten shilling and pound notes and stacking the shillings, florins and half-crowns into neat piles; she didn't seem to notice that Rosie looked somewhat dishevelled

'It's a bit late to be clearing the day's takings, isn't it?' Rosie stood by the connecting door, frowning. 'How come you didn't do it earlier?'

'I didn't think there was any need,' Sylvia said. 'We haven't had a particularly busy day today so I thought I might leave it till the morning. But then I had a call from your father to say he's coming home.'

'At this hour? I thought he was out of town?'

'So did I, but it seems he came back earlier today.'

'Where's he been till now?' Rosie asked.

'The pub most like, from the sound of his voice, but not a pub round here, I bet. He hasn't shown his face here all week, as you well know.'

'Why's he coming home all of a sudden?'

'He says he needs to see us – well, me really. Says he's got something important to tell me.'

'Like what?' Rosie said.

'If I knew that I'd be clairvoyant and I wouldn't have to wait till he got here to know, now would I?' Sylvia seemed to be looking over Rosie's shoulder. 'Talking of which, where's our Claire? I thought she was out with you?'

'No, I've been for a walk with Trevor. Maybe she went to Penny's?'

'I think she'd have told me . . .' Sylvia looked concerned.

'Why's it so important anyway?' Rosie asked. 'It's not as though it's late, even if she did go out.'

'I like to know where she is, that's all.' Sylvia hesitated, then, 'She's never seen your dad when he's in one of his . . . tempers. I thought it might be kinder to warn her to take no notice if she hears a bit of shouting. I'd hate her to walk in to the middle of something by accident.'

'Maybe she's upstairs,' Rosie suggested. 'You know how she often likes to go and lie on the bed and read.'

'Go and see for me will you, love, while I deal with this? I'd really rather know where she is.'

Rosie caught the panic in Sylvia's voice and she was relieved the spotlight was not on her. At times like this she actually felt a great deal of compassion for her mother, though there was nothing she could do to help her. She followed Sylvia upstairs and watched as she took the day's takings to her own bedroom, no doubt to add it to the savings she had managed to squirrel away in the special box she kept hidden in her wardrobe. To Rosie's relief, Claire was in bed fast asleep, snuggled under more than her fair share of the blanket. She was about to go to tell her mother that Claire was safely at home when she heard the back door slam shut and she realised she was too late. The only thing she could do now was to slip into bed beside Claire and pull a pillow over her ears to shut out the worst of the noise.

Sylvia barely had time to hide the glove box under her winter boots before she heard her husband shout her name from the bottom of the stairs. She locked the wardrobe door and slipped the key into her pocket.

'Come down here, woman! Why are you hiding?' he yelled.

'I'm not hiding.' Sylvia braved to go as far as the top of the stairs, trying desperately to keep her legs from trembling as she carefully made her way down.

'Have you eaten?' she said as pleasantly as she could when they drew level.

'They do a halfway decent cottage pie at the Three Jolly Tars,' Archie said. 'We should go there sometime, really.' His tone was genial but Sylvia was not so easily fooled.

It was obvious he had been drinking – she could see most of the usual telltale signs, like the way he fixed her with a glass-like stare and ambled aimlessly and unsteadily about the room. But for once his speech wasn't slurred and his clothes looked reasonably pressed and presentable.

'What do you need to tell me that couldn't wait till tomorrow?' Sylvia asked, wanting to get this over with. 'Do I need to sit down?' She wasn't sure why she added that but she caught him smiling.

'That's up to you and how you take the news.'

'Why? Bad news, is it?'

'Depends which way you look at it.'

'Are we going to play games all night or are you going to tell me?' Sylvia's anger gave her false courage.

'Oh, I'll tell you all right. I've come to pack my bags. I've decided not to wait for conscription. A mate of mine said that if I volunteer I'd be able to choose what service I go to. And as I've always fancied seeing the world – preferably at someone else's expense – I've signed up for the Merchant Navy.'

Sylvia gasped. 'But you can't swim!'

'Better to drown than be stuck in a muddy trench, like them poor buggers in the last war,' he said.

'Where will you be going?'

'I've no idea and I don't really care. I'm just looking forward to getting away.'

Now Sylvia looked at him pityingly. Was he really so stupid? Did he really think going to war would be that simple? 'When do you leave?' She was trying not to show her relief.

'Tonight. I'll be stopping over with a mate of mine for a few days and I have to report on Wednesday. You won't see me round here for a bit and I bet you won't be sorry.' He gave a chilling laugh.

She was afraid to answer as he was so close to the mark so she said, thinking that the occasional letter in his direction would be a small price to pay, 'Shall I write to you? Do you have an address?'

'I'll let you know as soon as I find out, then you can send me food parcels – decent ones, like.'

Sylvia couldn't help raising her eyebrows at that but thought it safer not to respond directly. 'How long is this war business going to last, do you think?' she asked. 'That's assuming it really does get started.'

Archie shrugged. 'Dunno. But I might find that I like travelling the world so much I'll not want to come home.' He chuckled, but Sylvia should have known better than to relax her guard for his hands suddenly shot out towards her like the poisonous fangs of a snake. Sylvia automatically recoiled but not quickly enough. Archie encased her chin painfully in the palm of her hand. 'Will you miss me?' He leered at her as his hands gripped her jawbone and spitefully pinched her cheeks.

'Of course I will.' She struggled to speak and hoped she sounded convincing. 'You'll let me know you're all right?'

Archie didn't reply but suddenly let go of her and ran up the stairs. She could hear him moving about in their bedroom and when he came down he was carrying the large duffle bag he usually kept on the top of his tallboy; she could see that it was stuffed full.

'The girls are in bed, I take it?' he said. 'Say goodbye to them for me. I never did get to know my niece. Some other time maybe. But let me give you something to remember me by. It might be the last time for quite a while.'

To Sylvia's horror he grabbed at her once more but this time his arm encircled her waist so that it was more difficult for her to avoid being caught in his grip. She did manage to twist partway out of his grasp but she was too slow to turn away completely and he caught hold of her as soon as she put one foot on the stairs. As he pulled her back down, she could hear the ripping sound of her skirt. This time he held on to her tightly with one hand as he popped the buttons of her blouse with the other before sliding his hand inside her underwear. Then he undressed himself only as far as necessary before he slammed his body into hers.

It was some time later, when she was convinced that Archie was long gone, that Sylvia finally stirred and painfully made her way up the stairs. But the sight that greeted her in the bedroom made her sit down heavily on the bed and weep. The lock on the wardrobe door had been prised open, leaving the doors hanging at an uncertain angle. Her shoes and boots were scattered across the floor together with her clothes, but most upsetting of all was when she trod on something hard and felt it snap beneath her foot. She looked down to see what had once been a sturdy cardboard lid and she realised that her precious glove box was empty.

Rosie hardly noticed that her father had gone because she had seen so little of him lately and no one talked about him either at home or in the shop. She wasn't sure what Claire had picked up about the night of his departure but neither she nor her mother referred to it or mentioned his name.

After the summer house debacle, Rosie worried that Trevor might not want to see her again and she spent time thinking of ways in which she might be able to make the first move to approach him. But before she had devised a workable plan she was surprised at the end of a shift to find him loitering by the wall the way he had when she had first come to work at the factory.

He was standing in among a crowd of his mates, on the same spot where she had first seen him, and she had the distinct impression that she had been the topic of their conversation. As soon as he saw her, Trevor detached from the pack and approached her with his arm outstretched. His fingers held a lit cigarette that he was shielding with his palm and he held it out towards her like a peace offering. She took it without comment and inhaled deeply.

'Were you waiting for me?' she said.

'Sort of,' he said. 'Though I wasn't sure if you were in today. Shall I walk you home?'

'That would be nice,' she said, smiling coyly, glad that he had made the first move and they walked on in silence for a while.

'I didn't think you'd want to see me again,' Rosie said eventually, hoping that the colour of her cheeks was not giving away the turmoil that was whirling in her head.

Trevor shrugged. 'Why not?' he said. 'I told you I love you, didn't I?'

'Yes,' she said. 'You did.'

'And you said you loved me,' he countered.

'That's right, I do.'

'Well, then, how about we . . .?' He put his arm round her and gave her a squeeze, while at the same time brushing her lips with his.

'Oh, aren't you the daring one?' she said with a smile.

'I've told you before, I'd like to show you how daring,' he said flirtatiously, 'if only you'll let me.'

Rosie stopped. 'I'm sorry,' she said, 'but I told you, I don't intend to let *anyone* . . . Not until we're married, and I mean it. So you can stop calling me a tease.' Her face creased into an exaggerated frown.

Suddenly she felt a rush of heat to her cheeks as she realised it sounded as if she was actually proposing and she was glad there was no one else nearby to hear or see them. She pulled her shawl more closely over her shoulders and continued walking in the direction of home. She was pleased when Trevor ground out what remained of his cigarette with the metal cap of his shoe and followed her.

'Why do we need to wait till we're married?' He quickly caught up with her. 'I've already told you I love you. Isn't that enough?'

He stepped in front to face her and Rosie looked into his eyes. They were still the same steely grey with the provocative glint that always made her blood race faster and right now they were issuing a challenge.

'I really don't understand. You say you love me and yet you're not willing to prove it,' he said. 'If you really loved me you'd want to please me.' He reached out and took her hand in his, then he began rubbing his thumb across her palm. 'Like I want to please you . . .' He had to clear his throat. 'A piece of paper, a ring, they're not going to make any difference to how I feel.'

'No, of course they're not,' she said, 'but they tell the world I'm respectable and that you have honourable intentions.'

Trevor didn't say anything but began to inspect his fingernails. Then he spread his hands, palms upwards and shrugged. 'If it's that important to you, why don't we get married then?' he said.

Rosie looked up and her hand flew to her mouth. 'Oh, but I didn't mean—' she gasped, and looked flustered. She shifted her feet awkwardly as she looked down at the pavement.

'Yes, you did. Don't start pretending otherwise. But we could get married if you wanted, you know. There's nothing to stop us.'

Rosie began to tremble at the enormity of what had just happened. It wasn't very romantic, but she didn't care.

'What with all the talk about war and bombs and the like, who knows what might happen,' Trevor said. 'So it might not be such a bad idea after all.'

'Do you think you might be called up into the army?' Rosie asked, terrified by the thought.

'Could be, I suppose. Though don't forget I've got a very important job helping to keep the factory going. But it makes sense that we should grab what we can, while we can.'

'Even if it's isn't very romantic?' The words were out before she could stop them.

'I'll get down on one knee if that's what you want?' Trevor said and suddenly he knelt down on the paving stones in front of her. Rosie was embarrassed and glanced desperately about her, but fortunately there was no one else on the street. Trevor grasped hold of both of her hands. 'Will you marry me?' he said, his voice pleading.

'Do you really mean it?' Rosie gasped.

'Why should I not mean it?'

He remained down on the ground.

'Then yes, I will.' Rosie whispered the words as if afraid to say them out loud and Trevor got up with a bright smile. He put his arms round her and kissed her lips briefly and Rosie felt her stomach turning familiar somersaults. This was the moment she had dreamed of so often . . . and yet, now that the moment had arrived, she didn't know whether to laugh or cry.

'What will my mother say?' she said at last, trying to picture announcing her engagement at home.

Trevor put his arm round her and pulled her close. 'If you're worried, don't tell her,' he whispered into her ear. 'I shan't be telling mine. It can be our secret.'

'For how long?'

'Until I've saved up enough for a ring.'

'Yes, that makes sense,' Rosie said, finding the idea of a secret engagement strangely appealing.

'*We'll* know we're engaged which is the most important thing after all. We can make it official once we've got the ring.'

'Yes, I'm dying to show that off,' Rosie said her voice full of excitement. 'And I know my mum will love me to have one.' She remembered her mother's pawnshop story and resolved that she would keep a firm grip on hers.

'Do you think she might offer to pay for the wedding, then? It doesn't have to be anything fancy.'

'Hmm,' Rosie said, thinking about the recent events at home, 'what with one thing and another she might not be in a position to pay for anything, not now my dad's gone into the forces.'

'Oh well, all we need is to sign the register, have a bit of a knees-up afterwards at the pub and Bob's your uncle,' Trevor said.

Rosie didn't answer immediately. It sounded so stark. She had always imagined she would have a big church wedding with all the trimmings to show off to the world that she was as good as any of the other girls in the street. She felt her eyes moisten. There was time to think about that. She held up her left hand and inspected her slender bare fingers; the first thing to do was to get a ring.

She stopped and looked back at the pavement they'd been walking along, trying to fix a picture in her mind of the actual spot where Trevor had proposed. 'There's a jewellery shop opposite the library, isn't there?' she said brightly. 'There's no harm in us having a look in the window next time we pass, is there? As you say, it doesn't need to be anything fancy.' And she slipped her arm through his once more and gave it a squeeze.

# Chapter 19

After their fishing trip, Vicky came in from Roger's car and sat down heavily at the kitchen table. The evening shadows were lengthening but she didn't bother to turn on the light. She was glad her father was out and she was free to sit and ponder on the events of the day. She felt as if Roger had managed to destroy all the pleasure she had taken from the whole day's outing when he had asked her to go to the Ritz, although she could hardly blame him for her reaction. It wasn't his fault that she had been so upset and, if anything, he deserved an explanation. He didn't know the bittersweet memories that had been triggered by the mention of the well-known dance hall. He had no way of knowing that that was the very place where she had first met

Stan, the place the two of them had returned to on Saturday 8th August, 1936. She would have to pluck up the courage to tell him that that was not a day that she was likely to forget, and that the ballroom was not a place to which she was eager to return.

The year 1936 had been a year of peace in England and Vicky had assumed Stan had asked her to go dancing at the Ritz in order to celebrate the six-month anniversary of their meeting. It would also provide an opportunity for them to discuss in more detail the engagement and wedding they'd begun to plan. She enjoyed dancing and had readily accepted his invitation. She was looking forward to an evening of romance and fun. Vicky also had her own reasons for celebration, although she hadn't told Stan yet, but she intended to before the night was out. However, halfway through the evening she'd found out that Stan had more serious things on his mind than anniversaries, none of which were romantic.

They both began the evening in a bright and cheerful mood and they hadn't missed a dance from the moment they'd arrived, wildly jitterbugging and Charlestoning their way through the big-band section of the programme until they were forced to pause when the band took a break for a drink.

'This is such fun! A great way to celebrate our anniversary.' Vicky beamed at Stan. 'Though I am ready for a sit down.'

'Oh dear, I'm afraid I didn't realise it was our anniversary,' Stan said. He had to raise his voice in order to be heard above the general hubbub and he looked genuinely apologetic. 'Still, I'm glad you're enjoying yourself, because it might be a while before we can do anything like this again.'

Vicky looked at him, puzzled. 'Why's that?' she asked. Alerted by the serious tone of his voice she felt a sense of foreboding and she was inexplicably doubled over by a sudden stitch in her side. She felt an overwhelming need to sit down and Stan guided her to one of the tables surrounded by red velvet upholstered chairs that stood vacant in a quiet corner away from the dance area.

'Can I get you anything, some water?'

Vicky shook her head. He sat down opposite her and reached out to cover her hands with his. 'Are you sure you're all right?' he said, his voice full of concern.

'I'll be fine. Just give me a minute.'

'I'm sorry to do this to you, but there is something that I've urgently got to talk to you about; that's why our anniversary went clean out of my head, I'm afraid.'

Vicky frowned. She could see he was serious. Thankfully, the pain in her side had receded and she was able to take a deep breath. 'I'm listening,' she said.

'I know you've always thought I was kidding whenever I've tried to talk to you about the war that's going on in Spain right now,' he began. 'You've never taken me seriously whenever I've tried to talk about the possibility of going over there to fight . . .'

'That's because I've never understood why it's so important when Spain is so far away—'

'It's important because it's critical for our future – if we're to have a future,' he said, cutting across her and Vicky was alarmed; he looked so earnest. 'In fact, it's vital that we stop the march of the fascists in Europe, otherwise they'll be invading us next.' He leaned forward. 'It's so important that I've signed up. I'm going to Spain to fight.'

Vicky gasped. Above the din she thought perhaps she hadn't heard him right, but Stan gazed intently into her eyes and tightened his hold on her hands. 'I feel I've got to go to help the cause.'

Vicky stared at him in disbelief. She'd always believed that boys like him were not born for soldiering; they were too gentle and peace-loving to willingly hurt others. Maybe she'd got it wrong.

'You can't really be serious?' was all she said as she scoured his face, but she could see from the steel in his gaze that he was.

'You should know me better than that,' he said. 'It's not something I would joke about,' he went on, though he gave a nervous laugh. 'Several of the lads from the mill have already gone. We might have missed out on the Great War, but now we've got the chance to show that Franco what we're made of.'

Until that moment, Vicky had hoped that he might only be posturing but she couldn't deny the determined look on his face or the strength of his grip.

'The problem is, I'm afraid it's all ending up being a bit of a rush,' Stan said, 'although that might be a good thing.'

Vicky frowned. 'Why? When are you going away?'

'I've to report for training tomorrow morning and then—'

Vicky pulled her hands free and quickly covered her mouth. 'But you can't!' she blurted out, her voice breaking. 'I thought we were supposed to be engaged to be married?'

'Yes, we are,' he assured her. 'Nothing's changed.' He reached across the table, trying to brush back the curls from her face. 'The only thing is that we'll have to put off the actual wedding for a few months. But that doesn't matter. There's no rush.'

'Oh yes there is!' Vicky cried out involuntarily. She could feel the blood draining from her face and she began to weep silently. 'I'm carrying our baby,' she sobbed.

Stan sat back and she was surprised to see that his first reaction was to smile. 'And you've been doing all that wild dancing? I think this deserves a proper drink.'

Vicky shook her head. 'Maybe a glass of water for now, that would be nice.'

'Oh, darling,' he said. 'Am I allowed to say that it's

wonderful news? Just bad timing that's all. I'm very excited, but are you sure? Have you been to the doctor?' The words all seemed to tumble out at once.

Vicky nodded. 'Dr Buckley confirmed it this morning.'

Stan sprang back. 'Roger Buckley? Isn't he your family's doctor?'

'Yes, and he's been very kind and understanding.'

'But does that mean he's told your father? We haven't even told him we're engaged yet.'

'No. My father doesn't know. Dr Buckley has promised to keep it a secret for now and I'm sure we can trust him. I told him we'd be getting married soon anyway, and . . .' she hesitated. 'Of course I didn't know anything about Spain then. I thought we'd have plenty of time to—' Her voice broke and she couldn't go on. 'If my father finds out before we've had a chance to get married he . . . he'll throw me out of the house!' She was overtaken by tears.

'Damn! It really is rotten timing,' Stan said, 'but honestly, Vicky, I'm sure your father will see sense when he knows we're serious about getting married.' He took her hands in his once more. 'We'll do it as soon as I'm home on leave. We'll get a special licence and get married immediately, you can promise your dad about that.'

The tears were still flowing freely but somehow Vicky managed to smile at the same time. 'So, you did mean it?' she said, the relief evident in her voice.

Stan clasped both of her hands in his once more and reached up to brush away the tears.

'Of course I meant it. I love you, never forget that, and I give you my word that we'll do what's best for our baby.'

Vicky hiccupped something that sounded halfway between a chuckle and a sob.

'I'll make an honest woman of you before your dad has time to line up the sights of his shotgun,' he said, and Vicky smiled at that.

Stan put his finger under her chin and tipped her face towards him. 'Hey, there's no need to look so worried. Your dad will understand. I'll write to him to explain the situation. I'll do it tomorrow.'

Vicky smiled more broadly this time, knowing that Stan would not let her down.

'Tell me more about the baby,' Stan said. '*Our* baby. I want to know all the whys and wherefores.'

Vicky laughed at that. 'I think you can work out the answers mostly for yourself. The only thing I can tell you is that I have another six months to go.'

'Plenty of time for us to get married then. How are you feeling right now? I'm not at all sure about all that dancing. Shouldn't you be sitting with your feet up?' Stan said with sudden concern and he stood up as if they should prepare to leave.

'No, really, I'm fine,' Vicky said, pulling him back down again. 'And I feel better now having told you.

But look, the band's back and they're playing much softer music now. It's all slow stuff. I think I'd like to dance some more before we go home.'

'So long as you think it's good for you – and the baby,' Stan said and he came to her side of the table and gave a mock bow. Vicky stood up and she let him gently guide her onto the dance floor.

'It's a shame we can't tell your dad tonight,' Stan said as the bus pulled up outside the Post Office door a little later. 'It would have been good to be able to deal with it while we're here together.'

'I'm afraid he must be asleep by now,' Vicky said, 'and the last thing we want to do is to wake him up, believe me.'

'Never mind,' Stan said. 'We'll do the deed just as soon as I can get home on leave and we'll have a big party . . .'

Vicky remained with her memories, seated alone at the table in much the same way as she had on that fateful August night almost three years previously, only then her father had been sound asleep upstairs. She sighed loudly as she remembered Stan's promise and the tender way he had kissed her before he'd rumbled off home on his motor bike.

How was she to have known then that, for them, there wouldn't be a next time?

# Chapter 20

Claire didn't know what to do. She had never lied to her mother and she didn't want to start now, but she was finding it more and more difficult to send a letter home that was filled with truthful banter and light-hearted news. There was only so much she could say about the knitting patterns she'd sold or the alterations she was making to customers' clothes. It was not always easy to sound cheerful but she didn't dare to admit to feeling as miserable and lonely as she did now, because that would reflect unfairly on her aunt's hospitality when she knew Sylvia was trying her best to make her feel at home. What she really wanted to write was a list of questions regarding the family's history, but she knew that under the present circumstances it wasn't a good idea to put into writing things she suspected might be happening within the family she was now living with. But each week, as she desperately tried to find something to write about, she feared she was edging closer to betraying someone in the Barker household.

It had been clear from the beginning that there were deep-rooted problems between her aunt and uncle and she had actually heard the two of them fighting on several occasions, though she usually pretended to be asleep; but that wasn't something she could tell her mother about, even if she had known all the details. Thankfully, life had become less tense for everyone recently since her uncle Archie had left to join the navy and that was something she could write home about.

What Claire really wanted was to ask her mother to let her go home, but as more and more Anderson shelters began to appear in people's gardens, together with instructions for what to do in the event of an air raid, she knew that the possibility of her returning to London in the near future was becoming more remote. She would have to continue to put on a brave face and try to find something that she could tell her mother each week. Though it was a surprise to find Rosie providing her with the most interesting news for her next letter.

Rosie had been out most of the evening as usual and when she finally clattered into the house it was time for her to say goodnight and go straight to bed. Her hair was down around her face, the original curls having dropped from their carefully pinned positions so that they hung limply and looked as if they might still be attached to their overnight curling rags. Rosie's cheeks were flushed, her eyes looked unusually animated, and Claire noticed she was giggling as if she'd been drinking as she hung her jacket over the bannister.

Sylvia raised her eyebrows. 'You could invite whatever his name is to come here for a nightcap, you know, instead of always wasting money in a pub. We don't bite.' She glanced at Claire who shrank back into her chair, not wishing to be drawn in to this conversation, though she could see Sylvia's point of view. 'In fact, I'd love a chance to talk to him properly; I'm supposing he's the one I met briefly before?'

'Ta, I'll tell him. I'm sure he'd love to come here sometime,' Rosie said, not without sarcasm and she gave a wink in Claire's direction that her mother couldn't see.

'What kind of a boy is he anyway, who's always taking you to pubs? I presume that's where you've been till now?' Sylvia didn't want to let it go. She stood up and wrinkled her nose as she confronted her daughter. 'Between the cigarette smoke and the beer fumes it smells like you've been there some time.'

Rosie ignored the barb and gave an exaggerated yawn. Then she ran up the stairs before her mother could ask any more awkward questions.

Claire followed shortly afterwards and was surprised to find Rosie was still very much awake. She was sitting up in bed reading a magazine and, as Claire entered the room, she actually looked pleased to see her. Rosie's cheeks were still glowing pink and she wriggled her legs under the bedclothes, setting the magazine aside.

'You'll never guess what happened tonight!' Rosie's eyes were shining brightly.

Claire waited, knowing better than to attempt a guess.

'You know Trevor?' Rosie said.

'You mean the boy who took you to the funfair?'

'Yeah, that's the one,' Rosie said. 'Well, he's only asked me to marry him.' There was an excited chuckle in her voice and she held up her left hand where what looked like a paper tie had been secured onto the third finger.

'No!' Claire was startled into a reaction and peered closely at the tie.

'Very definitely, yes! What do you think to that?' Rosie said. 'That thing's only pretend for the moment, till we can get the real thing.' She withdrew her hand hastily and hid it under the covers.

'I'm very happy for you, Rosie. It sounds wonderful,' Claire said. 'I wish you all the very best of everything. But why didn't you say something downstairs? Aren't you going to tell your mother?'

'No, it's not official yet,' Rosie said. 'I'm only telling

you because I've got to tell someone or I'll burst. But it's to be a secret from everyone else until Trevor can get the ring.' She bounced up and down with excitement.

'Gosh, I-I'm honoured that you've told me,' Claire said uncertainly.

'You are indeed. And I'm trusting you not to tell a soul.'

'But I thought your mum had already met him anyway?'

'She did, very briefly. Not enough to say that she knows him, though, and she's bound to disapprove of him on principle.'

'I'm sure that's not true. You know she has your best interests at heart,' Claire ventured, 'and I think she'd love you to be engaged.'

'That's probably true, but she always asks so many questions,' Rosie argued. 'I accept that not everyone takes to Trevor immediately. Mostly they're plain jealous, though not Mum, of course. But I don't want to push my luck and have her misunderstanding his motives.'

'Like how?' Claire said.

'Oh, I don't know,' Rosie was vague. 'But promise you won't tell her.'

'I promise,' Claire said solemnly. 'When will the wedding be? Have you set a date?'

'Not decided yet, but I'll let you know,' Rosie said, picking up her magazine again and hugging it to her chest.

Claire took the hint and, as she climbed in between the sheets, she curled up with her back to Rosie and pulled the blanket over her head. She knew it would be a quite some time before she fell asleep.

Rosie saw the ring the first time they looked in the jeweller's window.

'That one near the back in the black velvet box,' she said, pointing to what looked like a ruby-red chip of a stone set in a nest of tiny pearls. 'Don't you think it's pretty?'

'I thought engagement rings had to be diamonds?' Trevor said. 'Or at least bits of glass that look like diamonds.'

'Not necessarily,' Rosie said. 'You can have whatever you want and I happen to think coloured stones can look just as nice.'

'That's a relief, then, though that one looks expensive,' Trevor said. 'Do you think it's real?'

'I don't know, but it does look nice. I could see something like that on my hand, couldn't you?' She had abandoned the paper tie and she held up her ringless hand as if expecting him to admire it.

'Is there a price on it?' he asked. 'Then we'll know if it's real or not.'

'No, there isn't, but we can find out easily enough,' Rosie said, though secretly she hoped it wasn't expensive so that Trevor could never be tempted to put it in hock. 'And there's nothing to stop us going in and trying it on,' she went on, pulling at his arm. She had suddenly realised that she was really excited at the thought of being properly engaged and she hoped it wouldn't be too long before she would have a ring on her finger – maybe even that one.

Trevor laughed as he resisted. 'What? And find out how many years of saving it will take before I can afford it? I'm not sure I want to know. I'd like to get married before I'm an old man.'

'Don't be so pessimistic; it might not be so bad as all that,' Rosie said, and she nudged her shoulder against the door.

'What a pity, they're closed,' Trevor said, pointing to the sign Rosie in her eagerness had missed. 'We'll have to come back another time.'

'Preferably before you're an old man!' she said.

'OK then, I'll make you a promise,' he said. 'We'll get married as soon as I've paid for the ring.'

# Chapter 21

Tension had been mounting throughout Britain, acknowledging the inevitability of the country being plunged into another war and no one was in any doubt about the devastating impact that it would have on the whole country in general and on a small community such as Greenhill in particular. Despite Prime Minister Neville Chamberlain's optimistic announcement of 'peace in our time' on his return from Munich in September 1938, his policy of appeasement was proving to be unsustainable and ineffectual and it was becoming apparent that the Nazi war machine, having rolled through Czechoslovakia, was now amassing troops on the Polish border.

But Vicky had been trying not to think about the

impending war, or about her brother Henry who was poised to be shipped out with a British expeditionary force when war was finally declared. She was still thinking about that afternoon's fishing trip: the delight of a little girl over a jar of muddy tadpoles, her own pleasure at spending time with Julie and her father, the simple picnic they had enjoyed together, and her ultimate disappointment that the day had not ended well. She didn't know how long she had been sitting at the table when there was a knock at the back door and she was surprised to find Roger standing on the step.

'Sorry if I'm interrupting anything,' he said.

'No, not at all. My father seems to have gone out and I was just sitting, thinking. Do come in.' She held the door wide.

'I really did need to get Julie home before I could think of anything else,' Roger said. 'She was spark out. But I wondered if now might be a good time to talk?' He peered into the living room.

'Yes, do go through, I'm on my own,' Vicky said. 'And I was wanting to talk to you as well, to apologise for dashing off like that without thanking you properly for such a lovely day. The least I can do is to explain why I can't – or should I say *won't* – go with you to the Ritz.'

'I'm afraid I didn't handle things well in the car,' Roger said, 'and . . . well, I'm sorry if I sprang it on you about the dance. I had meant to talk to you properly first, so it was no wonder you looked so surprised.'

'The thing is—'

'I wanted to say—'

They began to speak at the same time and they both laughed.

'You first,' Vicky said, glad the tension had been broken momentarily, although she still wasn't sure how much she should tell him.

'I wasn't being totally fair about the dance invitation,' Roger began. 'I don't know if you've seen the posters?' Vicky looked uncertain. 'The point is,' Roger said, 'it's a special farewell get together for the next round of soldiers who are going off for their initial training.' Vickie froze. She'd seen the posters but once she'd noticed the venue she hadn't read the details and as Roger spoke she was hit by flash of déjà vu.

'Soldiers? Are you . . .?' She felt the blood drain from her face.

'That's what I was really wanting to tell you, but the thing about the dance slipped out first.'

'You mean you've . . .?'

'I seem to have got things the wrong way round,' Roger apologised. 'But the answer is, yes, I've enlisted. I reckoned that once the war actually begins they'll start conscripting men of my age. And there's no doubt they'll be needing qualified medics . . .' He didn't need to finish the sentence.

Vicky could feel tears prickling. 'Sadly, that's what war is all about.' She was barely able to get the words out.

'I don't really hold with fighting,' Roger said, 'but I can't claim to be a conscientious objector. I can't stand by and do nothing. I can't let people like Hitler and his fascist supporters march into any country they please. If we don't stop them they'll soon be trying to take over the whole world.'

Vicky sat down. Weren't these the same arguments – almost the same words – she'd heard before? Isn't that exactly what Stan had said before going off to the Spanish Civil War? When would the fighting ever stop? Vicky felt as if her brain had seized up and she wanted to stop listening. *How many more people have to die before men learn that wars are not the answer?* she wanted to scream. All she could think about was that she couldn't go through it all again. Then she realised Roger was still talking.

'From a purely selfish point of view, it's a rotten shame it's such bad timing. I felt you and I were just beginning to get to know each other and I was hoping – that is, I was going to ask you if . . . may I write to you?'

Vicky stared at him, too stunned to speak. *Bad timing?* When had she heard those words before? The pain was almost physical. She covered her face with her hands. 'I – I'm afraid I wouldn't make a very good correspondent,' she said at last, though she didn't look at him. 'I couldn't promise to write back.'

She glanced up and his face registered his disappointment, but that couldn't stop her saying what she had to say next. She took a deep breath. 'I'm sorry Roger, but if you're going away it would be better if we make a clean break,' she said, her voice barely above a whisper. She tried hard to smile but didn't quite manage it. 'You should go to the dance though.' She did her best to keep her voice light. 'You never know, you might find someone there who'll make a far better pen-friend than me.' Now she did manage a smile, despite the accumulation of tears, but Roger didn't engage or smile back and for a moment they sat in silence, each wrapped up in their own thoughts.

'What about Julie?' Vicky said eventually, struggling to keep her voice steady. 'Have you told her you'll be going away?'

'No, not yet. I shan't tell her until the last minute,' he said. 'My parents will look after her, of course, and at least it's a relief to know she won't have to be uprooted or evacuated to live with strangers. And before you ask, my father will be taking over my general practice.' He managed a chuckle. 'He already knows most of my patients, so people like your father will probably get better attention than I give them. Treatment is bound to include the odd game of cards.' He said this jokingly but Vicky didn't join in with his laughter and for a few moments there was an awkward silence.

'Can I ask when you are going?' Vicky said eventually.

'I have to report to the training camp at the end of next week. Soon after the dance really.' He stood up.

'I don't suppose I can persuade you to change your mind about that, if not about the letter-writing?'

Vicky shook her head. 'No, I'm sorry. That place holds too many memories of Stan.' She gave an involuntary shudder.

Roger drew in a breath sharply. 'Yes, of course. I'm sorry, I hadn't thought. There's not much else to say then,' he said.

At that there was the sound of a key being turned in the lock of the back door and a second later Arthur walked into the room as if on cue.

'Roger was just leaving, Dad,' Vicky said pointedly as the two men shook hands. Vicky also put out her hand. 'I wish you all the very best of luck, Roger,' she said softly and she turned away as her eyes misted.

'Good heavens! What was all that about?' Arthur said when Roger had gone. 'Did I come in at a bad time?'

Vicky frowned.

'You wouldn't have guessed you two were friends,' Arthur said, 'you both looked so glum. I thought you were supposed to have been out for the day. Didn't you have a good time?'

'Actually, we did, thank you,' Vicky responded automatically. 'We had a lovely time.'

'Then why the long faces?' He jerked his thumb in the direction of the closed door.

'Roger wanted me to go to the Ritz in Manchester

next week for some special dance and I told him I can't go.' She tried to sound casual.

'That's a shame. It's not every day you get the chance for a night out like that. Couldn't you change your arrangements? It might be fun.'

'It's nothing to do with my arrangements.' Vicky lowered her voice. 'That place has bad memories for me and I've no intention of ever going back there.'

'Ee, lass . . .' Arthur shook his head. 'Don't you think it's time to give up on your memories? Either tell them to get lost or lock them away somewhere. They're a thing of the past and that's where they belong.'

'That's easy for you to say,' Vicky retorted.

'You can't let them keep getting in the way of your life, now.' Arthur sat down and put his head in his hands, his breathing sharp. 'And here was I thinking the two of you were really beginning to get somewhere at last, like.'

'It's not as simple as that, Dad.' Vicky cut in. 'The dance is for soldiers, essentially to say welcome to the new recruits who are stepping up for training so that they'll be ready to go when the war really gets started. What Roger came to tell me is that . . .' She hesitated before saying the words. 'What he couldn't tell me this afternoon in front of his daughter was that he's joined up.'

'Oh. I see.' Arthur sat back and looked at her sadly. 'I suppose it's only to be expected, a young man like him, and a fully trained medic. It's a shame, though. Just when you were getting along so well.'

'Yes, it is a shame, but life's like that, isn't it? I think I'll ask for "Bad Timing" to be carved on my gravestone.' Vicky got up. 'Shall I mash us some tea?' she called behind her as she stepped into the kitchen to put the kettle on. 'I don't know about you, but I've a real thirst on.' She rinsed out the teapot. 'And it must be a while since you've had your dinner, so what can I get you for your tea?'

'I'm not hungry, thanks,' Arthur mumbled. 'Just come back in here and sit down and tell me what's really bugging you. There's got to be more to it than you turning down an invitation to a dance.

'Nothing's bugging me, as you so delicately put it,' Vicky said, as she came into the living room and placed two steaming cups of tea on the table.

'But if the look on that young man's face was anything to go by, I'd say you sent him away with a flea in his ear.'

'No, I didn't,' she protested.

'Then why did he look like that? I've never seen him looking so miserable before.'

Vicky sat down again at the table and stared into her lap. 'It's probably because I told him we had no future,' she said softly. 'And I told him I wouldn't write to him.'

Arthur's eyebrows shot up in surprise. 'Why did you do that? I thought the two of you were—'

'Because we don't *have* a future,' Vicky interrupted again. 'We've got no chance of getting together and I don't want him hanging on to any false hopes that we do.'

'Do you not like him?' Arthur frowned. 'Is that it? Only, I thought . . .'

'No, I do like him, but that's the problem.' She drew a deep breath that sounded more like a sob. 'Don't you see? I can't let myself fall in love with someone else who in all probability's going to be killed. I just can't.' She let out what sounded like a strangled moan. 'I couldn't stand losing one more person I love to another stupid war! The very thought of it tears me apart.' She squeezed her eyes shut but it didn't stop the tears spilling onto her cheeks.

Arthur said nothing. He looked at her as if he was seeing her for the first time. The room was quiet save for the steady ticking of the clock on the mantelpiece and Vicky's heaving sobs that she was desperately trying to bring under control.

'I've never heard you talk like this before, Victoria,' Arthur said eventually. 'You don't know that he's going to be killed. Just because Stan was unlucky. Roger's not going to cop it any more than . . . any more than our Henry.'

As he said the words they both stopped, but then Arthur ploughed on, 'You of all people should know how unpredictable life is. We can't say for certain what's going to happen to any one of us.'

'Yes, Dad, I do know that, and that's what upsets me so much.'

'Then you also know that some of us do come back.' He took a deep, rasping breath, 'Even if we're damaged.'

Vicky rushed over to him and embraced him in a huge hug. 'Oh, Dad! I'm sorry, I didn't mean . . .'

'Would you have written me off before I went? Or perhaps you'd rather I'd not come back once I'd been injured?'

'No, of course not. Don't be silly!'

'What if your mother had given up on me when I signed on because there was a chance I could come back like this? I shudder at the thought.' He shook his head and began to cough. It was several minutes before he could continue. 'And would I not have married her knowing that she wasn't going to survive long after the war?' he said at last.

Vicky didn't say anything and she went back to her seat, but she couldn't look at him as she sat down again at the table.

'You know your mam and I didn't have very long together, but I would rather have had them few years with her than to have missed out on what we did have together, including bringing you and our Henry into the world.' He chuckled and his face broadened into a smile.

Vicky fumbled in her pocket for her handkerchief and blew her nose loudly.

'We none of us know anything about the future, Victoria,' Arthur went on. 'And mostly we don't get any choice.'

'No, I suppose not, when you put it like that,' she said.

'That's why we've got to grab with both hands anything that we do get. Think about it,' he said. He reached out across the table and took her hand in his. 'Now tell me honestly: do you like him?' He stared into her eyes.

Vicky lowered her gaze. 'Yes, I do. I like him very much,' she whispered. 'I think I love him.'

'Then I'd have thought you should try to seize every chance of happiness that might come your way, without trying to second-guess how long it might last for. First love doesn't have to be last love, you know. Of course it's tough, but perhaps it's time you accepted that your Stan's long gone.'

Vicky began to cry again. 'But I can't go through it again, Dad. I'm not strong like you. I don't think I can survive losing anyone else that I love and it's not fair to ask me to.'

At this Arthur gave a wry smile. He took out a freshly ironed handkerchief from his own pocket and passed it across the table without comment. 'We never know how much strength we actually possess until it's put to the test,' he said. 'And then we're often surprised.'

'Is this supposed to be my test? Is that what you're saying?' Vicky said. 'I'd have thought I'd had my fair share of trials already.' She sat back in her chair for a moment, thinking about when she had last been tested on what she considered to be the worst day of her life. It was the day she really had hit rock bottom, the day she'd lost everything, and it had begun when she'd received The Letter.

It was Stan's parents who had written to her. She'd been well into her pregnancy by then and had already fallen in love with the new life that she could feel stirring within her, knowing it was as much half of Stan as it was half of her. It had not been easy for her since Stan had gone to Spain. As Stan had suggested, she had tried desperately to convince her father that, even though she was pregnant, she was still respectable, just unfortunate, and that Stan had honourable intentions.

'I promise we're getting married, Dad,' she had pleaded with her father, 'and Stan told me specifically to tell you that he promises too. He was going to write to you but as you must know from the newspapers the post from Spain is very uncertain. But we'll be married the minute he sets foot on English soil again. We don't want our child to carry an illegitimate stigma all its life, any more than you do. We'll get a special licence.' It was then she had resorted to tears. 'Please don't throw me out onto the street; I've nowhere else to go.'

At first her father had been adamant. 'No daughter of mine is going to become an unmarried mother. I'll not stand for it. And I'll not have any so-called grandchild of mine born out of wedlock. If you're going to give birth to a bastard, you'll have to put it up for adoption. I want nothing to do with it. Mind, I'll still want you out of this house. You've brought shame on the family. I'm only pleased your mother isn't here to see it.'

Vicky had been heartbroken at that. She was sure her mother would have understood. But it was young Dr Buckley, as she had thought of him then, who had finally convinced Arthur not to act on his cruel words and he'd made a special visit to their home one evening.

'If you throw her out onto the street, Mr Parrott, you'll be forcing her into the kind of life no young girl should have to live. She doesn't deserve that. And think of the poor baby. Whether you like it or not it will be your grandchild. What kind of a start will he or she have in life? Do you really want to punish an innocent child because its father was courageous enough to go away to fight for a cause he believed in?' Roger Buckley had stood his ground and eventually Arthur Parrott had relented. That was why it had felt particularly cruel, as she had stood reading the letter, for Vicky to realise that, despite his honourable intentions, Stan would not be coming back to marry her and he would never get to see his own child. The tears welled as she thought of her plight. She had tried to fight it but she knew at that moment that for the baby's sake she would ultimately have to give in and agree to an adoption.

But as she had stood reading the short letter, over and over, Vicky's knees had suddenly given way and she'd sunk to the ground, feeling as if her life's blood was draining away. The young Dr Buckley had been sent for and he'd insisted on immediate bed rest.

'It's the only chance you have, I'm afraid, of saving the baby,' he'd told a stricken Vicky. But the shock of Stan's death and the continuing arguments with her father were too much for her and Vicky had suffered a miscarriage. She lay in bed for several weeks, knowing that mentally as well as physically she had reached her lowest ebb.

Ironically, it was Roger who had arranged for her to be cared for and Roger who had persuaded her father to allow her to come back home afterwards, in an attempt to start rebuilding her life. Perhaps it was the memory of that that made her father want to champion Roger's cause now, for he had not only saved Vicky's life, but had saved the Parrott family from complete disintegration. His warmth and his compassion were certainly among the attributes that had drawn Vicky to him, for he had never passed judgement, had never referred to that day or those difficult times ever again – and he had never betrayed her trust. Having played such an important part in her young life she had only recently realised how much she had been enjoying getting to know him, adult to adult. And it was those same qualities that had made her realise now that she actually loved him. But in her mind that was all the more reason why she had to let him go, for she knew she would not be able to bear it if anything happened to him now.

# Chapter 22

Sylvia asked Rosie so many times to invite Trevor round for Sunday tea that Rosie found it impossible to keep making excuses.

'I think it's high time I really met this young man you seem to be walking out with,' Sylvia said on several occasions, until finally she would be put off no more. 'I'm beginning to think you have something to hide, Rosie. How about we agree on next Sunday?'

'OK, I'll ask him,' Rosie said, not at all sure how Trevor would react and she was relieved that Claire immediately offered her apologies that she would not be available to join them.

'Oh, Claire, you don't have to go out just because Rosie's young man is coming, does she darling?' Sylvia said, looking directly at Rosie. 'After all, you are part of the family. Wouldn't you like to meet him too?'

Rosie didn't endorse the notion and Claire was quick to confirm that she had already made arrangements to meet Penny on that day. 'I'm sure there'll be other opportunities to meet him,' Claire said with a knowing look to Rosie.

'What time will he be coming?' Claire asked Rosie afterwards, when the two girls were alone. 'I'll make sure to be gone well before then.'

'Thanks Claire, I do appreciate that; it will certainly make life easier if I tell him there's only my mum he has to deal with. I'll do as much for you some day,' Rosie promised. 'And there'll be no need for you to hurry back, unless you feel the need to grill him too.' She grinned and Claire laughed. 'Is that what you're expecting your mother will do, grill him all afternoon?'

'What else are mothers for? She sees it as her God-given right,' Rosie said with a sigh, and she turned her gaze heavenwards and said a silent prayer of thanks to whoever might be residing up there that Trevor wouldn't have to meet her father until the couple were safely married.

'And you still don't intend to tell her you're engaged?' Claire asked. 'Not even when he comes here?'

'Certainly not.' Rosie was adamant. 'I've told you, not until Trevor can get me a ring. That's the only thing that will be really meaningful to her.' Claire lifted her hands, palms upwards, then pressed her index finger firmly against her closed lips.

On the Sunday, Sylvia took out and washed the best china from the glass cabinet, together with the silver cream jug and sugar bowl, the only items of any value that she'd managed to salvage from what was left of her inheritance from her mother. She always liked to produce them on the rare occasions she had visitors, and despite Rosie's arguments to the contrary she was eager to treat Trevor like a special guest.

'It's important that he should see that you come from a nice, respectable family,' Sylvia said when Rosie tried to let her down gently that such an honour would be lost on Trevor. She didn't want to tell her mother about the rundown back-to-back cottages in the poor end of Greenhill that Trevor had told her he came from.

The afternoon went better than Rosie might have hoped, with Trevor being more polite than she had ever seen him. She was surprised at how he seemed to know exactly how to flatter Sylvia, so that she was soon fluttering round him like a butterfly, even offering him cigarettes that Archie had forgotten to take with him from his best box of Navy Cut, and by the time the tea was over it was obvious that her mother was impressed with him. Rosie was almost sorry she had agreed to keep their engagement secret.

'It sounds like you have an important and responsible position at the factory,' Sylvia said when Trevor had outlined, with only minimal embellishment, some of the jobs he was expected to cover on the factory floor.

'Indeed I do,' Trevor said proudly. 'So much so that it's unlikely I'll get called up into the forces if they begin conscription if we really do go to war.'

Sylvia was keen to hear more, but the more he elaborated, the more anxious Rosie became that her mother would soon be angling to ask him what his intentions were towards her daughter. She knew he would have no wish to divulge their secret but she preferred not to open up too many opportunities for telling lies.

'What time is your meeting at the WI tonight?' Rosie asked Sylvia pointedly when she felt the questioning was becoming a little too personal.

'Goodness, is that the time?' Sylvia said, checking the tiny fob watch she had pinned to her blouse. 'I don't know where the afternoon has gone. Would you think me very rude if I had to go out? I'm sure you won't mind if I leave you two alone?'

'Not at all. There's no need to fret,' Trevor said, a little too eagerly.

'And you don't have to worry about the washing-up, Mum,' Rosie added, smothering her smile. 'I'll be happy to do that if you need to get off. I'd hate you to be late.'

To her astonishment, Trevor added, 'And I can always help her.'

'I'm really sorry to have to leave you like this,' Sylvia said. 'I honestly thought I still had lots of time.'

Sylvia suddenly began rushing about looking for her coat. 'I don't know where the afternoon's gone,' she said when Trevor helped her on with it and she turned and patted his hand. 'Thank you for the kind offer to do the dishes, Trevor, but you mustn't dream of it. In this house guests never do the washing-up, do they, Rosie?' And she gave the tinkly laugh she usually saved for Archie when he was in a playful mood.

Rosie didn't say anything as Sylvia was still gushing. 'But please feel free to stay as long as you like, Trevor. I won't be gone long, but I'm to become the chairman of our local Women's Institute group next week and tonight's an important meeting as it's the last one before the handover. And what with'—she waved her hands in the air—'all the talk about war and the special measures that will have to be implemented, there's a lot of decisions to be made and items to be voted on.'

'I'll be glad to stay and keep Rosie company,' Trevor said. 'What time will you be back?' he asked with an air of innocence that suddenly made Rosie suspicious.

'I can't promise. But I'm sure I'll be back by eight at the latest.'

'Oh, that's fine. I'll be gone by then.' Trevor smiled broadly. 'So I'll say goodbye now and thanks for my tea.' He put out his hand. 'It was very nice to meet you properly at last.'

Trevor hardly waited for the back door to close than he was behind Rosie, urging her to turn the key in the lock and hurry back to the living room. He steered her towards the couch and gave her a forceful shove onto the cushions.

'What are you doing? I can hardly breathe,' she gasped, completely winded. In an attempt to flop down beside her, Trevor had almost landed in her lap. He quickly shifted his bulk and put his arms around her.

'Well, she's gone,' he said with a broad grin, 'and you heard what she said; she'll be back by eight so we'd better get a move on.'

'Doing what?' Rosie struggled to sit up.

'Use your imagination, girl.' Trevor grinned as he pushed Rosie back down again, more gently this time and smothered her lips with his. She could feel his hands beginning to move swiftly all over her body.

'Hey,' Rosie protested, 'what do you think you're doing?' She had been taken by surprise by the speed of his movements and protested more out of habit, not wanting to admit that she was enjoying it.

'You have got expensive tastes, my darling,' Trevor said, nuzzling her ear. 'I don't know if you realise it, but it's going to take me quite a while to save up for the kind of ring you want. You don't expect me to wait that long before we can have a bit of fun, do you?'

Rosie was nonplussed. She hadn't thought of that.

'So I thought it might be a far better idea to take advantage right now of your mother's hospitality, especially now that she's had the foresight to go out for an hour or so. What do you say?' But he crushed his lips onto hers before she could say anything.

'You know what I say!' Rosie managed to get the words out finally when he surfaced for air. 'I've told you on several occasions and I've no intention of changing my mind.'

Trevor smiled. 'Oh, come on, be reasonable,' he wheedled. 'What difference will it make if we do it before you actually get the ring, rather than after? We know we're officially engaged to be married. Between the two of us we don't even need a ring.'

'I think I am being perfectly reasonable,' Rosie protested. 'I'm also being sensible. We'd be taking an awful chance trying to do it here, and now.'

'Why's that?'

'What if Mum comes back early? She could, you know.'

'Oh God, this is hopeless!' Trevor sighed as he climbed off her, shoulders slumped. For a moment Rosie felt a flutter of fear, thinking of her father, but Trevor merely went to Archie's cigarette box that stood on the sideboard and helped himself.

He lit up two automatically before handing her one without comment. Rosie sat up. She was beginning to feel frustrated and disappointed that being engaged wasn't all she had thought it would be. For starters, she was no longer as sure as she had been about what she wanted. She had always been clear in her own mind that she intended to save herself for marriage, but when Trevor's hands had started wandering . . . well, she hadn't expected to feel like that.

Trevor came back and sat down on the edge of the couch beside her.

'So, how long is this going to go on?' he said.

'What do you mean?' Rosie turned to look at him.

'I mean, there must be some time when we can guarantee we'll not be interrupted.' Trevor's voice was cajoling again as he moved closer so that she could feel the heat as the sides of their thighs touched and Rosie could sense that his frustration matched her own.

He put his arm across her shoulders and his hand began to play with the curls in her hair.

'What are you thinking?' he asked.

Rosie shrugged.

'I'll tell you what I'm thinking,' he said, his voice soft and persuasive. 'I'm thinking, why don't we fix up a special time . . .'

Rosie giggled. 'You mean, like, make an appointment?'

'Why not?' Trevor said and he picked up her hand and kissed the tips of her fingers. 'At least if we plan it properly so that we can guarantee no one will interfere we'll both be able to relax and enjoy it and you won't be worried about your mother coming back in the middle and spoiling everything.'

Rosie looked thoughtful, enjoying this moment as he began to stroke her hair again. 'Next Sunday Mum said she'll be at the WI all afternoon and evening, didn't she?' she said eventually. 'They'll be doing that handover thing she was talking about and I think they're planning to have a party afterwards. That should be a safe enough time; she'll be gone the better part of—' Rosie stopped. She couldn't believe she was being complicit and was actually saying the words. But it was too late to back out now. Besides, a part of her was excited at the thought.

'You do know that as far as the rest of the world is concerned none of this really matters, don't you?' Trevor said suddenly. 'Nobody else cares what we do, or when, or even how many times we do it. We're engaged. In fact, we're as good as married, if that's what you're worried about so it makes sense that we should be allowed to act as if we *are* married.' His voice was smooth and calming.

'There is something else . . .' Rosie said, though she actually hadn't wanted to put voice to the words.

'Oh yes, and what's that?' he said.

'You know . . .' She lowered her chin, unable to look at him and took a tiny puff on her cigarette. 'The obvious,' she said. 'What do all girls worry about?' She could see from out of the corner of her eye that he was looking directly at her, and she could feel him smoothing her hair off her forehead and pulling the curls out of her eyes. She could feel her face redden as she stared down into her lap. It was as if he was forcing her to say it. But still she couldn't.

'You *do* know,' she said again.

And this time he smiled. 'If you're afraid of getting pregnant, why don't you say so? If that really is the only thing you're worried about then all I can say is that you'll have to trust me.' He put his hand on her leg and gently squeezed.

He was right, of course, that was exactly what she was scared of and somehow hearing him say the words only served to remind Rosie how frightened she was of the reality and how little she knew about how to prevent the worst from happening or what to do about it if it did. She began to breathe more easily when she felt the reassurance of his touch, though she didn't want to consider the implication behind his statement. She assumed that he was far more knowledgeable about these matters than she was from the confident way he had said it and she had no wish to go into any more detail. But she realised with horror that she really knew very little about even basic contraception. She'd heard talk of French letters that she knew were available at barbers' shops and chemists and she wished she had asked her mother more about them when she had had the chance, for she didn't really know how they worked. But it was too late to be asking now without giving the game away. If she was going ahead with their plan, as she now felt she was committed to do, she would indeed have to rely on Trevor.

* * *

During the next few days, Rosie's mood fluctuated like a roller-coaster ride: one minute she was high with emotional excitement, the next consumed with physical dread at the thought of what she and Trevor were about to do and she worried that she might regret having made him such a promise. But she knew she couldn't back out now. She also knew that she would have to say something to Claire if she was to guarantee that she and Trevor would have the house to themselves next Sunday afternoon. It was vital that her cousin understood that she must stay away at the appointed time, but she didn't know how she was going to tell her.

# Chapter 23

'You're planning on doing *what*?' Claire all but exploded when they were next together in their bedroom and Rosie had finally plucked up the courage to tell Claire why she needed her to be out of the house the following Sunday. They were getting ready for bed.

'Shhh,' Rosie cautioned. 'You know how thin these walls are. You don't want to alert my mother into asking awkward questions.'

'Sorry. But seriously, Rosie.' Claire resorted to whispering, 'I know it's none of my business but are you really going to lie down and let him have his way?'

'You make it sound disgusting and totally one-sided,' Rosie protested. 'As though I have no say in the matter. I want this as much as he does.'

'Really? Are you sure about that?'

'Of course I'm sure. I like to think of it as making love – and that's a beautiful thing.' She looked away with a dreamy look in her eyes that reminded Claire of a film she'd seen recently. And when Rosie stared off into the middle distance like several actresses she could name, Claire wanted to laugh. 'I do love him, Claire. You seem to be overlooking that fact,' Rosie said.

*Now she sounds like one of those cheap actresses*, Claire thought, and that made her feel even more sceptical. 'But it's such a huge step you'll be taking,' Claire said, not knowing how much she dared to say. 'Not one to be taken lightly. Have you really thought about it?'

'Believe me, I've considered it very carefully,' Rosie said, 'but it's not as if we aren't getting married soon, so what difference does a piece of paper make, or even a ring for that matter?'

Claire couldn't help wondering if those really were Rosie's words as she began to get undressed and ready for bed. She felt she could only challenge so far and was not sure what else she could say; it was obvious Rosie had made up her mind. 'I know it's none of my business,' she said eventually, 'but have you thought about the possible consequences if things go wrong?'

'Really, Claire! There's no need to be so pessimistic.' Rosie pouted with a false bravado. 'I'm not completely naïve.'

Claire pulled her flannelette nightdress over her head and tied some rags into her shoulder-length curls; her hair had really grown since she had come to live in Greenhill. 'All I can say is I hope he loves you as much in return – enough at least to justify what you're sacrificing.'

'You make it sound very dramatic,' Rosie said and she gave a little laugh.

'In my book what you're planning is pretty dramatic,' Claire said as she climbed into bed.

'So, does that mean you won't . . .?' Rosie's brow suddenly wrinkled as she turned to look directly at Claire.

Claire sighed. 'Don't worry, I'll get out of the way and leave the coast clear for you. I don't agree with what you're doing, but word of honour, I won't give away your secret.'

Claire, however, had been greatly disturbed by their late-night conversation and when she thought about it later she was sorry she had made the promise to Rosie. She lay awake most of the night worrying whether there was something else she might say that would stop Rosie making what she saw as such a huge mistake. Her aunt was the only person who might be able to prevent Rosie from going ahead with her plan but Claire had promised not to say anything to her and she couldn't think of anyone else she could confide in. It would feel like a complete betrayal if she said something to Penny as her new friend lived too close to home. No, Claire decided, there was nothing more she could do, but that didn't stop her spending the rest of the week worrying.

It was a relief on Saturday morning when Penny dropped in to Knit and Sew for a chat and to pick up some knitting wool, and Claire was delighted when her friend asked if she would like to go to the pictures that night. It would be good to have something to take her mind off her worries about Rosie.

'I thought we might go to see *Goodbye Mr Chips*,' Penny said.

'Yes please. I've been dying to see that,' Claire said. 'There's hardly been a customer in the shop who hasn't recommended it since it opened at the Odeon.'

'It starts at the Plaza on Saturday when the programme changes,' Penny said. 'I thought we could go there, though on a Saturday night we might have to queue to get in.'

'How's about we have a bit of a picnic first, if the weather's nice?' Claire suggested and Penny readily agreed.

It was bright and sunny all day on Saturday and, when Penny arrived to collect her, Claire asked Rosie if she would like to join them.

'Thanks, but Trevor's taking me dancing tonight,' Rosie said with a happy smile, and she gave a twirl to show off the fullness of her semi-circular skirt – what she called her dancing skirt. 'It should be fun,' she said, and behind her mother's back, she winked at Claire.

'Enjoy yourself, anyway,' Claire said. She and Penny set off to stroll up to the park together with their small basket of food and they sat on a bench by the children's swings to eat them. But all she could think about was Rosie and her plans for tomorrow.

They arrived at the cinema well before the programme's showing time to find two queues had already formed on either side of the box office. The longer line was for the cheaper seats and it stretched down the gable end wall of the picture house and round and back on itself in front of the cinema. The shorter queue was for the more expensive seats which usually meant the back rows where mostly courting couples went and that only stretched halfway down the wall on the other side.

'Sixpence or ninepence?' Claire asked as they made their way halfway round the cinema.

'Cheapest available,' Penny said.

'Do you think we'll get in? The queue's longer than I thought it would be.' Claire sounded anxious as they joined the end of the longer line.

'Oh yes, it can curl back on itself a couple of more times before you can't guarantee getting a seat, although even then you might be able to get one on the front row.'

Claire glanced over to the shorter queue, wondering if it might be worth splashing out for a ninepenny ticket but then she gasped and looked away quickly. Immediately behind the barrier at the front of the line marked ninepence was a man who looked exactly like Trevor. She had only met him once and that was in the dark, but he was tall and there was something distinctive about the wildness of his thatch of hair that made her certain it was him. She looked along the line, searching for Rosie. Meanwhile, the young man was animatedly talking to a pretty dark-haired young woman who was standing beside him and there was no sign of Rosie. Claire was about to say something to Penny, who knew Trevor from work, but her friend had already seen him.

'Well, well, well!' Penny said, before Claire had a chance to say anything. 'Is that who I think it is? It's your Rosie's lad. I thought he and Rosie were going dancing tonight? They are still stepping out together, aren't they?'

'That's certainly what Rosie seemed to think not more than half an hour ago,' Claire said, shocked now that Penny had confirmed her suspicions. 'She was waiting for him when I left the house and she was expecting them to be going dancing.'

'Well, now it looks like he's with Phyllis Whatshername. I forget her surname, but she used to work at the old mill, in accounts.'

At that moment, two young girls in smart maroon uniforms appeared in the cinema foyer and unhooked the plaited ropes that had been blocking the entrance.

Almost immediately the queues began the slow shuffle towards the box office, putting an end to any kind of private conversation.

'He's taken her to the back row,' Claire whispered as the usherette flashed her torch, illuminating one of the few remaining pairs of sixpenny seats and she and Claire had to concentrate on pushing their way past a row of people without treading on anyone's toes. Claire's mind was reeling and all she could think about was what had happened to Rosie? She was worried about what she should say regarding Trevor when they got home. She turned to Penny to say something, but before they even had a chance to sit down, the adverts were flashing onto the screen followed by miserable black-and-white pictures of German tanks practising manoeuvres in unidentified countryside as the Pathé newsreel recounted the latest European news, and it became impossible to talk over the soundtrack.

'Would you like an ice cream or a drink?' Penny asked in the interval after they had somehow endured the whole of the second feature. It was supposed to be a comedy but neither of them had laughed and Claire was hoping some refreshments might help lift the sombre mood that had descended on them both.

'I'll get them,' Claire offered and she stood up, as much for a chance to have another look at Trevor and the dark-haired girl as anything.

'Are you going to tell Rosie that you've seen him?' Penny asked as they unwrapped their choc ices.

'I have to,' Claire said, 'though I've no idea what I'll say. But I can't let her—' She'd been thinking about what was supposed to be happening tomorrow and stopped herself just in time from blurting out Rosie's secret. 'I wonder what excuse he gave her?'

'If he bothered giving one at all,' Penny said, and before Claire could challenge what she meant, the lights dimmed and the censor's certificate announcing the main feature flashed onto the screen.

Claire sat glumly through the whole film, hardly even registering when it was over.

'We can go home now.' Penny leaned over and whispered to Claire. 'Unless you want to sit through the whole programme again?'

'Sorry, I didn't mean to spoil it for you,' Claire said.

'You didn't, though you were obviously not in the mood.'

'No, I wasn't. My apologies, because I didn't realise that I wasn't. To be honest, I've been worrying that much about what I should say to Rosie that I found it hard to give the film much mind.'

'I tell you what we could do, because I've an idea,' Penny said when they were back in the foyer watching the people lining up for the second house. 'Why don't you come back to my house now for a cup of coffee? I think it might help if you talked to my sister, Stella.

I bet *she* can tell you what you should say to Rosie.'

'What's it got to do with your sister? Why would she know anything about it?' Claire asked.

'I'm not going to say anything more,' Penny said, tapping the side of her nose. 'You'll see.' And the two girls linked arms and began to walk home.

'I don't know why she wanted to get mixed up with the likes of Trevor in the first place,' Penny said when they were clear of the cinema. 'I did warn her when she first started working on our bench at the factory and he came sniffing round her because I'd had dealings with him before and I knew he was trouble. The only thing was, she didn't seem at all pleased that I was poking my nose in where it wasn't wanted, as she so delicately put it. So I butted out and decided not to say any more. She's a grown lass and she can do what she likes. But then, when something like this happens, I can't stand by and watch him—'

'Do you know who that was?' Claire interrupted. 'The girl who was with him tonight? You did say but I've forgotten.'

'Phyllis somebody. I don't remember her last name, though. As I said, she used to work in accounts at the old mill but I don't think she transferred when it became the munitions factory. I actually thought her family had moved out of the area.'

'Did they look like a couple to you,' Claire said, 'the way they were acting?'

'Yes, they did, but does it make any difference? They were sitting in the best seats – in snoggers' paradise – and it certainly didn't look as though this was the first time they had been out together.'

'Do you think I should tell Rosie I've seen him out with someone else?'

'I'm not going to say anything more until you've talked to Stella,' Penny said. 'I'm going to leave it to her because she'll help you decide. Believe me, she'll tell you a thing or two about Trevor Jones.'

It was late by the time Claire got home. Her head was spinning, her thoughts flying off in all directions, and she had quite overlooked the time. Her Aunt Sylvia had nodded off in her chair, and her head, which had been lolling towards her shoulder, shot back up when Claire opened the door. A look of relief flashed across her face.

'Where on earth have you been? Have you seen the time? It's not like you to stay out this late without telling me.'

'I'm really sorry Aunty Sylvia, I was only at the Downs's house. Penny asked me to come back for a coffee after the pictures and somehow we got talking and I didn't notice the time, but you're right, I should have dropped in to tell you where I was.'

'Well, I'm glad to see you're all right. I can go to bed now. Rosie's had a bit of a disappointment this evening and she went to bed early, said she'd got a headache.'

Claire was alerted. 'You mean about Trevor not showing up?'

'Yes. How did you know?'

To avoid answering, Claire went to hang up her jacket.

'He didn't turn up when he said he would,' Sylvia said, 'so not surprisingly Rosie was quite upset by that but she obviously wasn't going to tell me much more than that. You know what she's like. Maybe she'll tell you.'

I doubt it, Claire thought, not when she hears what I've got to say – or, more accurately, what Stella and Penny have to say.

Claire crept into the bedroom and though there was no movement from the bed she was convinced from the tensed-up stiffness of her position that Rosie was not asleep.

'Are you awake?' Claire whispered, even though she knew the answer. At first Rosie didn't stir. Claire put her cold hand on Rosie's bare shoulder that was exposed above the sheet and Rosie's automatic reaction was to turn over and lash out.

'I'm sorry,' Claire said, having provoked the desired reaction, 'but I thought you might want to talk.'

'About what?' Rosie sounded cross.

'You know very well about what – and I have to tell you that I know about it too.'

'What do you think you know, Miss Clever Clogs?' Rosie sat up and Claire could see her eyes were red-rimmed and they still looked watery.

'I know that you didn't go dancing tonight.'

'So, genius, I've had a less than satisfactory evening, of course you know. My mother waited up for you, didn't she?'

'Yes, but it's not because of your mother.' Claire saw her chance and she took a deep breath. 'It's because I saw him elsewhere and I know that he couldn't be in two places at once.'

'You couldn't have seen him because he was in bed with flu,' Rosie retorted.

'Is that what he told you?' Claire tried to keep the contempt from her voice. 'Well, how come I saw him at the Plaza? With another girl? In the back row?' She decided there was nothing else she could do but come out with it as quickly as possible. 'He was with someone called Phyllis something and, if you must know, they were snogging like there was no tomorrow.'

There, she had said it, and even she was surprised by how forcefully she had said it. Rosie's normally pink cheeks drained of colour.

'That can't be right!' Rosie laughed scornfully. 'Don't be ridiculous.'

'I'm afraid it is right. I saw him with my own eyes,' Claire said, not looking at her.

'Then how come . . .?' Rosie began, but stopped to think for a moment. She shook her head. 'No, you've got it wrong. You want to spread nasty tales because you're jealous that you haven't got a boyfriend and you can't bear that I'm engaged and about to be married. Trevor told me he was ill and he is. He was all muffled up and sounded full of cold. What he needed was a good night's sleep so that he'll be well for tomorrow, so you can keep your stories to yourself, thank you very much.' With that, she grabbed at the blanket and, pulling it across her bare shoulders, turned over, her back to Claire.

Ah, tomorrow, Claire thought, though she didn't say anything further. There might not be a tomorrow, at least not one like Rosie had been envisaging, but there was nothing more Claire could do tonight. She turned off the light and closed her eyes. She could see Penny and Stella, hear Stella's voice getting more and more upset as she had told her tale. Even after all this time, Claire thought. She was glad Rosie hadn't wanted to talk more now. Claire was glad to slow things down. It would be too much to hit Rosie with everything at once. What was that line from her favourite film? Tomorrow is another day.

On Sunday morning Sylvia left the house before either of the girls was up, leaving a note to say she'd gone. Claire helped herself to coffee and was attempting to spread some margarine in an effort to revive a rather dried-up piece of bread she had found in the bread bin.

'Shall I do a piece for you?' she asked Rosie when she appeared on the stairs.

'I'm not hungry, thanks,' Rosie mumbled.

'Your mother is out already.' Claire waved the note and Rosie smiled.

'Good for her. Glad she didn't suddenly decide to stay home. I trust you've made arrangements like you promised, too.'

'I shall be going to Penny's,' Claire said.

'I hope you didn't tell her anything – you know what a nosy parker she can be.'

'Actually, Rosie,' Claire said, 'Penny asked me to ask if you'd drop in for a coffee this morning too.'

Rosie frowned. 'Why on earth would I want to do that? These days she's more your friend than mine.'

'I know, but . . . but her sister . . .' Claire was annoyed with herself, knowing she didn't sound very convincing, but somehow what she was saying didn't sound like it had when she'd rehearsed it last night. 'It's her sister, Stella, as much as Penny, who wants to see you.' Claire tried again. 'She'd really like to talk to you because . . .' But then Claire froze. She was getting nervous as she could see Rosie was not taking the invitation seriously. 'The point is,' she tried again, 'I hope you'll come with me because I accepted on your behalf.'

'Well, you'll have to go and *un*accept then, won't you. I'm going to be rather busy today, remember?'

'Rosie.' Claire put out her hands in a conciliatory gesture. 'About that . . . I don't know how to say this, but I really do think you need to go and talk to Stella before you see Trevor this afternoon.'

'Oh God!' Rosie wailed. 'Not more of the stuff and nonsense you were trying to convince me of last night? You've not said anything to them about Trevor, have you?'

At that moment there was a knock on the back door. As Claire was the only one fully dressed, she went to answer it and was surprised to see Penny standing on the step with Stella behind her.

'I thought maybe we should come here, instead of the other way round, in case Rosie didn't want to come to our house today,' Penny said softly.

'Who is it?' Rosie called.

'It's vital that Stella talks to her before this afternoon,' Penny said.

Rosie had reached the door and she paled as Penny finished her sentence.

'You told her my secret!' Rosie gasped as she turned on Claire, and she glared at her accusingly. 'Claire, how could you?'

'I swear I didn't have to tell them anything, Rosie. They told me, because they already knew what was going to happen.'

'What are you talking about? How could they know? Unless you told them.' Rosie almost spat the words out in her anger.

'Please, Rosie, I beg you to listen to what they have to say before you blame me. Then you can judge.'

'What's so important that you have to come round here!' Now Rosie attacked Penny. 'You've never liked me, Penny Downs, and now you're trying to make trouble. I always felt I couldn't trust you.'

'Rosie,' Penny said, ignoring the slur, 'please can we sit down and talk like adults? Stella has something very important to tell you.'

Rosie looked at Stella in surprise, her expression doubtful. It was as though she had only just noticed that she had come too. But then she grudgingly stepped aside and indicated that the two girls should come into the living room to sit down.

'I'll let Stella start,' Penny said, when they were seated at the table, 'because it's her story and I think she needs to tell you this in her own words. Go on,' she urged her sister and Rosie sat down abruptly as the younger girl began.

'I once fell for Trevor Jones,' Stella said, not wishing to mince her words. 'I fell hard, because you've got to admit he's not a bad-looking fella.' She had taken a handkerchief out of her pocket and as if to distract herself began to roll the lacy edges between her fingers. 'We were stepping out together, doing a bit of courting, if you like. He'd been to our house and everything, met my dad. We were serious, as far as I was concerned, so I wasn't a bit surprised when one day he got down on one knee and proposed.'

Rosie stared at her, not sure whether to believe what she was hearing.

'He said we were engaged but he made me keep it

a secret – and that's when the trouble began. He started trying to persuade me that as we were engaged and as good as married, it was perfectly OK to act like we were married, if you know what I mean.'

Rosie's expression changed as she recognised the words.

Stella looked away. 'I was so naïve,' Stella said. 'I-I can hardly believe it now. It took me a long time to realise that he wasn't interested in marriage at all. All he wanted was to get me into bed.'

There was an uneasy stillness in the room as Stella stopped talking. Claire coughed but didn't say anything.

Then Stella said, 'I eventually realised that I was just one conquest on a whole list of targets that he had. Conquests that he wanted to boast about to his friends.' As her words sank in, the four girls sat for several moments in silence.

'Tell Rosie about the picnic,' Penny urged.

Stella looked at Rosie questioningly. 'Are you sure you want to hear this?' she asked. Rosie nodded as she steeled herself to listen. 'We went off to the moors one day, just the two of us,' Stella said. 'It was his suggestion that we should take a picnic. I said I'd bring the food and he was to bring something to drink. I thought the bottle was lemonade.' There was a sudden catch in her voice. 'But I'm sure it wasn't, though I could never prove it. All I know is that I had a very heavy head at the end of the day and that I was never quite sure about exactly what had happened after lunch.' She started to cry and wiped her eyes with the now well-scrunched handkerchief. 'But that was the end of it as far as he was concerned. The next thing I know he's dumped me.' She sniffled. 'He never gave me a reason, just stopped talking to me, but I then heard that he'd told his friends I was too easy and that I'd go with anyone. I was absolutely horrified when that got back to me, as you can imagine.'

'What did you do?' Rosie's voice was barely above a whisper.

Stella spread her hands and lifted her shoulders. 'What could I do? I denied it of course, but I couldn't actually prove my innocence. It was his word against mine. And as I say, I was never completely sure what he'd done . . .' She began to cry again.

Rosie sat perfectly still, staring at the wall behind Stella. Then she absently began drumming her fingers on the table.

'Do you understand what I'm trying to say?' Stella said, leaning in as she tried to make eye contact with Rosie. 'The thing is, I then found out it wasn't just me he'd tried it on with and that's why I'm trying to stop you make the same mistake.' Rosie didn't react so Stella went on. 'He loves the chase but he has no intention of getting married; all he wants is a notch on his belt, like the old cowboys always say in the Westerns.' Stella sat back, wiping the tears from her cheeks and Penny took over as if determined to make Rosie understand.

'We all worked at the mill in those days,' Penny said, 'before it changed and became the munitions factory, so lots of people knew him and he made sure that *everyone* knew about his so-called conquests. What most girls didn't realise, until it was too late, was that he was capable of ruining anyone's reputation.'

'I know I wasn't the only one,' Stella chipped in. 'I could write out a list for you now. But no one was prepared to accuse him in public. I felt like they were all pointing the finger at me because I dared to speak up. But somehow he managed to make it sound like it was my fault. It was dreadful. I couldn't take it and I had to leave in the end because it got so bad.'

There was a momentary silence then Rosie said, 'But he's not like that with me.' Her voice was barely above a whisper and she still refused to look at Stella.

'No, please don't tell me you're different,' Stella begged. 'That's what I used to believe. But it wasn't true, though it took me a long time to realise it. But that's how he operates and it was very painful to discover that. He's no more intention of marrying you than he had of marrying me, I'm afraid. You can be sure of that; it's happened to too many others for it to be a coincidence.'

Rosie finally turned towards Stella, although she still looked unsure, but it was Penny who spoke up now.

'Rosie, do you remember when I tried to warn you off him at the beginning when you first came to work at the factory?'

'Yes, I do remember,' Rosie said, her voice still quiet. 'I thought you were jealous.'

'And now? Do you believe me now?'

'I . . . I'm not sure,' she said and Penny sighed.

'Let me ask you something,' Stella said. 'Did you ever see an engagement ring you liked and he promised to get it for you? And then he said he'd marry you when he could afford to buy it but that it would take him a long time to save up? In the meantime, you weren't to tell anyone and you'd be secretly engaged.'

'Well, yes . . .' Rosie was beginning to go numb as Stella repeated Trevor's very words. She wasn't sure she wanted to hear any more but Stella seemed determined that she should.

'Don't tell me,' Stella continued. 'The next step was for him to say that as you were as good as married anyway there was no point in waiting for a useless piece of paper or even a ring before you could act as if you were married, so why not do it now? After all, life was too short, particularly with the threat of another war just around the corner.'

Rosie stared at Stella, a sudden sob catching in her throat. She had tried so hard not to take any of this on board but now she felt as if the blood in her veins was turning to ice and she sat stiffly in her chair. Now she had to believe.

'Are you still thinking I'm making all this up?' Stella asked.

'No, I think I'm beginning to understand,' Rosie said. She was crying now and sat for several minutes letting the tears flow unchecked. 'Did anything happen to you, after you . . . did it?' she asked Stella. 'Did you get . . . you know . . .?'

'No, thank goodness. I was lucky,' Stella said, 'but that was no thanks to him. He promised he would "take care of things" but when it came to it he said I shouldn't expect him to wear one of those johnnies, even though he'd said he would, as it spoiled his fun. I didn't want to stop and think about how he knew about these things, so I had to take my chances and I've since heard of others who weren't so lucky.'

'Really?' Rosie couldn't help shuddering.

'The trouble was,' Stella said, 'once it had happened I felt as if I couldn't say no the next time. Not that he hung around for very long once he'd got his way. He was more concerned with moving on to the next.'

'Did your father ever find out?' Rosie asked, suddenly picturing how she might fare if her father ever caught wind of what had happened.

'Unfortunately, yes.'

'What did he say?'

'I think you can imagine. But as there was no baby involved he didn't actually throw me out, though he threatened to.'

'I hardly want to boast but I think I may have had some influence there,' Penny said, grinning at her sister, and for the first time that morning there was a note of levity in the room.

'I think I should make us all a cup of coffee,' Claire said, getting up to stretch her legs, but no one wanted any.

'I was thinking that it would be really good if we could warn off his next target before things go too far,' Stella said. 'You know, the girl you saw at the cinema. What did you say her name was?'

Phyllis,' Penny said. 'Phyllis Murdoch. I've remembered her name. I wonder how many lies and false promises he's made to her already.'

'Do you think he's spinning her the same line?' Rosie said. She didn't want to admit it but she was feeling a little ashamed that she had been taken in so easily.

'I have no doubt,' Penny said. 'I don't think he can stop himself; that's how his mind works. And why should he change a winning formula?'

'I feel so helpless, but she deserves to be told, otherwise he'll keep getting away with it,' Rosie said.

'So you do believe me now?' Stella wanted confirmation. She turned to Rosie but it was Claire who spoke up first.

'I know I believe you,' Claire said, 'and I think Rosie has had a very lucky escape.'

Rosie nodded her agreement and Stella beamed. 'At least you're one person I've been able to save,' she said.

'Because that's how it feels, like I've been on a mission and I've saved your life.'

Rosie reached out and squeezed Stella's hand. She did indeed feel grateful, but she was unable to speak for the tears that were catching in her throat.

'Maybe there *is* something we can do that might save a few more girls in the future,' Penny said, looking thoughtful. 'He'll be expecting an evening of pleasure tonight, won't he?' The others turned to her with interest. 'There'll be no need to change any of the arrangements, then. The only difference will be that he'll find a larger welcoming committee than he bargained for when he arrives . . .'

Rosie greeted Trevor as she had originally planned, wearing the pretty, pale-blue lawn dressing gown her parents had given her for her eighteenth birthday. Fit for a film star, her father had said at the time. She had carefully pinned up her fair hair into the usual curls on her forehead, scooping the remaining ringlets into a roll that she pinned behind both ears and she was gratified to see his face light up when she opened the back door.

'Wow! You look terrific,' was his first reaction as he stepped into the kitchen and he eyed her from top to toe. 'Even more terrific than usual,' he added hastily when she frowned slightly. 'I hadn't expected . . .' He reached out to touch her gown. 'But first I've got a surprise for you,' he said, and he whipped out a bunch of flowers from behind his back and tucked them into her hand.

'Oh, thanks, they're pretty,' she said, deliberately off-hand, for she was thinking that they looked like he'd raided a neighbour's garden. 'I'll find a vase for them later,' she said and she stuffed the short stems into a jam jar that was standing in the sink.

'I've got a surprise for you too,' she said, making sure to meet his gaze and she beckoned him. Trevor peeled off his coat and threw it casually onto a chair. He took his jacket off and loosened his tie and was reaching out towards her when Rosie put a restraining hand on his arm.

'Let's not go too fast,' she said with a coy smile.

'Why? What do you mean?' Trevor frowned. 'I take it we're alone?' he said, lowering his voice. 'Didn't you manage to get rid of your mum and your lodger like you promised?' He sounded anxious as he scrutinised her face.

Rosie kept up the exaggerated smile and patted his hand. 'Don't worry, I promise this will be a very special evening,' she said. 'One that you'll always remember, just like you promised me.' Her hand was on the handle of the door leading into the living room and she turned the knob and flung it open. As she did so, four girls wearing heavily exaggerated make-up jumped up from where they had been squashed together on the couch and, lifting their arms high above their heads, shouted, 'Surprise!'

Trevor stepped back, clearly in shock; he was looking

from the girls to Rosie and back again. 'What's all this?' he cried. 'Who are you?' He anxiously scanned the faces of the girls and it was Penny who stepped forward.

'I'm sure you know who I am, Trevor, and you probably also know that I'm one of Rosie's friends. Well, we thought we'd get in first this time.'

Trevor looked puzzled.

'You know how you always like to boast to your mates?' Penny said. 'Well, we thought we'd let Rosie tell a few of her friends first, this time.'

'Who are all these people?' He turned to Rosie. 'Tell them what?'

Rosie didn't answer. Stella had moved to stand behind him and she spoke up next. 'You must remember me, Trevor,' she said, 'even though I admit it was a little while ago and I have grown up since then.' She tapped him on the shoulder and he swung round. 'You boasted about me for months; you can't have forgotten that.'

Trevor looked like he couldn't believe what was happening. His face one minute was white, the next pink with embarrassment as he switched his gaze from face to face in disbelief.

'This is Claire,' Rosie said, touching her cousin's arm. 'You have met her briefly before but, to set the records straight, she's my cousin from London, not just any old evacuee.'

Penny came forward then and took hold of his arm, forcing him to look at the fourth girl in the line-up who had so far remained silent. 'We thought we'd nip this one in the bud, Trevor,' Penny said. 'Before anything had time to get started. I'm sure you've not forgotten Phyllis Murdoch yet, now have you? I happen to know you were already lining her up to be next.'

'Hi Trev,' Phyllis said and she gave him a two-handed, Charleston-like wave. 'I think these ladies have saved me quite some bother, don't you? Not least a fight with my dad.'

Trevor stared at her as though he hadn't seen her before and looked round anxiously, searching for a way out.

'Haven't you got anything to say?' Rosie asked him. 'Sorry if you didn't like your surprise but I haven't had so much fun in ages. And I think you can rely on us to warn off any other potential Mrs Joneses should they appear on the horizon. We'll be delighted to sort them out and put them in the picture too.'

Rosie went into the kitchen and came back with Trevor's coat and jacket over her arm. 'I do believe these might be what you're looking for,' she said to Trevor, the smile back in place.

Trevor was standing in the middle of the room with his hands on his hips, trying to regain some dignity and he grabbed the items Rosie held out to him, quickly slipping his arms into the sleeves of his jacket. Then he stepped up to Rosie, putting his face as close to hers as possible without actually touching.

'So, the stories are true. I don't see any actual horns, but you Jews really are so sly,' he said, his lips twisting into a sneer as he stared down at the top of her head.

Rosie's eyes widened. 'I beg your pardon!'

'And you thought I didn't know!' His eyes flashed in triumph. 'Everyone warned me to watch out because there was no telling what a Jew might do. More fool me for not heeding them. But it seems you can't hide something like that for very long. Truth will out. Mean, grasping, and power hungry. Tsk.' He made a tutting sound. 'Thought you could land yourself an easy husband? Well, you'll have to think again. I would say Mr Hitler's got the right idea about keeping you lot in your place.' He looked from one to the other. 'You've no need to worry, I shan't be wanting anything to do with the likes of any one of you ever again. And I'll make sure none of my mates have anything to do with yous either. You're like witches, the lot of you.' He stood in front of Rosie, arms akimbo as he struggled to save face. 'You or your poxy cousin,' he said scornfully, eyeing Claire up and down. Then he turned to Penny. 'And you and your sister are no better, for sticking with them.'

'Do I look worried?' Rosie said, and she laughed loudly though her heart was pounding and her pulse racing. She had never been called names like that before and all she really wanted to do was to curl up into a ball, but she was determined not to let him see how much he had upset her.

'How about that for a performance, ladies? Penny said. 'What a nasty creature he turned out to be. Fortunately we can go back to our coven now,' she teased, as Trevor all but ran out of the door. Rosie closed it firmly behind him then leaned against it and closed her eyes. She felt as if she had been punched. 'See, Rosie, you should have trusted us sooner, but at least we were able to rescue you in time.'

'He's nothing short of a rotter. You're well rid of him,' Claire said with relief.

'I'm glad you finally listened.' Stella grinned.

'And thanks to you all for taking the trouble to find me,' Phyllis said. 'I feel like I really have been saved, thankfully before I got into trouble.'

'Delighted to have been able to help,' Penny said.

Rosie felt a hand touching hers and looked up to see Claire staring at her with concern. 'Are you sure you're all right?' she asked, squeezing Rosie's hand.

'I am now,' Rosie said. 'Thank you for helping to bring me to my senses.'

'Don't thank me,' Claire said. 'After all, I'm family so it's to be expected. I think you should be thanking your real friends.'

# Chapter 24

**September 1939**

Roger Buckley was home on leave when he heard the Prime Minister's declaration of war on Germany in the special eleven o'clock BBC news bulletin and he sat drumming his fingers in agitation on the leather arms of the old couch, anxious to get going. His bags were already in the hall, packed and waiting, as he had been due to go back to his unit that night. But now he'd been told there were extra trains being organised from Manchester to his base and there was a new urgency surrounding his return.

His company had been on standby at a base in the south of England where they had been preparing to be shipped over to France as soon as the call came, so he had been expecting to go back today but he had been alerted earlier that morning that he should be prepared to leave the country earlier than originally planned. He had already said his final farewells to the family; Julie, fortunately, didn't seem to understand that it might be quite some time before she would see him again. He was waiting now for the taxi to take him into Manchester.

When the broadcast finished, his father got up and switched off the radio.

'Here we go again,' the older man said. 'I never would have believed I would have to live through yet another war in my lifetime.' He shook his head in disbelief.

'The question is, how long will this one last?' Roger said.

'Shall we give it till Christmas?' his father said.

'Isn't that what they said about the Great War?' Roger said.

'I was being sarcastic,' his father said. 'Who knows?'

'Let's hope it's no longer,' Roger said, 'for everyone's sake.'

'Well, war or no war, I have work to do,' the older man said. 'Right at this minute I believe I have two new patients to see.' He got up and headed for the hall.

'Who's that?' Roger asked, frowning. 'Anyone I know? I didn't think anyone new had come to the village recently, unless it's a visitor I don't know about with an emergency?'

'No, I imagine it will be fairly routine.' He handed Roger the piece of paper he had picked up from the hall. 'Violet Pegg telephoned earlier this morning while I was out,' the doctor said. 'You know, the school teacher.'

'Yes, of course I know who Violet is, but she and her mother are already on the books, so who's new in their household?'

'I believe they've offered a home to two children who arrived on one of those special trains that came to London from Poland.'

'You mean the Kindertransport?' Roger said. 'I've been reading about that.'

His father nodded.

'Gosh, that sounds like quite an undertaking,' Roger said. 'What a terrific responsibility.'

'Yes, it is, particularly as I believe the children are very young and hardly speak a word of English. But people have been doing some amazing work rescuing these children from the horrors of what's going on over there.'

'Well, they couldn't be going to a better home. If anyone knows about kids, Violet does,' Roger said.

'She only offered to take one child initially, but she ended up agreeing to have a brother and sister who were desperate not to be separated. They've been in the country a few weeks already, in London, but they've only recently been sent north so they've not been with Violet very long. You can imagine the kind of paperwork that's attached to taking in kids like that. Anyway, she says she wants me to take a look at them and check out their general health, make sure they've not picked up anything nasty on their journey – which in itself sounds pretty horrendous. Apparently, the girl's had a bad cough since she arrived so I might have to try and trace some of the other kids who were on the train with her to make sure no one has any serious infection.'

'Poor kids. Tough enough to have been shipped off like that, leaving behind their families, without getting ill on top of everything,' Roger said. 'Weren't they checked out before they set off? I thought they had to be screened for things like TB.'

'From what Violet told me they only made it out of the country in the nick of time so who knows what tests got done and what didn't,' the older man replied. 'I believe they were among those who were on the last children's train out of Poland.'

'Let's hope they can be reunited with their family soon,' Roger said. 'Roll on Christmas!'

'OK, son,' his father said, and he came towards Roger with his hand extended. 'Let's not make this any more protracted than it needs to be. I'm going to see to Violet's new children, while you go and sort out Mr Hitler. I'm sure I can leave him to you,' he said and he left the room with a sardonic smile.

As he stepped out into the sunshine, a high-pitched whining sound screamed through the air.

'Oh, my goodness, what was that?' he called back into the house, and he shielded his eyes as he scanned the empty sky. 'I didn't expect the Jerries to be arriving this soon,' he said to himself and he shook his head and heaved a sigh. 'Don't panic!' he called out when he saw the front door opening wide. 'I'm coming back in. Everyone head quickly for the basement.' And he locked up the car and made his way back into the house.

When Vicky heard the siren going off for the first time she hadn't realised what it was and she had run around the Post Office trying to find out what alarm had been triggered to make such a noise, until her father had appeared at the top of the stairs.

'It's an air-raid siren, girl. We've got to get out of here,' he cried desperately. 'Blooming heck! We've only just declared war and they're sending planes over here already?' He was wheezing badly and shouting at her to get out to the shelter.

'You'd best get into that Anderson thing double-quick, girl, if you value your life,' he shouted anxiously.'

'I'll not go without you, Dad,' she said and she stood waiting for him at the bottom of the stairs.

'Is this what we've got to look forward to?' Arthur said, shaking his head, and he began to cough as Vicky took his arm and led the way to the shelter.

They made their way down the steps into the damp underground hole to find the neighbours they shared with were already there.

'Is this what it's going to be like from now on, alarms going off every five minutes?' Arthur grumbled.

'I won't mind so much, so long as we have time to get into a shelter,' Vicky said.

'Well, this suddenly makes it all very real,' Sylvia Barker from the Knit and Sew shop grumbled. 'Now we know we are actually involved in a war.'

At that moment, Vicky heard the door of the shelter rattle open and someone shout inside. She couldn't make out the words but a moment later a face appeared. With the light of her torch she made out Lawrence Boardman, the newsagent on the parade, looking very official with his ARP armband and his ARP warden's helmet and something that looked like a rifle that closer inspection revealed to be made out of wood.

'False alarm! False alarm! It's all right, folks, it was only a false alarm,' he was shouting. 'Someone must have panicked and pressed the wrong switch.' He tutted. 'It's just as well it was a false alarm because it seems that most folk didn't even know what it was anyway. They would all have been bombed in their beds.'

'Does that mean we can go back home, then?' Sylvia asked him. 'I thought they were supposed to sound the all clear?'

'I'm sure they will eventually. It's probably taking them a while to realise what's happened. Hopefully next time everyone will know what the alarm noise means,' Lawrence Boardman said. He tilted his helmet and scratched his head. 'We can't afford people thinking we're crying wolf.'

'I'm glad to see the Germans weren't so quick off the mark as I thought,' Arthur muttered. 'Let's hope we don't hear from them again for a long while,' and he slowly made his way back up to the garden.

Most of the shopkeepers on the Parade were already finding various items of their stock were in short supply and many food items in particular were becoming difficult to replace. The threat of rationing of items other than petrol, the first thing to be rationed, was becoming real.

Vicky was one of the few shopkeepers who could boast an increasing turnover as the number of letters, parcels, and small packages, and even telegrams, was growing exponentially as the number of men, and women, in the armed forces grew.

Even Arthur had taken up letter-writing regularly, replying to his soldier son, and he was always pleased to see another letter from Henry – although the news was usually scant – but it did help to keep him informed about the progress of the war and the posting of his son.

Arthur kept a close eye and ear on the news, avidly listening to the wireless and reading several newspapers each day, although at the beginning nothing much seemed to be happening and people didn't believe it was real. He was surprised, therefore, to hear from Henry that his outfit was likely to be shipped overseas soon as part of the British Expeditionary Force but he was upset to see that when he passed the news on to Vicky she actually flinched at the mention of her brother's name.

'Where exactly will he be going?' Vicky asked. The angry way she and Henry had parted was never far from her mind.

'He can't give us any further details other than "the continent" or the censor will black it out,' Arthur said. 'There's enough of his original letter missing as it is. But even from the little he's said about the organisation of the troops, I wouldn't be surprised if Roger gets shipped out soon too.'

Vicky started. It sounded odd to hear Roger's name like that in relation to the war. She hadn't heard from him, nor had she talked about him, since that dreadful night after the fishing trip. Now, as her father said his name, it was as if a lead weight had descended on her shoulders and she shivered as though someone had walked over her grave.

Since the war had begun, she had tried not to think about him, but the idea that he could be sent abroad without her knowing troubled her deeply and she was sorry that she had told him not to write. She had heard that he had completed his preliminary training course because several of her customers had news of him if she was within close enough distance to overhear. But her father's suggestion that he could be shipped off abroad without her knowledge had suddenly struck her hard and she spent the rest of the day feeling irritable and out of sorts.

# Chapter 25

After Trevor's downfall, as Rosie insisted on calling that fateful afternoon when she and her friends had done their best to humiliate him, she and Claire began to spend more time together. The pair were still squashed rather uncomfortably into Rosie's bed in Rosie's not-nearly-big-enough bedroom, but by the time war broke out they were no longer at loggerheads. More than that, they were the closest they had ever been to becoming good friends.

'I don't think I ever did thank you properly for your part in saving me from Trevor – or should I say saving me from myself, more like,' Rosie said when they were both sitting up in bed reading one night. Rosie liked to take the latest women's magazines to bed with her.

She would spend time checking out the latest make-up and fashion, seeing what tips were recommended for making-do and making the most of her existing wardrobe. Rosie, on the other hand, preferred to read one of the day's newspapers while she struggled to make sense of Britain's war-footing in relation to the situation in Europe.

'There's no need for thanks,' Claire said. 'I knew you'd listen to reason once you heard what Stella had to say.'

'If I hadn't been so pig-headed in the first place and had listened to Penny earlier I could have saved us all a lot of trouble,' Rosie said, putting down her magazine.

'Yes, but somehow life isn't like that,' Claire said and laughed. 'Do you think your mum guessed any of what went on?'

'If she did, she was wise enough never to say anything.'

'But she didn't seem too upset when you told her you weren't seeing Trevor anymore.'

'I suppose that sometimes she can be more perceptive than I give her credit for,' Rosie said.

'And I imagine she must be preoccupied with her own worries. She must feel sad, missing your dad.'

'I don't know about that,' Rosie giggled. 'I can never be sure how they feel about each other.

'But it must be hard with him being so far away at sea. Does he write?'

'I don't know about Mum, but he has written to me, yes. And I've written back to him, though I didn't tell him about Trevor. I don't even know if they can get letters at sea.' She thought for a moment. 'You know, in a strange way I miss him. Somehow I can't quite picture him on board a ship. But how about you? I know it's taken quite a while for you to settle, no thanks to me, and I'm sure you still miss your family, but are you enjoying it here, now?'

'Yes, thanks. I think you can safely say that I've finally settled in.' Claire grinned.

'I have to apologise that I wasn't very nice to you when you first came,' Rosie said, 'but if that business with Trevor has taught me anything, it's that friends and family are even more important than I thought they were.' She stopped and looked at Claire. 'And I hope we can stay friends even after you've gone back home.' She sat musing for a moment. 'I think Trevor did the best thing, leaving the munitions factory, don't you? Once the story spread it seems there were a lot of girls who'd had a hard time with him. He seems to have made a pass at every girl he met. They could certainly have made life difficult for him.'

'Thank goodness they felt as we did once they realised how he had used them, or it could have been awkward,' Claire said.

'Nobody likes someone taking advantage,' Rosie said. 'By the way, did I tell you the latest? The news is that he's signed up. After boasting that he would never be called up because his job was too precious, I believe he's now going to be some sort of mechanic in the army. I think that should suit him well,' Rosie said.

'And men in uniform never seem to have any problems finding girls,' Claire said with an ironic laugh. 'That bit will certainly suit him well.'

'My only hope is that the men he's with will cut him down to size,' Rosie said.

'At least all the young girls in this neighbourhood have been forewarned; I think he'd have trouble showing his face round here again,' Claire added and they both laughed.

Rosie picked up her magazine again and leafed through it, pausing at the knitting patterns then quickly turning the page. She needed to talk to Claire and she wasn't sure why she was finding it so difficult but she couldn't put it off any longer. She took a deep breath.

'I've decided I'm not going to work at the munitions factory anymore either,' Rosie plunged in.

Claire put down her paper and stared at her. 'You never said. How long have you been thinking about that?'

'A while, really, but I wasn't sure I'd be able to do anything about it.'

'Does your mother know?'

'I've hinted at it but I haven't told her for sure, though I doubt she'll be surprised.'

'What's brought this on, particularly now that

Trevor's gone? I should have thought things should be more bearable there.'

'Hard to say what made me come to the final decision. I like the money – who wouldn't? Particularly after working at the mill. But if I'm honest, I never did take to the work and I've known that from day one.'

'What are you going to do instead?' Claire asked.

'I don't know yet. I thought I might help you in the shop,' she said, raising her brows and grinning as she gave Claire a sideways glance. Then she patted her hand. 'Don't worry, I'm only joking,' she said. 'I'm sure you wouldn't want that, though I know my mum would like it. But it's definitely not for me.'

'What are you thinking about? You've got to have some sort of job,' Claire said.

'Of course I have, and that's what I've been driving myself nuts about. If I'm honest, what I really want – don't laugh – is to do something more directly connected to the war effort.'

'What's more connected with the war effort than making gun parts and ammunition?' Claire laughed but Rosie took no notice.

'I feel I'd like to be involved in some more personal way,' she said.

'You don't mean to join the services, do you?' Claire sounded shocked.

'No! That's going a bit far. I'm sure there's lots of other ways I could be gainfully employed.'

'Such as?'

'Do you know Violet Pegg, the schoolteacher?'

'I've met her once or twice in the Post Office,' Claire said.

'Well, she and her mum have taken in a couple of evacuees, two kids from the Kindertransport scheme who managed to get on the last train out of Poland.'

'Oh yes, I've heard about them,' Claire said, 'and of course I've read about the whole rescue operation. It's been going on for some months and it was quite amazing. They put on special trains to get as many kids as possible out of some of the danger zones.'

'They're Jewish kids who've been rescued, I believe,' Rosie said, 'and all kinds of people in England have offered them a home, but you probably know that?'

Claire nodded. Then she frowned. 'But you're not thinking of taking in a child, are you?'

Rosie smiled. 'No, but there's one thing I have talked to Mum about and that's about my religion.' She paused. 'I've decided it's time I owned up to being Jewish.'

Claire's brows shot up. 'Really?' she said. 'That's wonderful news,' and suddenly her eyes misted.

'Maybe Trevor did me a favour,' Rosie said. 'I've no idea how he found out but that doesn't matter now, does it? The point is that it's helped to put things in a different light.'

Claire dabbed at her eyes. 'I can't tell you why, but I'm really pleased,' she said.

'Mum agreed with me and she said she's prepared to be open and honest now too, and to tell everyone about her background and the fact that she's Jewish.'

'How do you think your dad will feel about that? Claire ventured.

'Mum said it's not a problem because my dad's always known and never been bothered.'

'Can I ask, why the sudden change of heart?' Claire almost whispered.

'It's not easy to hide when you keep hearing so much about Jews being persecuted,' Rosie said not looking at her cousin. 'I reckon we're very lucky in Britain and I feel I need to stand up and be counted.'

'Then I'm glad.' Claire smiled. 'And that makes it easier for me to talk about the fact that I'm Jewish too.'

'Anyway,' Rosie continued, 'I've talked to Violet about everything and she says there's plenty of children in the Manchester area who need help, not just with the provision of a home. And not only Jewish kids, but kids who've been evacuated into the countryside who need support for one reason or another. She wants to try and help them, starting with the two she's already offered a home to, and what I would really like to do is to help her in some way.'

'Doing what?' Claire was surprised and really interested to know more about her cousin's change of direction.

'Not sure yet, but as you know, kids who've been evacuated need help settling.' She grinned at her cousin.

'And it doesn't matter whether they come from Europe or from some remote part of Britain.'

'Like London, you mean?' Claire joked, but now Rosie looked serious.

'I suppose it doesn't matter where you come from; anyone would need help coming to terms with the fact that they may not ever see their families again. I can't begin to imagine how that must feel.'

'No, you're right,' Claire said. 'It was hard enough coming from London. My parents are still there and we are in touch regularly and there's every likelihood I'll see them again before too long.'

'Violet thinks there's a lot that we can do for these kids and I'm sure she's right. I believe there are societies and charities and the like, mostly in London at the moment, though I'm sure there are some in the north as well. She's thinking that maybe we could start some branch offices up here within an established organisation to help some of those who've moved north. I believe there are more kids who've become detached from their families than people realise and I can only see it getting worse as the war goes on.'

'It does sound like a worthy cause,' Claire said.

'I think so,' Rosie agreed. 'Particularly since I can now appreciate what a difference help and support from true friends can make.' She reached over and squeezed Claire's hand. 'And I intend to try, though I know I've got a lot to learn.'

# Chapter 26

**January 1940**

After war had been declared, it felt as if time was standing still, although Vicky never ceased to marvel at how there always seemed to be so much to do. The war itself did not appear to be moving and, after almost four months, it was being dubbed as 'the phoney war'. Christmas had come and gone and the battlefront was still notably quiet, but promises that the conflict would soon be over had long since been forgotten. What did seem remarkable was how easily the villagers of Greenhill settled into their new routines and accepted the new rules they were now expected to live by.

'Aye, it's surprising what you can get used to,' Arthur

Parrott said, patting his wheezy chest. 'You begin to take things for granted without thinking. Maybe it will all be over without ever really getting started.'

'Do you really believe that?' Vicky said.

'I don't know about believing, but I'm certainly hoping,' Arthur said, going into another coughing spasm.

But in the new year things suddenly began to change.

It was Arthur's job to sort the mail first thing on a Monday morning, ready for the delivery boys to distribute on their bikes. On this particular Monday, Vicky noticed he kept one letter aside that he later handed to Ruby. Not wanting to pry, Vicky made no comment on this rather unusual behaviour but later that day, when she found the torn envelope in the wastepaper basket, her curiosity was aroused and she couldn't resist picking it out to look at it. There was no return address but, with a jolt, she thought that she recognised the handwriting. She stood staring at it for several minutes, turning it over in her hand. She wanted to say something, though she didn't know what, but as the afternoon wore on, Ruby's demeanour seemed to change until she was no longer her bright and chirpy self but was short and irritable with customers.

Vicky was doing her best to ignore it when, without warning, Ruby suddenly burst into tears and rushed through the back door of the shop that led to the living room. Vicky was startled but made no attempt to follow her and she waited until the last customer had gone before she finally went behind the scenes. She found her father sitting alone at the kitchen table, reading one of the morning papers and sucking hard on his empty pipe.

'What's up wi' lass?' he said when Vicky appeared. 'She rushed straight through like a train and out t' lavvie as though a ghost were chasing her. I didn't know she could move that fast with that thing on her leg.'

'To be honest, I'm not sure what's up with her, Dad. Though I hope I'm about to find out.'

'What did you put in them sandwiches at dinner-time?' He chuckled.

Vicky ignored him. 'Any idea who her letter was from?' She tried to sound casual. 'That's far more likely to be the cause of the problem.'

Arthur frowned. 'I thought at first it might have been from our Henry,' he said.

'Henry? What would he be doing writing to Ruby?' Vicky was sceptical. 'They've not been corresponding, have they?'

'Not as far as I know, but it was definitely a military type of envelope.'

Vicky boiled the kettle and brewed a fresh pot of tea and when Ruby reappeared she handed her a cup without a word. At that moment, the shop bell tinkled. To her surprise, her father stood up.

'I'll take a turn,' he said, 'so you ladies can finish your tea in peace.' And as he turned away he winked in Vicky's direction.

When he had gone, Vicky patted the chair next to her, indicating that Ruby should sit down. She had been thinking about the letter, about the handwriting she thought she knew, and a sudden insight had clicked into place as a brief thought had flashed through her mind. Now her hands suddenly felt clammy as she tried desperately to work out what she might say. She sat back in her chair and decided to plunge straight in.

'You've a soft spot for Dr Buckley, haven't you?' Vicky said quietly. 'You must have been upset when he went away?'

Ruby looked up, surprised, tears instantly welling. 'Is it that obvious?'

'Maybe not to everybody, so you don't need to worry,' Vicky assured her.

'I don't want you to get the wrong idea,' Ruby said.

'And what idea's that?' Vicky said.

'That I'm a stupid kid with a childish crush, or anything like that.' She paused. 'The thing is that I do like him. I like him a lot.' She looked up and tears were streaming down her face. Vicky's heart went out to her, though she wasn't sure how to respond. But Ruby wasn't listening anyway. 'I more than like him,' she sobbed. 'I *love* him.'

'Ruby, I can see that,' Vicky began, 'and I'm sure he's very fond of you . . .' She had to force the final words.

'But that's not the same as love, is it?' Ruby cried. 'Fond is how you feel about kids, and that's how he thinks of me, I know. I've tried to tell him that what I feel is different, that it's proper grown-up love, but he fobs me off. He doesn't want to hear it.' Her tears were flowing profusely again. 'And now he's going away and he might not come back, so he's never going to know.' She let out a plaintive wail.

Vicky felt her stomach churn. 'What do you mean, he's going away?' she said.

'He told me, in the letter . . .' Her voice trailed off and she sniffled. 'I've been writing to him. At his base camp.'

'Did he ask you to write?' Vicky suddenly felt she had to know.

Ruby shook her head. 'Oh no, he wouldn't . . . he doesn't . . . that was purely my idea. I wanted to know where he was and what was happening to him so I asked his mother when I saw her in the shop and she told me where he was . . . and he did at least write back.'

'And what *is* happening to him?' Vicky forced herself to ask.

'Nothing much so far. He said in the letter how disappointed he was that he didn't go over to France with the first batch of soldiers.'

'Like my brother Henry,' Vicky interrupted. 'He was among the first to go.'

'Roger was complaining that they were kept hanging around so I think he's quite pleased to be moving at last. He'll be allowed to come home for a few hours for a very brief embarkation leave tomorrow and then he'll have to go back to camp so that the next day or the day after they can be shipped out to France.'

'Really? He's coming home?' Vicky caught her breath.

Ruby nodded. 'Only for a few hours. But he said he won't have time to see anyone. He made it quite clear he'd be spending the time with his parents and Julie. And then he'll have to go back south on the eight o'clock train from Manchester, London Road.'

Vicky closed her eyes, imagining the joy of seeing him again, but the image was fleeting and she was aware that Ruby was sobbing again.

'He said that I'm not to try even coming to the station to see him off as it will be chaos. And he says I shouldn't write to him anymore either, as he'll be far too busy to reply.'

'I . . . I'm sure it won't be that long before he's home again for good,' Vicky said softly, though she didn't really believe her own words.

'But that's no comfort if he refuses to understand how I feel about him. If he doesn't take me seriously, he may as well not bother,' Ruby said crossly. Vicky let her cry while she was lost in her own thoughts.

'How can I make him see me properly?' Ruby suddenly sobbed loudly. 'How can I make him love me? I want him to look at me the same way he looks at you!' she blurted out.

Vicky's eyes opened wide and she drew in her breath sharply. 'I . . . I don't know what you mean,' she said.

'When he looks at you it's like he really loves you!' Ruby exploded.

Vicky stared at her. That was not what she had expected and she didn't know what to say. But she did know she had felt a stab of something like jealousy when she had thought about the possibility of Roger loving someone else.

'I suppose you're going to tell me I'm being a silly kid after all?' Ruby said, sniffing as she patted her cheeks dry.

'No, please believe me, I'd never say anything like that to you, Ruby. But I think you need to understand that first love can often be quite painful, particularly if it isn't reciprocated, and it isn't always easy to get someone to love us in return, no matter how much *we* might love *them*.'

'You mean there's no hope?' Ruby said.

'I didn't say that. I . . . I can't speak for Roger,' she hesitated, 'but the thing to remember is that first love doesn't mean it has to be your last love.' Vicky couldn't believe that she had quoted her father. Maybe there was some wisdom in what he'd had to say after all. 'You're young, Ruby, and while that doesn't automatically make you foolish or even childish, it does mean that there will be lots more opportunities for you to love and be loved.'

Vicky wanted to smile as she spoke for she couldn't help thinking that Ruby's words had made her wonder if she herself had been too hasty in her own responses to Roger. She had revered Stan as if he was her first and last love and, in doing so, had perhaps spurned what could have been a second chance for her. Had this young girl unwittingly shown her the path to love?

Vicky reached out and, clasping both of Ruby's hands in hers, she smiled gratefully at the young girl without offering any further explanation. Then she glanced up at the clock. 'I think you should go home now, Ruby,' she suggested. 'It's been a long and tiring day.'

Ruby nodded. 'I think I will, if you don't mind.'

'One final thought,' Vicky said as they both stood up. 'It is also possible that he's not the right man for you. Have you ever thought of that?' Vicky smiled.

Ruby looked surprised. 'Do you think I might have made a mistake?'

'Go home and think about it,' Vicky said. 'You might find you view things differently in the morning. *Like I've finally seen things differently this afternoon*, she added silently. She had no doubt in her mind now that she had been blind when she had rejected Roger's love without really giving him a chance. Perhaps it was she who had made a mistake? And if that were true, was it too late to make amends?

# Chapter 27

Vicky had rarely seen her father cry before, even when the pains in his chest as he struggled to breathe must at times have been almost more than he could bear. The closest he had ever come to shedding tears was when he had told Vicky and Henry that their mother had died. But when she came down to breakfast the next morning, Vicky was shocked to see he was crying now. On the table was a letter and she was relieved to recognise Henry's carefully slanted writing. She'd never read any of Henry's letters – since their falling-out he had never addressed any to her and she relied on her father to keep her updated with her brother's news – but it was a comfort to know that he was alive and well.

Moments later, however, she saw that next to Henry's crumpled envelope was another letter with handwriting she didn't recognise but the name of an army captain had been given instead of a return address. It too was addressed to her father, but this time, as she picked it up to examine it, she was overcome by a sudden dread and stared at Arthur in dismay. Henry's letter remained sealed, telling her that it was something her father had obviously been wanting to savour later, but the contents of the mystery letter lay wedged on top of a single slice of toast, from where it was soaking up the melting margarine. Vicky slowly picked up the two pieces of flimsy paper, turning to check that her father didn't object. But he had been overtaken by a coughing spasm so deep-rooted that he wasn't able to say anything and fear clutched at her stomach as the bile rose in her throat.

*Dear Mr Parrott*, she read, *it is with the deepest regret that I have to tell you . . .* Vicky made no move to touch Arthur, who continued to struggle for breath and he stared at her blankly as she sank into a chair. Her worst fears had come true. They must have sat like that for some time, neither speaking, until Vicky became aware of someone knocking on the back door.

'Good morning.' It took a moment for Vicky to register that it was Lawrence Boardman, the newsagent, from next door, and she rapidly blinked away the tears that were misting her vision.

'Is everything all right, Vicky?' he said, 'Only, there's a queue formed to get into the Post Office and it doesn't seem to have been opened yet.'

'I'm afraid we've had some bad news, Mr Boardman.' Vicky struggled to control her voice. 'It's our Henry, you see,' she said, 'he's . . .' She didn't believe the words she was about to say.

'I'm right sorry to hear that, lass. That'll be hard on your dad.' He had stepped into the living room and stopped when he saw Arthur still sitting at the table, struggling to breathe. Lawrence raised his voice as if Arthur were deaf. 'I said I'm sorry to hear . . .' and he put out his hand, but Arthur, wheezing heavily, waved him away.

'Would you like me to contact the doctor, love?'

'Yes, please,' Vicky said. 'That would be very helpful. He'll know what to do. While I'd best go and see to the shop.'

Ruby, who hadn't yet been entrusted with the keys, was in the middle of the small crowd who were waiting outside, and once Vicky had opened the door she watched gratefully as the young girl automatically began weighing letters, filling out forms and issuing stamps and certificates 'as if she'd been born to it,' as she told her father later.

It was a relief when the day was finally over and Vicky could close the door on the last customer and go through to the back where her father looked as if he'd hardly moved all day. Since the doctor's visit, his breathing had become easier at least, but his eyes still had a glazed look and seemed to be concentrated on his dinnertime sandwich that was still sitting unappetisingly on the plate, the bread curling at the edges.

Vicky picked up Henry's letter that still lay unopened on the table and felt her own tears starting up again. 'We never did say goodbye properly, did we?' She spoke the words out loud and was aware that her father had turned to look at her.

'What a bloody waste,' he said, 'to have a bellyful of regrets.' He picked up the company captain's flimsy condolence letter that was grease-ridden and almost indecipherable by now and tossed it across the table. 'He never did become a hero, but at least I hope he managed to make the most of what little life he did have.' He seemed to be speaking into the air but then he suddenly pointed his finger at Vicky. 'Like I've been telling you to do. I hope you're listening at last, because this is what all that struggle boils down to.'

Vicky swallowed hard.

'Did you know he's been here today?' Arthur barked out the question.

'Who?' asked Vicky, thrown by his sudden switch of subject.

'Young Roger. Been here all day he has, by all accounts. Well, not at this house, but he's been in Greenhill, according to his father. He's being posted abroad, so they've given him a chance to say goodbye. More than my lad got. That's because the good doctor is an officer, most like. So, are you going to say goodbye?'

'What do you mean? Go where?'

'To his house. He won't come here, will he? You couldn't expect him to after the way you treated him. But it's my bet you'll live to regret it if you let him go without a proper farewell. Isn't it enough you've already done it to your brother?'

Vicky was appalled. '*I* did it? What about . . .?'

'Oh, stop gassing, lass, what does it matter who did what? All I know is your brother's gone and you never got to say goodbye. Don't let history repeat itself.'

Vicky was astonished to hear her father suddenly talking like this and without thinking she glanced up at the clock. Maybe he was right. It was something that had been at the back of her mind all day. She looked at the clock again; she hadn't registered it the first time, and she tried to remember what Ruby had said.

'Did the doctor say what time Roger's train was?' she asked, and for the first time that day she saw her father smile.

Arthur shook his head. 'All he said was that he'd saved petrol coupons specially so that he could take him down to London Road station in his car. I doubt they've left yet. Get on your bike and get over to his house. No doubt you'll catch him there.'

This time Vicky needed no second bidding.

She pedalled furiously all the way to Roger's house, laughing because she had suddenly realised that her father was right. It was time she let Stan go. Life was for living. It was as though she was being given a second chance and it was up to her to take it. She felt ready to grasp it in both hands. She pulled into the drive, unsure whether to go to the clinic or to use the family's front entrance, but as she stood there uncertainly the side door opened and Mrs Buckley appeared with Julie trailing after her. Julie ran up to Vicky and, clasping hold of her hand, stared up at her.

'My daddy's gone away and I don't know when he's coming back,' she said. Tears were forming in her eyes as she tried to suck comfort out of her thumb and Vicky thought her heart would break.

'He'll be back, my love, I'm sure of it.' She bent down to talk to the little girl face to face.

'Will you tell him he's got to come back?' Julie pleaded.

'I will if I see him, but you said he's already gone, so am I too late?'

'I'm afraid you are,' Mrs Buckley intervened. 'If it was him you were hoping to see.'

'I wasn't sure what time the train was . . .' Vicky's voice trailed off.

'The train isn't until eight, but his father was driving him all the way into Manchester so they left early,' Mrs Buckley explained. 'I'm afraid you've missed him, unless you want to ride down to the local station on your bike and catch the next train into Manchester. Then you'd be bound to make it in time.'

Vicky felt Julie tugging at her skirt. 'Will you go and see my daddy now?' the little girl begged.

'Yes, I believe I will,' Vicky said.

'You'd better let her get going or she'll miss the train,' Mrs Buckley softly admonished her granddaughter.

Julie tugged at her skirt again and Vicky bent down to the little girl's level once more.

'I'm not supposed to ask you this,' Julie said in a loud whisper, 'but will you be my mummy instead, now that Daddy's gone away? Daddy says you would make a very good mummy. Do you want to come and see my old mummy? I've got a picture of her on my wall.'

Vicky laughed and she caught Mrs Buckley's eye as she straightened up. The older woman was blushing, eyebrows raised. 'I don't know where she's got all that from,' she said.

'Out of the mouths of babes,' Vicky said, then she said to Julie as gently as she could, 'I don't think it works like that, sweetheart. You can't replace a daddy with a mummy like that, but I can certainly promise to be your friend.'

Roger and his father had had about a half hour start on her and Vicky practically flew all the way to Greenhill station. If she caught the next train into town she could be in Manchester at about the same time as it would take Roger to drive there with his father.

She sat in the almost empty carriage, urging the train to get her there in time. And when it did, it wasn't difficult to pick out the troop trains because soldiers seemed to be spilling out of every door and window. The problem was that all the men looked alike in their brand-new uniforms and Vicky didn't know where to look first. She could see it was going to be difficult to spot one lone soldier, even if he was as tall and good-looking as Roger. That thought made her spirits lift and suddenly she wanted to laugh as she began racing frantically up and down the platforms. To her astonishment, above the melee of steam engines and chatter, she thought she heard her name being called. It took her several minutes to pinpoint the source then a voice clearly shouted, 'Vicky! Can it really be you?' And she saw him dismounting from the train and come running towards her. They embraced spontaneously at the moment of impact but then stood diffidently, not knowing what to say.

'Get on with it, fella, you haven't got all day,' she heard a voice say from behind him and someone cuffed Roger playfully. 'Kiss her, you idiot! Can't you see that's what she's waiting for?'

Vicky laughed and seconds later she felt the light, feathery touch of his lips on hers. 'Only obeying orders,' Roger said as he looked up, and they both laughed. It was as if they were in their own private bubble, oblivious to the crowds milling across the concourse.

'I can't tell you how pleased I am to see you here,' he said. 'I wanted so much to ask you if you'd come but I didn't dare.'

'Oh dear! Am I that scary?' Vicky said. 'I'm sorry. But I can tell you another thing: I will gladly reply to your letters if you'll write to me. If you still want to, that is.'

'Try and stop me,' Roger said. 'Can we put the past behind us? Start a fresh sheet.'

'Of course,' Vicky said.

'I don't know what I can promise you by way of a future,' Roger said. He frowned but Vicky smiled. 'Let's not worry about that now. Let's agree to live for today. And today we are here, together.'

Roger kissed her again. 'Can I ask you a favour?'

'Of course.'

'Will you call in occasionally on Julie? She's very fond of you and I know she would like that.'

'She's also way ahead of you,' Vicky said with a giggle, and she told him of her visit to his house.

At that moment there were several loud whistle blasts.

'Oops!' Roger said, 'I'd better get back on that train or it will go without me. My dad is over there, under that recruitment poster,' Roger pointed to the far wall and waved. 'He said he would see me off from a safe distance; he didn't want to come right up to the train.

I'm sure, if you ask him nicely, you'll be able to cadge a lift home.'

'Thank you, I'll do that.' Vicky turned and waved in the same direction. 'Now go before you miss that train.'

'It's wonderful to see you. I'm so glad I caught you,' Roger said holding her close, not wanting to let her go.

'And I'm glad you caught me, too,' Vicky said. He kissed her again, only more deeply this time, and he held her head away from him in both his hands as if for inspection. As a piercing whistle blasted out one more long sustained note, he smiled and gave her the kind of look that finally made her understand what Ruby had meant.

# Postscript

It is ironic that it has taken a global pandemic, a tragedy that even as short a time ago as the beginning of 2020 could never have been conceived, that has allowed me to write this book; the book I have been waiting for years to write. It is a book about ordinary people living ordinary lives, the kind of people who populated the world I grew up in who nevertheless have a story to tell. Readers should rest assured, however, that the characters and personalities who inhabit these pages have arisen solely from my imagination.

Although this book has been germinating in my mind for some time, I didn't start writing it until the initial onslaught of the Coronavirus COVID-19 hit. When London, and then the whole country, was plunged into a total lockdown situation, I was a virtual prisoner in my own home—but for a writer what is new about that? Every time I write a book I am incarcerated for weeks or months at a time, virtually in solitary isolation. To be able to roll out of bed and onto the computer chair is part of a normal working day for me and I was glad to have something that I knew would so pleasurably occupy my time. No shopping distractions, no visitors and no visiting; a writer's dream. But sadly, no cinema or theatre visits to look forward to at the end of the day either, no dinners out with friends, no holidays, no weekends away, no excuse not to write . . . and write . . . and write.

As the characters developed and I became gradually more involved in their world, I started looking forward to being with them each day. And I began to understand what it must have felt like to be in northern England when the war began and people's lives changed forever. No one then knew how long the war would last or how the world would change as a result. They were unable to contemplate protracted hostilities and assumed there would be an end to it sooner rather than later; just as we assumed we would conquer the virus quickly, and yet here we are many months later still fighting it on all fronts. Our world has already changed and we still don't know how the story will end or what – as they say, is to be our 'new normal'?

Writing this book has given me insight into ordinary

people's lives and a greater understanding of what it must have felt like to live through the Second World War in Britain as my own dear late brother and parents did, even if I was fortunate enough not to have been born yet. If they had known when it first started that it would last for six years, might they have wanted to give up the fight before it even began? What would they have made of *their* 'new normal' if they had known at the beginning how it would be by the end?

But then I realized that the circumstances surrounding the two events were not completely comparable, for their pre-war world was part of what is for us a bygone era, and I came to appreciate that my own life had never been of that time. My world is in an age of great technological advancement where 'isolation' is different from what it would have been then. I can communicate with my editor, my publishers and my agent through a router, a wireless connection and the double click of a mouse. I can conduct research of all kinds without having to step outside my front door. And now in this time of quarantine and potential isolation I can still connect with friends and family all over the world. I may not be able to touch them, to hug them or embrace them in the flesh, but I can use Twitter and Facebook and interact with the whole world. I can see and hear my loved ones as if they were with me in my own living room thanks to the wonders of WhatsApp, FaceTime, or Skype, and I can connect with colleagues and attend all kinds of editorial and business meetings via Zoom. Thanks to this modern marvel, I have been to a wedding in Canada, a party and a book launch many miles from home, continued to attend my book group and sadly I have even attended a COVID-19-related funeral in another city. But the hands of friendship that have been extended during this dreadful time have been extraordinary and far from feeling isolated it has been a time for forging new connections, interacting with the neighbours, building new support systems, and consolidating old ones in new and exciting ways. All of these wonderful people are too numerous to mention, but you know who you are and all I can say is thank you for being there and for making this book possible.

# Acknowledgements

Although some parts of *The Postmistress* have been in my head for several years, this book actually began life over a seasonal celebratory lunch in a fashionable French restaurant in London and I have to thank my champion and editor, HarperFiction Editorial Director Kate Bradley who has supported all my writing endeavours with patience and care. Without her initial enthusiasm and the encouragement and support of Publishing Director Charlotte Ledger there would be no book and I am thrilled not only to be a part of the Harper*Collins* team but of One More Chapter as well. Special thanks also to my ever-supportive agent, the RoNA award winning Kate Nash for her faith and belief in me, her constant encouragement and her tireless work on my behalf. They have all played such an important part in helping me achieve my dreams.

I would like to thank my dear friends Jannet Wright and Ann Parker for their contributions to my research and for helping me surmount obstacles that at times may have threatened the writing process; they have always been there to help me scale the impossible walls thrown up by that process and to hand me down safely on the other side.

Thanks as ever to Sue Moorcroft and Pia Fenton (Christina Courtenay) for the generosity of their time and wisdom and for all their unstinting support and to the Finlay family for helping me keep in touch with the outside world.

And lastly thanks to all my friends and family for being so tolerant and for finally accepting that a deadline is a deadline.

If you enjoyed *The Postmistress*, read Maggie Sullivan's compelling and heart-warming Coronation Street series . . .

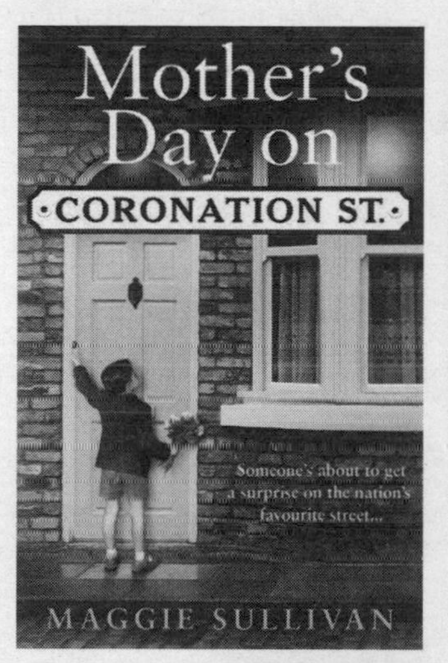